Praise for
THOSE SCAND

The Dangerous Mr. Ryder

"Allen's latest adventure romance is a roller-coaster ride that sweeps readers through Europe and into the relationship between a very proper baroness and a very improper spy. The quick pace and hold-your-breath escape plans turn this love story into a one-night read that will have you cheering for the appealing characters."
—*Romantic Times BOOKreviews*

The Outrageous Lady Felsham

"Allen's daring, sexy and, yes, outrageous spin-off of *The Dangerous Mr. Ryder* gently borders on erotic romance because of the manner in which she plays out her characters' fantasies (including a marvelous bear rug!) without ever losing sight of Regency mores."
—*Romantic Times BOOKreviews*

The Shocking Lord Standon

"Allen continues her collection of novels centering on the ton's scandalous activities with another delightful and charming Ravenhurst story of love and mayhem."
—*Romantic Times BOOKreviews*

* * *

Coming soon
**The Piratical Miss Ravenhurst—
September 2009**

Author Note

Lady Maude Templeton believes in love, as I discovered during the course of *The Shocking Lord Standon* when she refused to marry the hero because she just knew the right man was out there waiting for her somewhere.

And then she found him and fell in love instantly with Mr. Eden Hurst, who is not only resoundingly ineligible for the daughter of an earl, but is a man who most definitely does not believe in love.

Maude sets out to convince Eden that love does exist and that she is the woman he needs in his life. It seems a hopeless task, but Maude can be quite as shocking as any of her Ravenhurst friends when she puts her mind to it, and Eden Hurst soon finds that doing the right thing is harder than he ever imagined. If only he can work out what the right thing is…

There is one more Ravenhurst cousin still without the love of her life—Clemence Ravenhurst, far away in Jamaica. Little does she know it yet, but respectable Clemence is going to find her life turned upside down as she becomes *The Piratical Miss Ravenhurst* in the final episode of THOSE SCANDALOUS RAVENHURSTS. Coming September 2009.

Louise Allen

THE NOTORIOUS
MR. HURST

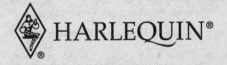

HARLEQUIN®

TORONTO • NEW YORK • LONDON
AMSTERDAM • PARIS • SYDNEY • HAMBURG
STOCKHOLM • ATHENS • TOKYO • MILAN • MADRID
PRAGUE • WARSAW • BUDAPEST • AUCKLAND

Recycling programs
for this product may
not exist in your area.

ISBN-13: 978-0-373-29555-5

THE NOTORIOUS MR. HURST

Copyright © 2009 by Melanie Hilton

First North American Publication 2009

www.eHarlequin.com

Printed in U.S.A.

DON'T MISS THESE OTHER
NOVELS AVAILABLE NOW:

#956 SIERRA BRIDE—Jenna Kernan

Sam Pickett is rich, powerful and used to getting his way. So he is baffled when stunning Kate Wells isn't remotely interested in becoming his latest plaything—despite the fact that she's poor, with an aunt and blind sister to support. Since striking it rich, Sam has felt a troubling emptiness and knows that his money can never fill the hole in his life where Kate now belongs....

He'll have the only woman he wants!

#957 THE VISCOUNT'S KISS—Margaret Moore

When Lord Bromwell meets a young woman on the mail coach to Bath, he has no idea who she is—until *after* they have shared a soul-searing kiss! The nature-mad viscount isn't known for his spontaneous outbursts of romance—and the situation isn't helped by the fact that the woman he is falling for is a runaway....

The Viscount and the Runaway

#958 REYNOLD DE BURGH: THE DARK KNIGHT—
Deborah Simmons

Tall, dark and handsome, Reynold de Burgh is nonetheless wary of the opposite sex—until he meets beautiful, young Sabina Sexton! That innocent Sabina fearfully begs his help to fight the "beast" terrorizing her village only makes the brooding knight more desirous of her.

The last bachelor of the de Burgh dynasty is single no longer!

RAVENHURST FAMILY TREE

Francis Philip Ravenhurst, 2nd Duke of Allington = Lady Francesca Templeton

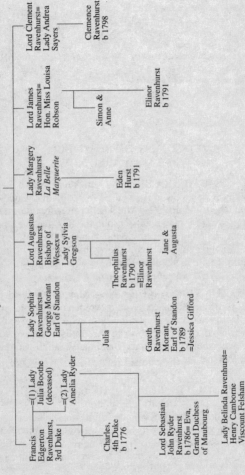

Chapter One

'And so, my false love—I die!' The maiden sank to the ground, a dagger in her bosom, her white arm outflung.

The audience went wild. They applauded, whistled, stamped and, those members of it who were not weeping into their handkerchiefs, leapt to their feet with cries of 'More! More!'

The dark-haired lady in the expensive box close to the stage gripped the velvet-upholstered rim and held her breath. For the audience who had flocked to see the final performance of *The Sicilian Seducer, or Innocence Betrayed*, the tension was over and they could relax into their appreciation of the melodrama. For Lady Maude Templeton, the climax of the evening was about to occur and, she was determined, it would change her life for ever.

'You would never guess it, but she must be forty if she's a day,' Lady Standon remarked, lowering her opera glass from a careful study of the corpse who was just being helped to her feet by her leading man.

'One is given to understand that La Belle Marguerite never

mentions anything so sordid as age, Jessica.' Her husband turned from making an observation to Lord Pangbourne.

'Fine figure of a woman,' the earl grunted. He was still applauding enthusiastically. 'Not surprising that she was such a sensation on the Continent.'

'And so much of that figure on display,' Jessica murmured to Maude, who broke her concentration on the shadowy wings long enough to smile at her friend's sly remark. The loss of focus lasted only a moment. Tonight was the night, she knew it. With the excitement that surrounded a last night at the Unicorn she had her best opportunity to slip backstage. And once she was there, to make what she could of the situation.

Then her breath caught in her throat and her heart beat harder, just as it always did when she glimpsed him. Eden Hurst, proprietor of the Unicorn theatre, strode on to the stage and held up both hands for silence. And by some miracle— or sheer charisma—he got it, the tumult subsiding enough that his powerful voice could be heard.

'My lords, ladies, gentlemen. We thank you. On behalf of Madame Marguerite and the Company of the Unicorn, I thank you. Tonight was the last performance of *The Sicilian Seducer* for this, our first full Season.' He paused while exaggerated groans and shouts of 'shame!' resounded through the stalls and up into the gods. 'But we are already looking forward to *Her Precious Honour* to open in six weeks' time and I can assure her many admirers that Madame Marguerite will take the leading role in this dramatic tale of love triumphant over adversity. Good night to you all and I hope to welcome you next week for our revival of that old favourite, *How to Tease and How to Please*, with the celebrated Mrs Furlow in the leading role.'

'Damn good comedy that,' Lord Pangbourne pronounced,

getting to his feet. 'I recall it when it first came out. In '09, was it? Or the year after?'

Maude did not hear her father. Down below in the glare of the new gas lights stood the man she desired, the man she knew she could love, the man she had wanted ever since she had first seen him a year before.

Since then she had existed on the glimpses she had caught of him. In his theatre she sat imprisoned, in a box so close she could have almost reached down and touched him. On the rare occasions he had attended a social function where she had been present he had been frustratingly aloof from the unmarried ladies, disappearing into the card rooms to talk to male acquaintances or flirting with the fast young widows and matrons. And even she, bold as she was, could not hunt down a man to whom she had not been introduced and accost him. Not in the midst of a society ball and not a man of shady origins who had arrived in England trailing a tantalising reputation for ruthless business dealing and shocking *amours*.

And last Season he had closed the Unicorn for renovations and returned to the Continent for a tour with his leading lady only months after they had arrived in England.

Standing there, he dominated the stage by sheer presence. Tall, broad-shouldered, with an intense masculine elegance in his dark coat and tight pantaloons, yet somehow flamboyant and dramatic. Maude caught the sharp glitter of diamonds at his throat and from the heavy ring on his left hand and recognised that his clothes had been cut with an edge of exaggeration that would be out of place in a polite drawing room. He was a showman, demanding and receiving attention just as much as the most histrionic actor.

'Maude.' Jessica nudged her. 'One of these evenings your

papa is going to notice that you dream through the performances and only wake up when Mr Hurst is on stage.'

'I don't dream,' she contradicted, finally getting to her feet
as Eden Hurst walked off stage to loud applause. 'I am watching
and I am listening. I have to learn how this place works.'

She had never managed to speak to him. The only words
he had spoken in her presence had been to a shopkeeper while
she, the bright, lively, witty Lady Maude had stood in Mr Todmorton's perfume shop, struck dumb by the sheer beauty of
the man. But three days ago, thanks to an overheard conversation at Lady Robert's otherwise dull reception, she had discovered that Mr Hurst had been making discreet approaches
to potential investors. And that, she realised, gave her the
perfect excuse.

Now she must have her wits about her as she followed her
father and the Standons down to the main lobby of the
Unicorn. Parties were gathering and chattering beneath the
famous clock that hung from the neck of the one-horned beast
charging out of the wall like a ship's figurehead. As she had
hoped, Jessica stopped to speak to a friend. Gareth, her
husband, waited patiently beside her while Maude slid
through the crowd to her father's side.

'Papa, Jessica invited me to drive home with her and to
spend the night,' she said as he clicked his fingers at the at-
tendant for their cloaks. It was quite true, Jessica had done just
that and Maude had thanked her nicely and explained that she
thought her papa would expect her home tonight.

Which was also true, so very gratifyingly she had told no
actual untruths. And she was, after all, a lady of resource with
money in her reticule who was perfectly capable of finding
herself a hackney carriage. Eventually.

'Very well, my dear.' Lord Pangbourne craned to see the

Standons in the crush. 'I'll see you at dinner tomorrow. Say all that is right to Lady Standon for me, won't you? I can't fight my way through this like you slender young things.'

'Yes, Papa.' Maude watched until he was outside and then slipped through the door to one side of the entrance. She was not certain where it went, other than backstage. But that was enough for her purposes.

'Can I help you, miss?' She was in a passageway, as brown and dingy as the lobby was brilliant and gilded. Maude dragged in a deep breath compounded of oil and dust, gas fumes, overcrowded hot people and greasepaint, and smiled brilliantly at the youth who had paused in front of her. His arms were full of hothouse flowers, an incongruous contrast to his shirtsleeves and baize apron.

'Mr Hurst's office, if you please.'

'The Guv'nor, miss?'

'Yes,' Maude said firmly. 'The Guv'nor. I have a proposition for him.'

Eden Hurst tugged his neckcloth loose from amidst the heavy ruffles of his shirt, flung himself into his great carved chair and put his feet up on his desk. Ten minutes of peace and quiet, he promised himself. Then back down the corridor to Madame's room to flatter and reassure in the midst of enough blooms to fill a conservatory.

Why she needed reassurance after a reception like tonight, Heaven only knew, but he had sensed a petulance that must be soothed. Ever since she had reluctantly agreed to return to England after years on the Continent she had been on edge, more demanding, more insecure, and the return tour while the renovations were carried out had only made things worse.

Perhaps the light of the new gas lamps was unkind when

her dresser finally creamed away the greasepaint. He would have the oil lamps on their stands brought back into her dressing room. Anything to keep the star of the Unicorn happy.

Feet still on the desk, he leaned forward and reached for his notebook to add *oil lamps* to the never-ending list of things to be done. His groping fingers nudged a pile of stiff cards, sending them to the floor. They lay face up, yesterday's social obligations.

Eden dropped his head back and stared at the ceiling, oblivious to the cracks that created fantasy maps over its grey surface. Was it worth it, allowing himself to be lionised by Corwin and his vulgar wife? He shut his eyes, annoyed with himself for revisiting a decision that had already been made. He needed an investor if he was to continue to make the improvements the Unicorn needed to keep it in the forefront of London's smaller theatres, and he needed a damned sight more cash than the gas lights had cost him if he were to finally persuade the owner to sell it to him.

Through his agents he had bought several small theatres around the country over the past two years as investments, leaving them in the hands of managers while he continued to tour Europe with Madame. Then had come word of the kind of theatre he had been dreaming of ever since he had stepped on to a stage, and he sold them all to raise the money to restore the Unicorn. It had meant coming to England and it had meant risking everything on a building that was not his own, but Eden Hurst had learned to trust his gut instincts in business and was prepared to be ruthless with himself, and with Madame, if necessary.

He could stomach Corwin, even Mrs Corwin in her purple toque, at a pinch. What was tightening his gut was the thought of the simpering Misses Corwin: Miss Calliope, Miss

Calenthe and Miss Coraline. One of them was the price Corwin was going to ask for his investment, Eden was sure. He'd marry a Corwin daughter over his dead body and he'd been certain of managing the thing tactfully in the end. Certain—until he'd heard the girls giggling and plotting together in the overheated conservatory.

No time to think about that now. He lowered his feet back to the threadbare Turkey carpet, twitched his neck-cloth into order and ran his hands through his over-long hair. Outside his office the corridor was deserted, with all the noise and the activity coming from the stage where they were striking the sets in one direction, and the Green Room where the actors were entertaining their friends and admirers in the other.

Eden took a deep breath and stopped. Gardenia was not a familiar scent in the utilitarian passage outside his office door. Nor was the rustle of silk skirts from the shadows expected. As he realised it, he saw her, an indistinct form in the alcove opposite. Young, slender—he could tell that from the way she moved, the glimpse of white skin at neck and breast.

Those accursed girls. He had thought himself safe for a day or two while they perfected their scheme to ensure that one of them was comprehensively compromised by him. But, no, here was the first of them, it was irrelevant which. If he pretended not to have seen her and went to the Green Room, she would be into his office, probably prepared to strip off for maximum effect when he returned, with or without a witness. And he was damned if he was going to stand here and shout for help in his own theatre, which seemed the only other option.

Or was it? Perhaps he could scare the living daylights out of her. Eden smiled grimly, took a long step forward and caught the half-seen figure by the shoulders. She came easily, with a little gasp, like a maid into her lover's arms, he thought with habitual cynicism, just before he took her mouth. Hard.

She had been kissed before. At the age of twenty-five, and after several Seasons energetically avoiding becoming betrothed, Maude had flirted with sufficient young gentlemen and had dallied in enough drawing rooms to have experienced everything from gauche wet ineptitude, to boldly snatched kisses, to shyly gentle caresses.

But she had never been kissed by a man who knew what he was doing and had no inhibitions about doing it thoroughly. How he managed it she had no idea, but one minute she was hiding in a dark alcove, poised to step forward and introduce herself, and the next she was moulded against the long hard body of a male who was quite frankly and obviously aroused, whose lips were crushed to hers and whose tongue was taking full possession of her mouth.

For a moment she froze, passive with shock in his grip. Then her mind began to work and caught up with her body, already pliant in his arms. It was Eden Hurst who was kissing her. She had dreamt of this for months and now it was happening. Hazily she acknowledged that he had no clue who she was and that he also appeared to be thoroughly out of temper, but just now that did not matter.

Maude found her fingers were laced in his hair, that romantic mane of black that gave him such an exotic appearance. Her breasts were pressed to his chest so that the swell of her bosom was chaffed by the brocade weave of his waistcoat and against hers his heart was beating, disconcertingly out of stroke with her pulse. But she was only peripherally aware of those tantalising discomforts. Her entire world was focused on what he was doing to her mouth and the devilish skill with which he was doing it.

Should a kiss make the soft flesh of her inner thighs quiver and ache? Should the insolent thrust of his tongue send shafts of desire deep into her belly, setting going an intimate pulse that made her want to twine her legs around his and press herself hard against him?

He growled, a warning she did not heed, was incapable of taking, then his hands slid to cup her buttocks and he pulled her up against him so that the ridge of his erection pressed into the delta of her thighs. Now she knew what her body was searching for. Roughly he pushed her back to the hard wall, letting the movement rock them intimately until she was moaning in total surrender against his mouth.

And then, just when she would have gone to the floor with him, done anything if only his mouth had stayed on hers, he released her, all but one hand, and stepped back. He reached behind him to fling open the office door and the light spilled out across her face when he tugged her into its path.

'Now let that be a lesson—hell and damnation,' Eden Hurst said quietly, loosing her wrist. 'You aren't one of the Corwin girls.'

'No, I am not.' *Thank God, I can still articulate.* She reached out one hand to the wall beside her, unsure whether her legs would be as obedient as her voice. 'I am Lady Maude Templeton, Mr Hurst.'

'Then why the hell did you let me kiss you?' he demanded with what she could only characterise as a total lack of reasonableness.

'One, you took me by surprise; two, you are somewhat stronger than I am; three, you are very good at it,' she said coolly. This was not the moment to cast herself into his arms and declare her undying love. Besotted she might be, but she had her pride. One of these days he was going to tell her he loved her, but he needed to find that out for himself.

'Well, I thank you for that last,' he said on a disconcerting choke of laughter. 'You are not inclined to slap my face?'

Maude very much doubted that her legs would allow her to take the two steps necessary to achieve that. 'No, I do not think so.' It was so long since she had been close to him that now it did not seem there was enough air to breathe. Or else that kiss had dragged the air from her lungs. 'Perhaps I should explain why I am here?'

'You want a job, my lady? I need a costume mistress and a scene painter. Oh, yes, and a couple of handmaidens for the farce.'

He kept his face so straight that she could not decide whether he was totally literal or had a nasty sense of humour. 'I doubt whether I would be suitable for any of those positions,' she responded, deliberately matching his tone. 'My sewing is poor, my painting worse and I would make a thoroughly heedless handmaiden. I have come to congratulate Madame Marguerite on her performance and to broach a matter of business with you, sir.'

'Business?' He studied her, expressionless. Maude was used to male admiration; this indifference piqued her, not unpleasantly. Her Mr Hurst was not in the common run of men. 'Well, shall we start with Madame and then we can agree a more suitable time for a meeting tomorrow?'

Maude would have thought him quite unmoved by what had just happened if it were not for the tension that seemed to flow from him, fretting her aroused nerves as though he had dragged a fingernail along her skin.

'You are without an escort, Lady Maude?'

'Yes,' she said, daring him with her eyes to make something of it. 'Perhaps you would be good enough to find me a cab later, Mr Hurst?'

'You are a practical woman it would appear, ma'am. And one with strong nerves as well as—' He broke off. Maude turned her head to follow his gaze. From the direction she had come there were soft footsteps and the sound of nervous giggling. 'Hell.' He caught her hand again and pulled her into the office, closing the door behind them.

'Mr Hurst, I declare you appear quite hunted.' Now she could see him clearly. The golden skin that always seemed lightly tanned, the dark brown eyes, the sensuous, sensual, mouth and the elegant, straight nose. She had been correct—those were diamonds in the pin at his throat and one old-fashioned cabochon stone in the barbarically heavy ring on his hand. And as he turned to face her, she saw another glinting in the lobe of his right ear. It should have looked effeminate, but it simply gave him the air of a pirate and she guessed that was quite deliberate.

'Truer than you know, Lady Maude. Perhaps you would care to sit? I fear you are about to be the audience for a private performance of a farce.' He gestured to a chair on one side of the desk and went to take the other, a great carved monstrosity of a throne with eagles on the back and lions' heads on the arms

The door inched open. More giggles, muffled, then a girl came in, her head turned to speak to someone outside. 'Oh Calenthe, I am so nervous!'

'But why should you be, Miss Corwin?' Hurst enquired in a voice like sugar soaked in aloes. 'You are amongst friends here.'

The girl gave a shriek and dragged at the door to reveal her companion just behind it. Maude blinked at the sight of two thoroughly overdressed young women clinging together on the threshold.

'Lady Maude, may I introduce Miss Corwin and Miss Calenthe Corwin to your notice? Ladies, this is Lady Maude Templeton. I fear I cannot offer you refreshment as Lady Maude and I are discussing business.'

Maude, who was beginning to get some idea what was going on, enquired, 'No doubt your mama is waiting for you close by?' Their faces were so easy to read it was almost laughable. 'No? Well, in that case I will take you home in my hackney, for you most certainly should not be out alone at this hour. Perhaps you would be so kind as to obtain one, Mr Hurst. I am afraid I must forgo the meeting with Madame this evening, but I do feel that seeing these misguided young ladies safe home must take priority. Shall we say eleven tomorrow to continue our discussion?' She knew she sounded about fifty, but her tone was certainly having a dampening effect on the girls.

'Certainly, ma'am.' He might not be a professional actor, but the manager of the Unicorn could dissimulate like a master. His face showed nothing but a slightly obsequious attention to Maude and a faint irritation directed at the two younger women, as though at the antics of a pair of badly trained puppies.

Maude swept out into the corridor, amazed to find her legs steady again. Who these two girls were she had no idea, other than that they were certainly not of the *ton*, but she had no way of knowing if they would gossip about her. It was imperative that she kept them on the defensive, more worried about their own position than speculating about what the daughter of an earl was doing unchaperoned in Mr Hurst's office at eleven in the evening.

He led them through a maze of corridors and out into the night. Maude drew her veil down over her face and raised the hood of her cloak to shield her face from the crowd of gentlemen who were milling around the stage door, inside and out, while the stage door-keeper produced a hackney with a blast on his whistle. She allowed Mr Hurst to seat her in the vehicle before he stood back to allow the Misses Corwin to scramble in unaided. 'Thank you, sir.'

'Thank you, ma'am. Until eleven, then.' He stopped to give the driver an address in the city, then turned away as the carriage rattled out into the late evening bustle of Long Acre.

Maude waited with interest to see what her two companions would say now they were alone with her. In the gloom of the carriage they fidgeted, whispered and eventually one of them blurted out, 'You won't tell anyone, will you, Lady Maude?'

'What exactly do you not wish me to reveal?' she enquired coolly, finding herself irrationally annoyed with the pair of them. Why she should feel so protective of Eden Hurst she had no idea. He was more than capable of looking after himself, if their encounter in the corridor was anything to go by. If he had pounced on one of these girls in that manner, she would have fled screaming, just as he intended, no doubt. They quite obviously had not got a *tendre* for him, either of them, so what on earth were they about, risking ruin like this?

'That we were trying to…um, encourage Mr Hurst into making an offer,' the shorter one ventured.

'For which of you?' Maude enquired, intrigued. Yes, he had known about this plot and had mistaken her in the gloom for one of these silly girls.

'With any of us. Mama thinks he will, because he wants Papa to invest in his theatre, but we aren't sure because he never takes any notice of us. We don't understand it,' she added naïvely, 'because we are ever so well dowered.'

'Perhaps Mr Hurst already has an attachment?' Maude ventured, finding her irritation turning into something more like amusement until she realised that might very well be the case. She had no idea—Eden Hurst was a very private man.

'Well, if he has, it isn't anyone from amongst the merchant families. Papa would know,' the taller sister offered confidently. 'And he can't marry anyone in society, because of being a bastard.'

That was a relief. Then Miss Corwin's words sank in. 'A…a what?'

'Bastard. Although Mama says not to use that word and say *love begotten*, instead. But it doesn't matter really, because his father was an Italian prince or something equally grand.'

That would explain his colouring, Maude thought hazily. *Was* Eden Hurst illegitimate? She had never heard a whisper, although it was not the sort of thing mentioned in front of unmarried ladies. Oh, Lord, if he was, that would be another obstacle to overcome. Trade was bad enough, the scandalous world of theatre even worse. Being the love child of an Italian prince was hardly going to make it any better. Papa was going to have palpitations, poor man, when he was finally presented with Eden Hurst as a son-in-law.

The hackney cab stopped. 'We're home.'

'And how do you propose to get in?' Maude enquired. They did not appear to be too worried by the prospect.

'Through the service area.' The girl hesitated on the carriage step. 'Thank you, Lady Maude.'

'Well, don't do anything like this again. If I were you, I would not talk about this little adventure to anyone,' she added repressively. 'And please tell the driver to take me to Berkeley Square.'

* * *

Maude was deep in thought when the hackney came to a halt again. The door was stiff and the light from the flambeaux either side of the Standons' house flickered wildly in the stiff breeze. She almost tripped getting down, then stood shivering while she fumbled in her reticule.

'All right, m'lady, Mr Hurst paid,' the man said, leaning round to slam the door shut.

'Oh. How kind of him.' Maude felt very tired all of a sudden. The shallow steps up to the front door seemed endless as she looked at them. Her hopes for the evening had been vague, beyond making contact with Eden Hurst, but she had not expected to be ruthlessly kissed and then find herself chaperoning two girls.

'He's come along to see you home,' the man added over his shoulder as the horse moved off.

As she stared across the corner of the square she saw another hackney drawn up, a tall figure standing by its open door. He raised a hand in acknowledgement as he saw her looking at him, then climbed back in. Maude drew her cloak around her and ran up the steps to Jessica's house, no longer tired.

Chapter Two

'Lady Maude, your ladyship.' Jordan, the Standon's butler, managed not to appear shocked by her unannounced arrival on the doorstep at almost midnight without so much as a valise about her person.

'Maude darling, I thought you said you couldn't come tonight.' Jessica put down her book, removed her stockinged feet from the fender and regarded her with mild surprise.

'I was trying not to tell an untruth to anyone,' Maude explained. 'Thank you, Jordan, a cup of tea would be perfect. And one of the special ginger biscuits if Cook has made any,' she added hopefully.

'You intrigue me vastly.' Jessica curled up in her chair and waved Maude towards the one opposite. 'You have been exploring at the Unicorn, I surmise?'

'How did you guess?' Maude kicked off her slippers and tucked herself up in the depths of the chair.

'Where else would you have slipped off to? Reveal all,' she commanded, reminding Maude that her friend had once been a governess.

'I told Papa that you had invited me and let him think I was coming back here with you directly after the performance. And I told you he was expecting me to go home with him, without actually saying that I did not intend to.'

'There is a word for that sort of thing. Devious.'

'I prefer to think of it as considerate. No one was worried.'

'Go on—' Jessica broke off as Jordan entered with a tray loaded with tea things, bread and butter, some tiny cakes and the famous ginger biscuits. 'Thank you, Jordan, that will be all for tonight. His lordship will let himself in.'

Maude waited patiently while Jessica poured two cups of tea and then pounced on a biscuit. 'I'm famished. Well, my intention was to visit Madame Marguerite in her dressing room and congratulate her upon her performance and while I was at it, just happen to encounter Mr Hurst and make an appointment to discuss a business matter.'

'And?' Jessica nibbled a triangle of bread and butter.

'I, er…encountered Mr Hurst first.'

'And he threw you out? You do look somewhat flustered.'

'He kissed me. Ruthlessly, indecently. Without mercy. Until I almost lost the use of my legs. The man is a complete rake.'

'Oh, my dear! How frightful, you must be devastated—' Her face full of concern, Jessica put down her cup and began to scramble to her feet.

'It was wonderful,' Maude finished. It was beginning to feel unreal, like an incredible dream. Only, her mouth still felt swollen and all those alarmingly wonderful sensations kept rippling through her whenever she thought about Eden's body pressed intimately to hers.

Jessica sat down again with a thump. 'Is that all he did?' she demanded. 'Kiss you?'

'Yes, although I don't think *all* is quite the word. But he thought I was someone else. He was extremely courteous afterwards and sent me home in a hackney. He followed in another one to see I arrived safely,' she added in an effort to reassure.

That a number of questions were fighting for priority in Jessica's head was obvious from her expression. 'Who did he think you were?' she asked eventually.

'One of the Misses Corwin, apparently. I've never heard of them, but their father is a merchant and he is about to invest in the Unicorn. The daughters are determined that one of them is going to marry Mr Hurst. Two of them arrived moments after he let me go, apparently hell-bent on getting the elder one compromised. I was able to foil that and escort them home, adding a warning about their behaviour while I was about it.'

'The pot calling the kettle black?' Jessica enquired.

'Not at all.' Maude frowned. She had been worrying about that as she drove back. 'I have no intention of entrapping Eden Hurst,' she reassured Jessica, and herself into the bargain. 'Only of giving him every opportunity to fall in love with me.'

'How can he resist?' teased Jessica, relaxing somewhat.

'Well, your darling Gareth could, very easily,' Maude pointed out.

'It was mutual, was it not? And I won't lecture you, I promise. How can I, given what I got up to disentangling you and Gareth?'

'You made a perfectly captivating loose woman,' Maude said, deciding she could, after all her adventures, manage a third ginger biscuit. 'Whereas I have no intention of doing anything more forward than making sure I am very much in Mr Hurst's life from now on. Sooner or later he will come to realise he cannot exist without me.'

'It did not strike him like a thunderbolt at your first en-counter,' Jessica pointed out. 'I might have been heavily veiled at the time, but I could see quite clearly and I have never observed a less struck man in my life. I described him to Gareth as an icicle, but an iceberg would have been more accurate. And he appears to have survived kissing you without falling at your feet either,' she added cruelly.

'He is probably racked with desire, the more he thinks about it,' Maude asserted. 'Another cup of tea?'

They drank in silence, the plate of biscuits mysteriously diminishing until Jessica said, 'You are sure, aren't you, that it isn't just his looks? I know I described him as an icicle, but he is also the most exotically beautiful man I have ever seen. It would not be at all surprising if you fell for that.'

'You mean, am I being extremely superficial?' Unoffended by the question, Maude brushed crumbs off her skirt and got up to place some more coals on the fire. 'You forget, I have grown up surrounded by men of character. Dearest Papa, Gareth, to name but two. I could not possibly love or marry a man without intelligence, drive, fine qualities. Yes, I was attracted to Eden Hurst because of his looks. But it was also his presence, his strength.

'And then the more I found out about him, the more I admired him. He has revived the Unicorn's fortunes in mere months in the face of the Patent theatres' opposition, created a vehicle in England for Madame Marguerite when she was known only by reputation. And everyone says he managed one of the most successful theatre companies on the Continent—and that cannot have been easy under the circumstances of the past years.'

'How old is he?' Jessica asked. 'Thirty, at least, I would have thought.'

'I do not know.' Maude frowned into the hot centre of the fire. 'I can't find out anything like that about him, who his parents are, where he was born, when.' She was not going to mention the rumour about his father. Time enough to cross that bridge when she had to.

'You don't think he and Madame are, er, involved…?' Jessica asked tentatively.

'Surely not?' Maude stared back, aghast. That had never occurred to her. 'She's *years* older than he is, surely?'

'Well, I have no doubt she's a creature of unrestrained passions, if her acting is anything to go by, and he is a very handsome man. Tell me…' Jessica leaned forward '…what was it like?'

Maude felt herself colouring up. 'Amazing,' she said finally. 'I have been kissed before, but this was quite unlike anything else. Is it *supposed* to make you feel odd all over?'

'The odder the better,' her friend said with a grin, uncurling from the depths of the chair. 'Time for bed, although I doubt you are going to get a wink of sleep after that.'

'Don't you think so?' Maude took the proffered candle. 'I was rather hoping I was going to dream.'

Eden waved the tired dresser out of the door and closed it behind him. 'I have called your carriage, Madame.'

'Call me Marguerite, darling. How many times do I have to ask you?' The actress fluffed at her hair petulantly.

'It does not feel right. Here, let me help you with your cloak.' He settled it around her shoulders as she stood, enveloping them both in a cloud of Attar of Roses, drowning the faint remembered fragrance of gardenias in his nostrils.

'Foolish boy.' She twisted round, her head on one side, and smiled. Always the coquette, always practising her charms. 'Are they all gone?'

She meant the swarm of admirers who had infested the

Green Room and queued, petulant if they were not given instant admission, at the stage door. 'All gone. I got rid of them at last.'

'They adore me.' It was a statement, but underneath he heard the need for reassurance. Always the need for reassurance.

'They worship you,' Eden agreed with a smile, his watchful dark eyes cataloguing the faint betraying lines beside her eyes, the slackening of the skin over the exquisite jaw line, the harshness of the dark hair tint. He knew he must begin to edge her towards the more mature roles. And how was that to be achieved without her throwing a tantrum to rival Mount Etna? He had witnessed the eruption in 1810, and the fiery image came to mind with increasing frequency whenever Madame was thwarted.

There had been a time, when she had first taken him from the palazzo, before he had learned to harness his emotions and not to entertain foolish fantasies about love, when he had hated her. Now, he thought he understood her, had come to accept her total lack of empathy for anyone else and to admire her talent, her sheer determination. But when he was tired it was still an act of conscious will to humour her.

'You must be exhausted after that performance,' he suggested, edging her towards the door. 'So much emotion.'

She lifted a daintily manicured hand and patted his cheek. 'Darling, you are cold.'

'I have been out, a small matter of business to take care of.' And if Lady Maude had not been there he would still have been dealing with it. The consequences of Corwin discovering that two of his daughters had been found, unchaperoned, in his office late at night would be the most almighty row and the loss of his most promising investor.

Eden smiled grimly, then caught sight of his saturnine expression in the big glass. Why the devil would a woman want to marry him in any case? Used to scrutinising the faces of actors at close quarters, all he could read in his own features was cold, hard ruthlessness wedded to the theatrical tricks of a mountebank—the earring, the hair. His profession and his birth made him ineligible to all but the merchant classes and below, and his character was surely something a woman would take on only in return for his money.

Which brought him back neatly to Corwin. 'What are you scowling about, darling?' Marguerite allowed herself to be guided out and towards the Green Room. The square chamber with its green velvet curtains, Turkey rug and motley collection of chairs, sofas and side tables was both the common room for the company and the reception salon after a performance.

Now, in the wake of Marguerite's admirers' departure, the room resembled the aftermath of a drunken party. Bottles were upended into ice buckets, flowers were strewn everywhere, empty glasses stood around and most of the company were sitting or reclining in various combinations of stage costume, street clothes and undress.

They struggled to their feet, or, in the case of George Peterson, the heavy who was already well in his cups, vaguely upright, as their leading lady swept through. 'Good night, darlings,' she trilled, blowing a kiss to the three walking gentlemen, the bit-part players, who swept her bows as she went.

Eden noted in passing that Miss Harriet Golding, the ingénue, was sitting almost on the lap of Will Merrick, the juvenile lead. That could spell trouble—Merrick was living with Miss Susan Poole, the lively soubrette who had apparently already left. He could well do without a love triangle in the middle of the cast, especially with a visiting leading lady next week. Madame would sail blithely through any amount of emotional turmoil provided it was not her own emotions at stake. Mrs Furlow could well find it most disagreeable. He dug out the notebook and added *Merrick/Golding/Poole* below the note on oil lamps. If this was serious, then Miss Golding would have to go; ingénues were two a penny.

'I am utterly drained,' Marguerite announced, draping herself across the gold plush of her carriage seats. '*Drained*. I have given my all for a month.'

'Well, you have two weeks when you need only rest and get up your lines for the next part, then rehearsals,' Eden soothed, the words forming themselves without any conscious work on his part. Then some demon prompted him to add, 'And I have an idea for the piece after that.'

'And what is that to be?' she demanded.

Eden knew he had been hedging round breaking this to her, seeking the right moment. Oh well, now, with no audience of dresser and sycophants to fan her tantrums, might be as good a time as any. 'Lady Macbeth.'

'Lady Macbeth? *Lady Macbeth?*' Her voice rose alarmingly. 'That Scottish hag? A mad woman? A *tragedy*? Are you insane?' She subsided. Eden braced himself; she was not finished yet. 'In any case, we cannot perform it. The Patent theatres have the monopoly on *legitimate drama*.' Her voice dripped scorn.

'Not if we introduce music, have a ballet in the background in some of the scenes. I have been working on it and we can scrape past the licence issues.'

'Why should we want to?' she demanded. Even in the dim light he could see the alarming rise and fall of her bosom.

'You do not want to do it?' Eden injected amazement into his voice. 'One of the great Shakespearian roles? The woman who is so seductive, so powerful that she can drive a great king to murder? Imagine the dagger scene. Every man in the theatre would take the knife from your hands and do the act if *you* commanded it. The sleepwalking scene—you, magnificent yet so feminine in your night rail…' He fell silent. She was already rapt, eyes closed, lost in her imagination.

Eden offered up silent thanks to whichever minor deity looked after theatre managers and sat back against the soft squabs. Finally, he could contemplate those hectic few moments in the corridor with Maude Templeton in his arms.

Thinking about it had the inevitable physical effect. He crossed his legs and tried to pin down the nagging feeling he had seen her somewhere before. It would not come and con-centrating was virtually impossible while the memory of the feel and the scent and the yielding of her filled his brain and agitated his body.

What business had she with him? he wondered. She was quick witted as well as beautiful, with a sense of humour that matched his own, he rather suspected, recalling her stated reasons for allowing him to kiss her. He did not believe for a moment that she had been subdued by his superior strength. Which left the flattering probability that she had enjoyed the experience.

And the not very flattering recollection that a second later she had been all business. Not that there was any legitimate business an unmarried *lady*, with the emphasis on lady, could possibly be transacting with him, which was puzzling. Eden found himself intrigued, aroused and curious, a combination of emotions that he could not recall experiencing before.

He indulged himself with the memory of her slender waist, spanned by his hands, of the slither of silk under his palms, the erotic hint of tight corseting as his thumbs had brushed the underside of her breast…

'I need a new carriage.'

Back to reality. 'This one is only eighteen months old, Madame. I bought it in Paris, you recall. I cannot afford a new one.'

'Why not? You are a rich man, Eden.'

'Yes. And very little of that is liquid just now. I invested heavily in the gas lights, as you know, to say nothing of all the rest of the renovations, the costumes, the props. Then the foreign tour while the work was being done was not all profit.' And just maintaining Madame Marguerite in gowns and millinery was a serious drain. His investments stayed where they were until the time was ripe for each to be liquidated. The bedrock of his hard-won fortune was not to be frittered to sate Madame's urge for novelty.

'Oh, fiddle! Cash some gilts or whatever those things are called. Or sell out of those tiresome Funds or something.' He could hear the pout in her voice. 'My public image is important, darling. I need to cut a dash.'

'You would do that from the back of a coal-heaver's cart,' he said drily. 'I am not touching the investments until I can get the owner of the Unicorn to talk to me about selling it. I need to invest in the place, but I am not spending any more now until it is mine.'

'Darling, I thought you were getting money from that vulgar little cit.'

'Corwin? Yes, I hope to. I just have to be sure I can keep him from interfering in the running as part of the deal.' Never mind the detail that Corwin would insist on making Eden his son-in-law.

'You are so stuffy, Eden.' She subsided into a sulk, leaving him once more free to contemplate Lady Maude and the inconvenient fact that, if he was going to have any hope of sleep tonight, a visit to Mrs Cornwallis's hospitable establishment was probably the simplest way of achieving it. Surely all he needed was the scent of another woman's skin, the heat of another smiling mouth under his, the skills of a professional, to rout the memory of innocently sensual beauty.

'Are you coming in?' They were already at the Henrietta Street house, pretty as a jewel box with the white porcelain flowers filling the window boxes and the shiny green front door flanked by clipped evergreens.

'No, Madame.' Despite the footman, he helped her down himself, up the steps to the front door, dropping a dutiful salute on her cheek. 'Sleep well.'

'Blackstone Mews,' he said to the coachman, climbing back in. Mrs Cornwallis would have some new girls by now. It was six weeks since he had last called.

Two hours later Eden lay back on the purple silk covers, his eyes closed. If he kept them closed, the girl probably wouldn't talk until he was ready to get up and go. He had already forgotten her name.

A fingertip trailed down his chest, circled his navel, drifted hopefully lower. His imagination made it Lady Maude's finger, with predictable results.

'Ooh!' she said with admiration that was not all professional. 'Why not stay all night?'

'I never sleep here.' Her voice chased away the image in his mind. Eyes open, Eden rolled off the bed and reached for his breeches.

'Oh.' Another woman who could manage an audible pout. 'But you'll ask for me next time?'

'No. I never ask for the same girl twice.' No entanglements, no expectations. No messy emotions on her part. Certainly no night spent with her in his arms, waking up off guard and vulnerable.

'But I thought you liked me…' And she had that wheedling tone off to perfection too. He kept his back to the bed as he fastened his shirt. Madame, cajoling over her millinery bill, actresses fluttering their eyelashes as they tried to persuade him to give them a role, those simpering Corwin girls in pursuit of a husband. Did every female in existence, he thought irritably, have to coax like that? It occurred to him that Lady Maude had been admirably direct. No simpering, pouting or wheedling from her. What, he wondered, did *she* want from him?

'Good night.' Eden did not look back as he went out of the door.

Chapter Three

Eden Hurst was pacing like one of the caged lions at the Tower. *No*, Maude silently corrected herself. Those animals were confined behind bars. However menacing they looked, with the muscles bunching under their sleek hides and the flash of white fangs, they were impotent.

This man was free. This man made things happen, just as she had sensed he would. He turned from checking a ledger someone had handed him and Maude moved back between the flats, stumbling slightly over the grooves they ran in. The paperwork dismissed, Hurst strode to the front of the stage and began a highly technical discussion with someone invisible in the pit about the placing of the instrumental players to achieve a certain required effect.

He had discarded his coat and rolled up his sleeves. There was no sign of last night's exaggerated tailoring, unless one counted the very whiteness of the linen shirt that made his skin even more golden in contrast and the expensive cut of his pantaloons and waistcoat. There were no diamonds in his ear today, just the ring to give emphasis when he swept a hand down in a gesture to reinforce his orders.

Maude found her eyes fixed on the point where his waist-coat had been laced at the small of his back, emphasising the balance between broad shoulders and narrow waist, slim hips and long legs.

Now he put his fists on his hips and leaned back to stare up into the gods to where a hand was shouting a query. The line of his throat was that of a Greek statue, she thought.

'Extraordinarily beautiful animal, isn't he?' a dispassion-ate male voice asked, just by her ear.

Maude felt herself colouring: she could hardly deny to herself how she had been looking at him. 'Mr Hurst appears very fit,' she said repressively, turning to find one of the walking gentlemen at her elbow.

'I'm not interested in him *that* way, you understand,' the man continued, still watching his employer through narrowed eyes. Maude tried to appear sophisticated and unshocked at the suggestion he might be *interested*. 'I just wish I could move like that. I watch and watch, but I'm damned if I can get it. New, are you? Nice gown, by the way. My name's Tom Gates, walking gentleman and hopeful juvenile lead if that clot Merrick upsets the apple cart.'

Maude regarded him with some interest. He looked about twenty-one, but from a distance, with make-up, she could see he could easily pass for a lad of seventeen. 'Thank you, it is one of my favourite gowns. I'm sure you'd make a very good juvenile lead. Is Mr Merrick prone to trouble, then?'

'He will be if he doesn't stop lifting La Golding's skirts,' Tom confided frankly. 'Either Susan Poole will run him through with a hat pin or the guv'nor will have his balls for making trouble in the cast. What's your line, then? Too classy to be a walking lady, I'd have said.'

'I am not an actress, I'm an investor,' Maude explained,

watching the blood drain from the young man's face as he realised his *faux pas*. 'I am early for a business meeting with Mr Hurst.'

'Oh. My. God.' He smote his forehead dramatically. 'Should I go and pack my bags now, do you think? Let me see, have I remembered everything I said that you'll be complaining about?'

'Lady Maude. Gates? Be so good as to explain what will cause her ladyship to complain to me.' Eden Hurst was standing right behind them, his expression one of polite interest. Maude thought that it was just how a shark would look before sampling one's leg.

'Good morning, Mr Hurst. There is absolutely nothing to be concerned over. I arrived somewhat early and Mr Gates has been so helpful in explaining things, but he seems conscience-stricken because he forgot to address me by my title. I do not regard it at all.' She shared a sweet smile between both men. Gates shot her a look of adoring thanks, Mr Hurst merely raised one eyebrow in a manner calculated to infuriate anyone else who could not manage the same trick.

'I'll get your coat, Guv'nor.' Gates shot across the stage like a retriever and returned with the garment, brushing it assiduously. His complexion had returned to normal.

'Thank you. Have refreshments sent to my office.' Hurst took her arm. 'Alone again, Lady Maude?'

'My maid is waiting in the Green Room.' Maude had left Anna there, wide-eyed in anticipation of witnessing some of the scandalous behaviour she was convinced must go on in such a wicked place. So far, Maude imagined she had been seriously disappointed. The language might be colourful, but everyone was focused totally on their work. Mr Hurst ran a tight ship.

'I will leave the door open, then.' He showed her in, gesturing to the chair she had sat in the night before.

'Why? Do you fear you may be unable to restrain your animal impulses again, Mr Hurst?' Maude sat and placed a folder of papers on the desk.

Behind her the door shut with a sharp click. She pursed her lips to restrain the smile; it was part of her strategy to keep Eden Hurst on edge and she did appear to be undermining that control, just a little. 'I was not failing, Lady Maude, and I was not acting upon impulse. I fully intended to do what I did. I always do.'

'Excellent. So do I. And I prefer to keep my personal business confidential, so do, please, leave the door shut.'

She waited, hands folded demurely in her lap while he circled the desk and sat down on his sorcerer's throne. He steepled his fingers, elbows on the carved arms, and regarded her in silence. The light from the window was behind him, no doubt intentionally. Maude, who had trained in the hard school of the Almack's patronesses, waited, outwardly unruffled. Inwardly her stomach was executing acrobatics that would have impressed at Astley's Amphitheatre.

'In what way may I help you, Lady Maude?'

She felt she had scored a point by not babbling to fill the silence. She wanted to babble. She wanted him to kiss her again. She wanted to climb into that big chair and curl up against him. 'By moving my chair to the side of your desk, Mr Hurst. I dislike holding a conversation with someone whose face I cannot see.'

Without a word he got to his feet, came round the desk again, waited for her to rise and then moved the chair. 'Here?' How many people challenged him on his own ground? Would it impress him or merely irritate?

'Excellent, thank you.' Unasked, he moved her papers too, then shifted his chair so he could face her.

'I wish to invest in the Unicorn, Mr Hurst.'

'Indeed.' *Damn him, he might at least look faintly surprised.* How many unmarried ladies did he have coming in offering him money? 'And what makes you think I require investors, ma'am?'

'I have heard some gossip to that effect and I should imagine all theatres need funds. And Miss Corwin tells me her father is thinking of investing with you.' His mouth twisted wryly for a second, whether at the thought of Miss Corwin or of her father, Maude was not certain.

'And what does *your* father think of this, might I ask?'

'I have not discussed it with him as yet. Mr Hurst, I am five and twenty and I have had control of my own money for some time.' An exaggeration—it was only since last year, in fact, when Papa had recognised that withholding control of it was not going to force her into the marriage with Gareth Morant, Lord Standon.

A gallant man would have exclaimed in surprise at her claiming such advanced years. It surprised Maude herself sometimes to realise how old she was and to acknowledge that most people would consider her almost on the shelf. Eden Hurst made no reference to her age at all. Now, was that galling or refreshing?

'I have always been interested in the theatre, so this seemed an obvious thing to do. I am not intending to over-commit myself, I realise this is a risky business, however well run.' That earned her an inclination of his head. Still no smile. The shark appeared to be circling, perhaps puzzled about what kind of prey had swum into its territory.

'You have been a leading light in country-house amateur

theatricals, no doubt, Lady Maude?' The way he said her name made her swallow hard, every time. It was difficult to define just why. Something about the deep voice, perhaps, the touch of mockery she sensed behind the respectful address. Or was it just that she was so close and they were, at long last, talking?

'I cannot act for toffee,' she admitted with a smile. 'As my family and friends always point out to me. No, my strengths lie in writing and producing dramas.'

'Well, you are not writing or producing any in my theatre, let us be quite clear about that.' So, the first sign of hackles rising. She was reminded of prints she had seen of Italian Renaissance princes, hard, handsome, elegant men staring out at the watcher in their pride and their power. Or perhaps, as those dark eyes narrowed and the sensual line of his mouth thinned, he was not an earthly prince, but one of the Devil's henchmen.

Yes, the Unicorn was very much Eden Hurst's theatre. 'I do not wish to, not here—I am quite clear about the differences between amateur and professional theatre. I propose investing a sum of money. Our respective men of business can assess it as a percentage of the value of the business and I will thereafter take the appropriate share of the profits.'

'Or losses.'

'Or losses,' she agreed equably. He had lowered his hands and now each curved over the lion masks at the end of the chair arms. He had big hands, she noticed, with long, elegant fingers. The well-kept nails contrasted with bruises and cuts on the backs of his hands, presumably from handling scenery. The contrast between strength and sensitivity was somehow arousing. Those were the fingers that had held her helpless with such negligent ease. Maude dragged her eyes away.

'So you do allow a man of business to act for you?'

'Of course. I believe in employing experts as I need them. Well? Does my proposal interest you?'

He did not answer her question directly. 'And what involvement will you require?'

'To see the books. To visit behind the scenes and watch rehearsals. To discuss policy and to put forward my ideas. But hardly to direct policy—you are the owner of the Unicorn, after all.'

There was a tap at the door and it swung open to reveal a large tea tray dwarfing the young woman who carried it. 'I've raided Madame's best tea, Guv'nor. Tom Gates said to make an effort.'

'Thank you, Millie. I am sure you have.' He waited until the door closed again. 'Perhaps you would care to pour, Lady Maude.'

He waited while Maude busied herself with the tea things, then settled back, his cup unregarded on the desk. 'How much, exactly, are you proposing to invest?'

She had given it a great deal of thought. Enough to make him take her seriously and to give her an entrée to the theatre and its management. Enough to give her every excuse to enter into his professional life on a regular basis. But not so much she would seem foolish or rash. Maude flipped open her folder and slid a paper across the table. 'That much.'

There was silence for a long moment. Eden Hurst picked up the sheet and tapped it thoughtfully on the desk. 'A not insignificant sum.'

'I am a wealthy woman, Mr Hurst. That is the maximum that will be available. I do not regard this as a frivolous amusement to be pouring money into, you understand.'

'I do. And you calculated your investment on your understanding of the value of a theatre I own.'

'Yes.'

'Then I am afraid your research was not thorough enough, Lady Maude. I am not the owner of the Unicorn.'

'You are not?' He watched with interest the effect surprise had upon her. Those delicately arched brows shot up, a faint groove appeared between them. Then he saw her begin to think and speculate, the big brown eyes alive with intelligence. 'It belongs to Madame Marguerite?'

'No. I have to confess I have no idea who owns it. I deal with their agents, I pay the rent, I observe the lease conditions and I am met with a very polite refusal when I ask to meet their principal.'

'How very mysterious.' Another expression, one of lively curiosity, flitted across her face. That lovely visage was as easy to read as a book, but only, he suspected, when she wanted it to be. He was convinced that last night, after he had kissed her, her feelings were far from being reflected in her expression. In fact, he was beginning to wonder if she used that openness as a weapon to make him underestimate her.

Her dazzling smile took him by surprise. 'Well, then, Mr Hurst, we must buy it.'

'What? The Unicorn? *We* must?'

'Can you afford it alone?' This was frank speaking indeed. Eden contemplated snubbing her by loftily remarking that he had no intention of discussing his financial position with her, then caught himself. He was enjoying this meeting. There was no one he could discuss business with, not on equal terms. Madame merely wanted to know if there was sufficient money to maintain her lifestyle; his banker and his solicitor expected only to take orders and to offer advice when asked.

The small circle of men he admitted to anything approaching friendship were either too interested in his business for comfort if they were from the merchant class or completely uninterested if they were gentlemen. He had become used to taking all decisions alone, arguing problems out with himself.

And now here was, of all things, a young lady. Bright-eyed, confident, interested and quite unabashed at being alone with a man, speaking of things ladies were simply not expected to understand. And, miracle of miracles, she did not simper, she did not wheedle and she most certainly did not try to cajole.

Eden smiled. Lady Maude blushed, which was unexpected. Hastily he resumed a straight face. The last thing he wanted was for her to think he was flirting with her. Not after last night. 'No,' he responded frankly. 'I cannot afford to buy it alone just now. At least, not without committing myself more than is prudent.'

'And are you always prudent, Mr Hurst?' There was a laugh lurking in her eyes. Was she thinking about last night? He wished he was not, it was too damn uncomfortable.

'With money, yes,' he admitted and the answering smile made the corner of her eyes crinkle. Yes, she had been thinking about last night. So why had she blushed earlier?

Eden was used, without vanity, to women reacting strongly to his looks, although he saw to it that they never got close enough to him emotionally to react to the man behind that handsome face. His appearance was nothing to be proud of, in his opinion. He owed his looks to the father who had refused to have anything to do with him. As for the rest, he took care of his body, exercised hard and spent more than he needed on his clothes.

But Lady Maude was not flirting. She had reacted to his kiss with a mixture of innocence and appreciation that was arousing, yet her response afterwards had been that of an assured young matron and now… Now he had no idea how to read her. Which ought to be infuriating, not intriguing.

He realised that he must have been silent, thinking, for over a minute. Unperturbed, Lady Maude had opened her portfolio and was scribbling energetically. When she saw he was back with her she smiled, the uncomplicated smile of a friend. 'I will need to rework these figures, for I am sure my banker will tell me I should not invest so much if you do not own the Unicorn. It is very vexing—you must press for information about the owner.'

'I have tried; it is not going to be forthcoming.'

She sent him a look that said clearly that he had not exerted himself sufficiently in the matter. She was wrong. Ever since he was fourteen he had wanted his own theatre. Not a little provincial playhouse, but a significant, fashionable, demanding theatre to satisfy the longing that had entered him the first time he had set foot on a stage, the sense that he had come home. He had found the Unicorn and had known that this was love and that this was the only passion he could, or would, ever trust. But he could not speak of that to a near-stranger, or try and justify an emotion he only half-understood himself.

'Lady Maude, have you considered what Lord Pangbourne is going to say when he knows what you are doing?'

'Of course. He said I was old enough to make my own mistakes with my own money.' She hesitated, her eyes sliding away from his. 'Some time ago…he wanted me to marry someone; he had wanted it for years, in fact. Neither the gentleman nor I wished for it and things became—' she broke off, searching for a word '—*complicated*, before Papa understood how things were. He has always been somewhat unconventional in his attitude to women's education and freedoms. What happened has made him somewhat indulgent in many ways.'

So, not only was she intelligent, but she was also strong

enough to stand up to parental pressure over her marriage. And now, at twenty-five, the Marriage Mart would consider her on the shelf, or almost so. Or was the daughter of an earl, wealthy in her own right, ever on the shelf? Perhaps she had grounds for her confidence.

'He may be indulgent about how you invest your money, but he is not going to be so if he knows you are alone with me in my office, is he?'

That appeared to amuse her. 'Do you imagine he will call you out, Mr Hurst?'

'I imagine he will want to horsewhip me. I am not, after all, a gentleman, and therefore would not merit a challenge.'

Maude looked at him, her eyes wide and steady. 'Yes, you are, in every way that counts. Or I would not be here.'

Her certainty knocked the breath out of him. He was accepted, to a point, in society as an intelligent, personable exotic. He could imagine the reaction if he so much as flirted with one of the young ladies on the Marriage Mart. And they, he was quite certain, would have had him pointed out by their mamas as completely ineligible, if not dangerous. Yet Lady Maude appeared to have no such scruples.

'I will speak to my man of business tomorrow and amend my figures,' she continued. 'Would it be convenient to call in a few days' time?'

'I should not—' He meant to say, *I should not be doing business with you*, but it came out differently. 'I should not expect you to come here. Could I not meet you at his office? It would be safer, surely?'

'For whom?' she enquired, suddenly very much Lady Maude and not the unconventional young woman conducting her own negotiations. 'I feel quite safe. Are *you* frightened of something?'

Eden drew in a deep breath, ignored the interestingly unsafe suggestions his body was making. 'For myself, I fear nothing and nobody, Lady Maude.' He let a chill harden his voice. He could not act, had never wanted to, but he had grown up surrounded by good actors and learned a trick or two. When he wanted to, he could intimidate and he found that useful.

Her lashes swept down to hide her thoughts, and he thought he had shaken her. Then she lifted her eyes and murmured, 'Good. I will hold you to that.' She closed her portfolio and got to her feet, smiling with ladylike composure as he rose to open the door. 'I will send a note and come back here next week to discuss how to proceed.'

'You will attend the first night of our new play?'

'On Monday? I am looking forward to it. You will be putting on a ballet and a farce for the intervening nights, I assume?'

'Yes. Trifling things, but I do not care to have the theatre dark.' He looked down at her and knew he had to take control of this situation, whatever it was. 'Lady Maude. Unless you tell Lord Pangbourne of your intentions, I must decline to discuss this matter further with you.'

For a moment he thought she would admit defeat and did not know whether to be relieved or disappointed. 'You make terms, Mr Hurst?' she asked, her face unreadable.

'That is what businessmen do.'

She stood there, one hand in its tight kid glove resting on the door frame, quite clearly thinking. 'Mr Hurst, do you want me to take my money and go away?'

'It would be safer for your reputation and it would certainly make life simpler,' he said honestly.

'That is not what I asked you,' she said, managing to look down her nose at him, a considerable feat considering their respective heights.

'No,' Eden said, surprising himself. 'No, I do not want you to go away. After all, I have so little in my life to worry about as it is. You will doubtless be the grit in my oyster.' She glared in response to his sarcasm. To his horror he found himself thinking about kissing her face back into smiles. 'But I mean it. Tell Lord Pangbourne before this goes any further. I want your word on it.'

'My word, Mr Hurst?' Her chin came up as she gathered her skirts in one hand. 'You have it, sir. Good day to you.'

Chapter Four

Maude cupped her chin in her palm and regarded her father thoughtfully. For once they were both at the breakfast table at the same time, he having declared that he was not going to the House that day and she deciding it would be good tactics to forgo her usual early morning ride in Hyde Park in order to speak to him about the Unicorn.

She had spent an uncomfortable night fearing Eden's scruples had overturned all her plans right at the outset.

'Papa?' He seemed to be in a good mood. His perusal of the *Morning Post* and *The Times* had provoked only half a dozen exclamations of wrath and he had not yet screwed up any of his morning correspondence and lobbed it at the fireplace.

'Yes, my dear?' He folded his paper and laid it beside the plate. 'When your mother addressed me in that tone, she usually had some fixed purpose in mind.'

'Well, and so I have. You recall saying I might have the control of my money unless I wanted to do something foolish with it and you would rely on Mr Benson to warn you if I did appear to be doing just that?'

'I believe I said something of that nature,' he responded,

wary. 'Rainbow, that will be all. I will ring if I need anything.'

The butler bowed, nodded at his subordinates to follow him and left them alone.

'Tell me. I am braced for the worst.' Lord Pangbourne folded his hands over his stomach.

'You know the Unicorn theatre?'

'I should do, since you rent a box there and we have visited regularly since it reopened.'

'You will have noticed that it is one of the best of the non-Patent theatres and that the manager, Mr Hurst, has been improving it.'

'The gas lighting, yes.'

'I wish to invest in it.' She sat back and tried to look calm, as though she had asked if she should buy government bonds, or some rental property in a good area. Her fingers hurt; she found they were knotted into her napkin. Maude frowned at them and made herself relax.

'In gas lighting? I believe that could well be the coming thing.' He lifted the newspaper. 'There are some companies advertising here, in fact—'

'In the Unicorn, Papa.' Time for complete frankness. Almost. 'I wish to invest a sum in the theatre and to take an interest in its overall policy. I find it most interesting.'

'The theatre? But, Maude, that is not at all a respectable world, not on that side of the curtain. It is inhabited by the demi-monde and frequented by gentlemen who are not there because of their interest in the dramatic arts—I am sure I need not say more. For a woman to be connected with the stage is to court ruin. It is quite out of the question.'

'I do not want to appear *on* the stage, Papa,' Maude said. 'That *would* be a scandal indeed—think how bad my acting is! And I most certainly do not want to be behind the scenes when the gentlemen come calling in the evening. I can quite see what a risk that would be.'

He was frowning at her, bless him. He did try so hard to let her be herself. Maude knew she was indulged, far beyond what most single young women of her background were. And she knew too that her position meant that what would be condemned as outrageously fast if done by, say, the daughter of an obscure baronet, could be carried off with dash by the daughter of an earl.

'What about your charity work?' Lord Pangbourne asked. 'Are Lady Belinda's wounded soldiers no longer absorbing your time?'

'Of course, I have a committee meeting this afternoon. But it is hardly a full-time occupation, Papa.'

'And the Season will soon be in full swing,' he pointed out.

'Yes. And neither is that all consuming, at least, not during the day. I like to be busy, Papa, and to use my brain.'

'I would like it if you just stood still long enough for a nice young man to catch you,' Lord Pangbourne said with a sigh. 'I suppose you want me to say that Benson should call on this manager chap—Hurst, is it?—and suggest a basis for your investment.'

'Yes, Mr Hurst. But I have already called upon him and proposed my scheme.'

His lordship choked on his coffee and put his cup down with enough force to rattle the saucer. 'Called on him? My God, Maude, of all the shocking—'

'I took my maid, Papa, and called at the theatre in the morning, not at his home, naturally.' Maude knew she couldn't act, but she felt fairly confident in her expression of outrage.

'It is still most unwise. The man is not a gentleman. And the theatre of all places!'

'Well, his behaviour was most gentleman-like,' she asserted. 'I felt quite comfortable. I was served tea and waited upon by a maid.' That was doubtless stretching the description of the lass who was probably the general dogsbody. 'And everyone there was behaving most decorously.' If one disregarded Mr Gates's indiscretions, of course. 'Would you meet Mr Hurst and judge for yourself? I thought perhaps we could invite him to our box in the interval on Monday. You do want to see the revival of *How to Tease and How to Please*, don't you, Papa?'

It would allow Papa to judge Eden face to face and it would reassure Eden that she had spoken to her father. He would not take kindly to being summoned to the house to be inspected, she was sure of that, but on his home ground he might be less prickly. She would order champagne with the refreshments and think carefully about who to invite to join the party for the evening. No one who would be shocked by a man wearing a diamond ear stud, that was for sure.

The committee for Lady Dereham's Charity for the Employment of Soldiers Disabled by the Late War—or Bel's Battalion, as her husband irreverently referred to it—was somewhat diminished in numbers that afternoon. Bel's cousin Elinor was on the Continent with Theo Ravenhurst, her new husband; Elinor's mother Lady James Ravenhurst was studying Romanesque churches and the Grand Duchess Eva de Maubourg, a cousin by marriage, was at home in Maubourg and not expected in London until early March.

Jessica had been welcomed into the committee on her marriage. It was a positive coven of Ravenhurst cousins, her husband Gareth Morant, Earl of Standon—himself a cousin— had joked. Maude would have become a Ravenhurst if her father's intention to marry her to Gareth had come to pass and she had known most of the family since she was a child.

The Reverend Mr Makepeace, Treasurer, was already seated in Bel's dining room, fussily arranging his papers on the long mahogany table while assuring Lady Wallace, a lady of a certain age and indefatigable energies, that the money she had extracted from her long-suffering husband had been safely banked. Mr Climpson, Lady Wallace's solicitor, and legal adviser to the charity, bowed punctiliously to Maude and pulled out a chair for her while Jessica waved gaily from the other side of the room where she was talking to Bel.

The minutes read, and matters arising dealt with, they sat through Mr Makepeace's interminable report. Maude surfaced from a daydream involving Eden Hurst and herself alone in her box at the Unicorn to discover that the charity was in excellent financial health.

'In fact, our only problem at the moment appears to be finding other sources of employment for the men on our books,' Jessica remarked. 'We have bought three inns now, which employ all those suited for the various roles those offer.' She scanned the lists in front of her. 'We have placed sixteen men with various craftsmen and a further twelve in domestic service or stables, but there are still fifteen unsuited and, as you know, more come to us every week, despite the war being over now for almost two years.'

'What about theatres?' Maude asked, the idea coming straight out of her daydream. 'Stage-hands, door-keepers, scene painters, carpenters—there must be many types of work the men would be suitable for.'

'Excellent,' Lady Wallace applauded, shushing Mr Makepeace, who started to say something about immorality. 'What a clever idea, Lady Maude.'

'But however will we find out what is available?' Jessica asked, all wide-eyed innocence. 'Who can we *possibly* ask?'

'It just so happens,' Maude said, attempting to kick her friend under the table and painfully finding the table leg instead, 'I know someone who might be able to help.'

'I was going to ask you and Gareth to join me in my box on Monday,' she said to Jessica as the others departed. 'And then you could have met Mr Hurst because he is taking champagne with Papa and me during the interval.' At least, she hoped he was; she hadn't written to him yet. 'But if you are going to be so unkind as to tease me, I will ask Bel and Ashe instead.'

'Ask us what?' Bel came back into the room and eased herself down on a chair. 'Oh, my feet! I have been playing with Annabelle all morning and I am quite worn out with that meeting on top of it.'

'How exhausting can playing with a baby be?' Maude demanded. 'She's tiny.' A doting expression came over Bel's face, so she added hastily, 'Anyway, will you and Ashe be able to come to the theatre with us on Monday?'

'We'd love to. Your box at the Unicorn? Do you mind if we bring another gentleman with us? Ashe has a navy friend coming to spend a few nights.' She looked up, obviously making connections. 'Is that where you think you may be able to find employment for some of the men?'

'Possibly. I am intending to invest in the theatre and Papa wishes to meet the manager before he will support me.'

'I should think he does.' Bel narrowed her eyes. 'You are up to something, Maude Templeton.'

'As I said, investing. Of course, it *is* somewhat unconventional,' Maude said airily.

'And of course Mr Hurst of the Unicorn is very good

looking,' Jessica added slyly. 'Gareth and I are definitely coming on Monday. I'm not missing this for anything.'

'No!' Bel sat up straighter, weariness forgotten. 'Hurst? But surely I have heard of him.' She bit the tip of her finger in thought. '*Eden* Hurst? But he is notorious for his *affaires* with married ladies! Ashe warned me about him, although I gather he is hardly predatory; he just stands around looking handsome and they throw themselves at him as they did at Byron. But Maude, even if he is a lay preacher in his spare time, he still has to be utterly ineligible, you wicked woman. Darling, I don't think this is sensible; he's received, but that doesn't mean you can't be ruined by associating with him.'

'I wish to invest in his company,' Maude protested, flustered that Bel had immediately leapt to the conclusion that she wanted Eden Hurst. As for his reputation—well, she refused to think about that just now.

But Bel had seen Jessica's face and Jessica knew only too well what she wanted. 'Oh, very well, Jessica will tease until you know it all anyway. I intend making Eden Hurst fall in love with me. He is intelligent, charismatic, dynamic and beautiful. When I talk to him it is not like any other conversation I have with anyone. I was right when I sensed he was meant for me; when I am with him I feel more alive than you can imagine. There is so much passion in him, so tightly controlled. Passion for the theatre, I mean,' she clarified as Jessica rolled her eyes.

'He just doesn't know yet that I am the woman for him. I intend to give him every opportunity to realise it.'

'Goodness,' Bel said weakly. 'And then what? You cannot *possibly* marry him. Think of his reputation.'

'If he marries me, he will not be having *affaires*. And why should he not marry me?' Maude demanded. 'He is very well off. And his father, I believe, was an Italian prince.'

'But was he married to Mr Hurst's mother? That's the point,' Jessica queried. 'Hurst is not exactly a Italian name, now is it?'

'Er…no.' She turned in a swirl of skirts and plumped down in a chair. 'It is no use the pair of you looking at me like that. You don't have to tell me it is going to be difficult. I want to marry an illegitimate, half-Italian theatre owner with a reputation. He is quite a *rich* illegitimate theatre owner,' she added hopefully.

'Maude,' Bel said gently. 'Money is not going to be the issue. Breeding is.'

'I have enough breeding for both of us, and he is a gentleman, even if society won't see it,' Maude declared, beginning to be alarmed despite herself. She had expected Jessica and Bel to support her.

'Yes, but what does he think about this?'

'Nothing at all, as yet, other than I am very unconventionally intending to invest with him. I have been cool and businesslike. I intend to grow upon him.'

Jessica snorted inelegantly. 'Maude, I am your friend, so I can say frankly that you are a very beautiful woman. The man has kissed you—passionately, by all accounts. And you are waiting to grow on him? I should imagine your financial assets are the last thing on his mind at the moment.'

'He has done what?' Bel's face was a picture.

'Kissed me. By accident. He thought I was someone else,' Maude explained patiently. 'It was wonderful, but he appears more than capable of restraining his animal passions when I am alone with him, believe me.'

'Oh. That's not very encouraging,' Bel said, then caught herself. 'I mean, what a good thing. To be fair, according to his reputation he does not appear to be dangerous to virgins.'

Maude determinedly ignored contemplating who else Eden

Hurst might be dangerous to. 'Well, I am not concerned. I want him to fall in love with me, gradually. Not lust after me. That, too, of course, in time, but I am sure desire clouds men's brains. Love first, then lust.'

'It doesn't work that way round,' Bel observed, smiling. Jessica nodded in agreement as she continued, 'I'm afraid the poor weak things work on the basis that anything female between the ages of sixteen and sixty is looked at with the eye of lust. One's finer features, such as your mind or your skill at the harp, or your lovely nature, have to grow upon them.'

'Oh.' Somewhat daunted, Maude regarded her two friends. 'I wanted him to be so passionately in love with me that he would disregard the difference in our positions.'

'Not if he has the gentlemanly instincts you say he has,' Jessica pointed out with depressing logic. 'If he loved you, then he would sacrifice himself by refusing to see you any more. As Bel said, he does seem to restrict himself to married women, so he has some scruples.'

'And anyway,' Bel added, 'it isn't what *he* thinks about your respective positions, it is what society thinks.'

Maude fell silent, wrestling with the conundrum. The only possible solution appeared to be to become his lover, then hope he fell in love and realised that, having hopelessly compromised her, he must marry her. But what if he did not fall in love and felt he had to offer anyway?

'This is 1817,' she said, raising her chin and meeting their sympathetic looks with determination. 'Things are changing, men with wealth and intelligence are breaking into society.'

'Merchant bankers and nabobs, maybe,' Jessica said doubtfully. 'But the theatre is simply not respectable. Not for marriage.'

'In that case,' Maude declared, getting to her feet, 'the Unicorn is going to become the first respectable theatre in the country.'

'The evening post, sir.' Eden's butler proffered the laden salver. 'Dinner will be served in thirty minutes, sir.'

'Thank you.' Eden took the pile of letters and began to flick through them. He was dining at home, alone, for the first time in weeks and finding it hard to relax. His brain was still working on too many levels. There were the remaining issues with the staging for *How to Tease*, there were the tactics to persuade Madame to take the role of Lady Macbeth and, if she did, the problem of producing a version that would not bring down the wrath of the Patent theatres and the Lord Chamberlain for performing 'legitimate' drama without a licence.

Ways of improving the scene shifting were beginning to form at the back of his mind, there was the situation between Golding, Merrick and Poole to resolve and decisions about investments to make.

Investments. He tossed the letters down on to his desk unopened. They were not normally a problem. His instructions to his broker were straightforward enough, he simply had to decide on one or two points and send a letter to the man. No, it was Lady Maude Templeton and her hare-brained desire to invest in the Unicorn that was baffling him. And Eden Hurst did not like being baffled. Challenged, yes—he enjoyed a good fight. But not baffled by a brown-eyed lady with a pointed chin, a cool manner and a staggering disregard for convention.

He wanted to make love to her. Oh, yes, he most definitely wanted that. His imagination had no trouble conjuring up the image of her naked on his big bed upstairs, that thick hair tumbling around her shoulders, her hands gripping his shoulders as he sank into the tight wet heat of her. But he also, oddly, wanted to get to know her. Understand her, not simply discover why she had come up with this madcap scheme. And why should he want to do that?

Eden gave himself a brisk mental shake and returned to his post. Bills, letters from aspiring players, the opening scenes of a play written in odd green ink… He really should get a secretary for all this.

One plain white wrapper of fine quality paper, sealed with a crest pressed into the dark blue wax; that looked more interesting. He cracked the seal and spread out the single sheet.

Lord Pangbourne requests the pleasure of Mr Hurst's company for refreshments during the second interval at the Unicorn on Monday next.

'My God, she *has* told him.' Eden stared at the invitation, reluctant admiration stirring. No sign of a horsewhip, not yet at any rate. Perhaps the earl was as unconventional as his daughter, or perhaps he thought to show her just how unsuitable a person Eden was for her to associate with by putting him into a social situation.

That was the logical answer. And in order to remove the puzzle of Lady Maude from his life, all he had to do was to turn up and act as Lord Pangbourne would expect. Eden toyed with the combination of clothing and manner that would make him appear louche, dangerous and entirely impossible.

His on-stage style was already established; he just needed to develop that to the point of caricature. He had seen enough old-school actor-managers to be able to assemble the worst characteristics of all of them. And then even the most indulgent father would take fright and bundle his daughter off out of harm's way, leaving Eden to manage his theatre in tranquillity.

He picked up the paper and as he did so the faint scent of gardenias wafted to his nostrils. So, this firm black hand was not that of the earl or his secretary. Lady Maude herself had penned it. Eden smiled thinly. Was her father even aware he was going to have a visitor to his box on Monday night?

Chapter Five

'It is fortunate that the private boxes at the Unicorn are spacious, for this one seems very full of large men tonight,' Jessica remarked to Maude on Monday evening as the Derehams entered with their guest. Lord Pangbourne, with Gareth at his side, was greeting them, giving the friends the opportunity to study Ashe's naval acquaintance.

'Why not fall for *him*?' Jessica whispered. 'He looks so distinguished in that uniform and he is very good looking and not too old either. Not more than thirty, do you think? A younger son, of course, but excellent connections. Your father would be delighted.'

'I have no interest in other men, as you very well know,' Maude hissed back, too tense to enjoy being teased. The officer was tall and rangy in his dark blue uniform, his hair close cropped, his eyes, as he turned to be introduced to the two young women, a deep and attractive blue against weather-tanned skin.

'Lady Standon, Maude, this is Captain Warnham. My lord—Lady Standon, my daughter Lady Maude.'

Greetings exchanged, the captain settled his long frame

between Maude and Jessica. 'It is a long time since I have been inside an English theatre,' he commented, looking around with interest. From the boxes opposite came the flash of light on lenses as opera glasses were raised to scrutinise comings and goings. It would be all round the *ton* before long that a handsome naval officer was newly in town.

'You have been at sea for many months?' Maude enquired, fanning herself. The theatre was crowded and the heat rising from the gas lamps added to that generated by the crowd and her own anxiety.

'Three months in the South Atlantic, ma'am. I am back for some weeks before sailing for Jamaica on another mission.'

'The West Indies? How fascinating, I have always wanted to go to those islands.' Maude, her twitching nerves over Eden momentarily forgotten, leaned closer. 'They always sound so romantic and exotic.'

Captain Warnham smiled. 'They have their charms, I am sure, but they also have slavery, hurricanes, tropical disease and pirates.'

'And sunshine and blue seas and parrots and waving palm trees,' Maude said wistfully, thinking of the drizzle that affected London.

'My husband and Lady Belinda have a cousin in Jamaica, do you not, Bel?' Jessica raised her voice to catch Bel's attention.

'Jamaica? Yes, Clemence Ravenhurst. We are expecting her father to bring her over to England this summer to stay so she can have an English come-out next Season. I expect your ships will pass in mid-Atlantic, Captain.'

They began to chat, Bel and Gareth explaining what they knew about their youngest uncle, a highly successful West Indies merchant.

Now he *is in trade*, Maude thought resentfully. *The*

youngest son of a duke and no one thinks the worse of him for it. But, of course, Lord Clement Ravenhurst was a very successful man and did not soil his own hands with the details of his luxury goods business. Presumably wealth and birth wiped out the stain of trade, if you had sufficient of both.

'What a pity he will not be at home when you are there, Captain Warnham,' Bel concluded. 'We would have given you letters of introduction.'

The orchestra began to file into the pit and tune up, earning catcalls and jeers for the cacophony from the common folk up in the one-shilling gallery. The noise gradually subsided back to the usual hubbub and then the lights were dimmed and the curtain rose on the first piece of the evening, a short farcical item featuring the company heavy as a strict father, thwarted at every turn by the ingenious antics of his daughter's suitors.

'I have every sympathy with the fellow,' Lord Pangbourne remarked as the furious father chased a young man over a balcony while, behind his back, another rake took advantage and snatched a kiss from the daughter. Maude recognised Tom Gates, the ambitious walking man, who whisked out of sight behind a convenient curtain in the nick of time.

'It is an ingenious piece,' Captain Warnham agreed, laughing at the business between the cast, the maid changing clothes with her mistress, while the two young men dressed as footmen and the baffled father searched frantically for his daughter. In a few minutes the happy couple escaped down a rope ladder, the remaining suitor consoled himself with the maid and the curtain came down on appreciative applause.

There was a short interval before the next piece, a ballet. Maude reviewed her preparations for the main interval: canapés, champagne, two small tables to be brought in and the seats rearranged. But who to place where?

She wanted her father to appreciate Eden's strong points, not be distracted by long hair or diamond ear studs or over-emphatic tailoring. Perhaps best not to place him next to the clean-cut Lord Warnham in his dress uniform. Between Bel and Jessica then…

'You are muttering,' Jessica said.

'I want you and Bel to sit either side of Mr Hurst,' Maude whispered back. 'I don't want him sitting next to Captain Warnham and making Papa think of haircuts.'

'I think the length of his hair is the least of his problems.'

One step at a time, Maude told herself, sitting through the ballet in such a state of abstraction that she would have been hard pressed to say whether there had been dancers or circus horses on stage if questioned afterwards.

Eden's note in response to the invitation had arrived, punctiliously prompt and formal. But would he really come?

The waiter came in with the refreshments and, on his heels, a tall figure, dark against the brightness of the open doorway.

'Standon, my dear fellow, would you—?' Lord Pangbourne broke off in confusion, realising that the man he thought he was addressing was still seated to his left. The figure moved, the light fell across his face and Maude let out a long, inaudible sigh. Eden.

Her father got to his feet, ponderous and, for all his formal good manners, wary. 'Mr Hurst?'

'My lord.' He came in, as the waiter closed the door behind him, and inclined his head to his host.

'Allow me to make you known to Lady Dereham, Lady Standon, my daughter Lady Maude—'

Papa is pretending we have not met, Maude realised, returning the bow with slight curtsy, while her father completed the introductions and waved Eden to the chair by his side.

And then she realised what was different about him. Gone was the exotic theatre manager, gone too was the working man in his shirtsleeves, and in their place was a perfectly conventional gentleman in well-cut evening formality, a modest ruffle on his white shirt, the dull sheen of garnet satin on his waistcoat and just a hint of sparkle in the strange old ring, his only piece of jewellery. Even his hair had been ruthlessly pomaded and brushed into a fashionable style that distracted the eye from its length.

He is making an effort, she thought, astonished. It had never occurred to her that Eden Hurst might go out of his way to impress her father. Was it because he needed the money, or because he did not want to lose her as…as what? An investor? That was all she could be to him at the moment, surely?

Lord Pangbourne, nobody's fool, even though he cultivated an appearance of bluff and bluster, had apparently realised that he could hardly explain to a boxful of guests, one of whom was a virtual stranger, that he had invited Mr Hurst there to interview him as a potential business partner for his daughter. He had also, while introductions had been made, managed things so that the men were all sitting to one side of the box and Maude was safely trapped between the other two ladies.

She realised, with sinking heart, that Bel and Jessica had not exaggerated the unconventionality of what she was doing. Gareth and Ashe were regarding Eden with expressions of politely neutrality, but she knew them both too well to be deceived. They were watchful and suspicious and, she feared, disapproving.

'Good of you to join us,' her father remarked, pouring champagne. 'I'm very interested in this new gas lighting you have here. Thinking of installing it myself. What do you think?'

'I would not put it in my own home, not just yet.' Eden took the glass, but did not drink. Close to the naval officer's tanned skin his colouring seemed less exotic. He looked and sounded just like the rest of them, yet he was the focus of more than polite attention. 'There is an odour, and it is dangerous without proper ventilation. But, in a year or two, I think it will replace oil everywhere.'

Captain Warnham, for whom this was apparently the first sight of gas used inside, joined in the conversation with a remark about the gas lights installed on Westminster Bridge in 1813 and all four men were soon deep into the technicalities.

Maude rolled her eyes at her friends, but Bel smiled and nodded encouragement. And, yes, superficially it was a success. They could have been any group of gentlemen engrossed in discussion, but she sensed relief all round at such a neutral topic that could distance the men from the ladies.

Eden, she realised, had muted his forceful character. He deferred to the older man, held his own with the others, yet it was as though he had turned down the wick on the lamp of his personality.

Clever, Maude thought. He is adapting himself to his company, blending in. She met his eyes across the table. His expression hardly changed, yet she sensed rueful amusement. He knew exactly what he was doing, but he did not seem entirely happy that he was doing it. And he sensed the raised hackles of the other men.

'We are neglecting the ladies,' he remarked, bringing all eyes to where his gaze was resting, her face.

'But I am *fascinated* by gas lighting,' she said sweetly, all wide-eyed feminine attentiveness. His lips were definitely quirking now. It was infectious. She bit the inside of her lip to stop herself smiling back. 'Still, we do not have that much time before the curtain rises again. Will you not tell us about the next piece? My father saw it the last time it was produced in London.'

'In 1810 at Covent Garden, my lord? We have had to adapt it here, of course, because of the licence, add a short ballet, and some songs, hence our choice of Mrs Furlow in the lead; she has just the voice for it. Still, it is very much the same comedy you will recall from before.' He uses his voice like an actor, Nell thought, listening to how he spoke, not what he said. It was a deep and flexible voice, shaded with colour. He seemed to have it as much under his control as his face, betraying only what he wanted to show.

Her father was relaxing now; she saw his shoulders shake as he recounted some piece of amusing business from the production he remembered.

The conversation moved on while she was brooding. Gareth must have asked Captain Warnham about his new ship. 'Do you welcome another commission so far from home?'

'I am a career officer, I go where I am ordered and may do most good, but in any case I could not turn down the opportunity to make war on pirates. They are everything I loathe.'

'But are there any left?' Maude asked. 'Enough to be a problem?'

'Not so many now, we have them under control in many areas. But those that remain are the worst of them. And like rats they know we almost have them cornered and that makes them the more vicious. They used to take prisoners for ransom; now they cut their throats and throw them overboard.'

The party fell silent, chilled, Maude sensed, not so much by the horror of what he was describing, but the controlled anger with which he said it.

Bel, the more experienced hostess, picked up the thread of the conversation after a heartbeat had passed and moved them on to safer ground. 'I love to read the shipping news in the daily papers,' she remarked. 'It is so fascinating to see where they have come from to reach us, bearing our luxuries all that way.'

All those luxuries, Maude thought, unfurling her Chinese fan and looking at it with new eyes, brought over huge distances at such risk. She looked up and found Eden was still watching her and was visited by the odd idea that he knew what she was thinking. Then the imagined look of understanding was gone and he rose to his feet.

'You will excuse me, my lords, ladies. The curtain rises soon.' He bowed and was gone, his champagne untouched, leaving the crowded box feeling somehow empty.

'What a pleasant man,' Bel remarked, carefully not looking in Maude's direction. 'Not at all what I would have expected of a theatre proprietor.'

'Indeed not,' Jessica added. 'One can only think that the theatre is becoming so much more respectable these days.'

'Superficially, perhaps. But it is scarcely eight years since the riots over the changes at Covent Garden,' Gareth countered. 'Nor can one call that sort of thing *respectable*.' He nodded towards the box opposite where a party of bucks were becoming very familiar indeed with three young women whose manners and clothing clearly proclaimed them to be of the *demi-monde*. Gareth appeared quite unconscious of the dagger-looks his wife was darting in his direction.

'And matters will be laxer on the Continent, I have no doubt,' Ashe added, his eyes resting on the door as though he could still see Eden.

'Oh, look,' said Maude with bright desperation, 'Here come the string players.' Across from her, Lord Pangbourne appeared sunk in thought.

* * *

'What did you think, Papa?' Maude ventured as the carriage clattered over the wet cobbles on its way back to Mount Street.

'Excellent production. In my opinion, adding the songs helped it. It was a lot livelier than I remembered.'

'Not the play, Papa, although I am pleased you enjoyed it. Mr Hurst.'

'Surprising chap. Not what I expected.' Lord Pangbourne fell silent.

'And?'

'And I need to sleep on it.' He sighed gustily. 'Confound it, Maude, I know I promised you more freedom, but I don't know what your mother would say if she were here.'

'*Yes*, probably,' Maude ventured. 'She was very unconventional, was she not, Papa?'

'Very fast, you mean,' he said, but she could hear he was smiling. 'Your mama, my dear, was a handful. And so are you. I don't like refusing you anything, Maude; I promised your mother I would never make you feel as she did as a girl— caged. But I don't want to see you hurt too.'

'Hurt?' She swallowed hard. He realised her feelings were involved?

'By any kind of scandal. You can ride out a lot in your position, but that's an uncommon man you'd be dealing with.' *He certainly is…* 'I'll sleep on it,' he pronounced. And with that she knew she would have to be satisfied.

It was not until she was sitting up in bed an hour later that what he had said about her mother sank in. *I don't want to see you hurt too.* Mama had been hurt? But by what? Or whom?

Breakfast was not a good time to ask questions about the past, Maude decided, pouring coffee and schooling herself to patience. It would take three cups and the first scan of *The Times* before she could expect anything from her father.

'Well,' he said, pushing back his chair at length and fixing her with a disconcertingly direct look. 'I was impressed by that Hurst fellow, despite myself. You may invest in that theatre, to the limit that Benson advises, and not a penny more. You will not go backstage after four in the afternoon and you will always, *always*, go there with a chaperon. He might be a good imitation of a gentleman, but he's young, he's ruthless and he's unconventional. A chaperon at all times—is that clear, Maude? I see no reason to be telling all and sundry about this involvement of yours either.'

'Yes, Papa.' *Oh, yes, Papa!* 'Thank you. I do believe this will be a worthwhile investment.'

'It will be if it makes you happy, my dear. Just be prudent, that is all I ask.'

Prudent. That was what Eden declared himself to be, with money at least. Men seemed to set great store by prudence. Maude's lips curved. Now she had to teach him to be imprudent with his heart. This morning she would write and tell him she had her father's approval, make an appointment to call with Mr Benson.

Chapter Six

Papa had not been speaking lightly when he had insisted upon a chaperon, Maude thought, torn between amusement and annoyance. Anna, her Sunday best hat squarely on top of her curly mop of hair, was seated in one corner of Eden Hurst's office, an expression of painful intensity on her face.

As they had alighted from the closed carriage—the one without the crest on the door, Maude had noticed—the maid had assured her, 'I'll stick like glue, never you fear, my lady.'

'Like glue?' Maude paused on the step up to the stage door and stared at the girl.

'His lordship said so. He told me he was relying upon me to maintain the proprieties.' Anna nodded earnestly, her face pink with combined delight at having been spoken to so and alarm at her responsibilities.

'Indeed.' Thoughtful, Maude walked in and smiled at the door-keeper. 'Mr Hurst is expecting me. There will be a gentleman as well.'

The man consulted his ledger. 'Mr Benson, ma'am? Came in five minutes ago. I'll take you through, ma'am, if you'll just wait a minute while I get the boy to watch the door.' Maude shook her head.

'No, it is quite all right, I know the way, Mr—?'

'Doggett, ma'am.'

'Mr Doggett. This is my maid, Anna—you will probably be seeing quite a lot of us from now on.' The man knuckled his forehead and grinned, revealing several gaps in his teeth, as they walked past.

'The stage door-keeper is an important man backstage,' Maude explained as they walked along the corridor to the Green Room. This passageway had been painted green up to the dado rail, then cream above with prints of theatrical subjects hung on the walls, no doubt in acknowledgement of the class of visitors to the Green Room. 'You will need to speak to Doggett when you want to call the carriage, or if you need to go out on an errand for me. He keeps an eye on things and makes sure no riffraff come in.'

'Yes, my lady.' Anna nodded solemnly. Maude hoped she was absorbing the idea that it would be all right to leave Maude from time to time. It was going to be impossible to establish any sort of relationship with Eden Hurst with the maid always at her side.

'You'll be able to reassure his lordship about how well run and respectable things are here,' Maude continued chattily.

'Oh, yes, my lady. I'll do that.' So, she was expecting to report back.

Bless him, Papa was no fool, however indulgent he might be, Maude thought, half her mind on the proposals Mr Benson was outlining, half on her tactics for dealing with Anna.

Eden Hurst was silent, listening. His head was bent over his hands clasped on the desk, his eyes apparently fixed on the gold tooling around the edge of the green leather top.

Benson put down his pen and sat back, too experienced to prolong his presentation.

'Reduce the return by one percent and I will consider it,' Eden said at last, looking up, his eyes clashing with hers, not the attorney's.

'By one quarter of one percent,' Maude said promptly.

The dark eyes looked black; there was no softening tilt of the lips or warmth in his voice as he responded, 'Three quarters of one percent.'

'Half.' She felt as though she had been running, the breath was tight in her chest and it was an effort to keep her voice cool and steady. This was, somehow, not about the money.

She was meticulous in keeping all hint of feminine charm out of her voice, her expression. When she was buying supplies for the charity or coaxing donations from patrons she would use whatever pretty wiles worked—wide-eyed admiration, a hint of chagrin, a touch of flirtation. But with this man she sensed they would not impress and he would think less of her for it.

'I will meet you halfway,' she added.

'Will you indeed, Lady Maude?'

'But no further.' Beside her Benson shifted, uneasy. She did not turn her eyes from Eden Hurst's face. It was like trying to outstare ice. Then slowly, subtly, she was aware of heat and realised she was blushing and that those cold, dark eyes were warming, smiling, although the rest of his face was impassive. There was no air left in her lungs now, but she was not going to give in, she was not…

Anna coughed, Benson put his pen down and the spell was broken. Which of them looked away, Maude had no idea, but Eden was on his feet, his hand extended across the wide desk. 'Come, then,' he said. 'Halfway.'

No man had ever offered her his hand to seal an agreement before. It was not done. A gentleman told her what he would do and she took his word for it. A tradesman agreed a price and bowed her from his premises. Men shook hands on deals with other men. Some instinct made her pull off her glove as she stood and took his hand. It was warm and dry and she could feel calluses on the palm as it closed around her fingers, firm, positive, but careful not to squeeze hard as it enveloped them.

A lady allowed her gloved hand to remain passive in a man's for a few seconds while he bowed respectfully and then released her, or placed her fingertips on his forearm so he could escort her. A lady did not grasp a man's hand in hers and return pressure with her naked fingers as she was doing now. He must be able to feel her pulse thudding, she was certain.

Mr Benson cleared his throat, her hand was released and they sat down as though nothing had happened. She had finalised a business arrangement—why did she feel almost as disorientated as she had when he kissed her?

'I will amend the documents now.' The attorney produced a travelling inkwell and pen and began to alter the documents before him. Maude sat silent while the nib scratched over the paper, occupying herself with removing her other glove and tucking them both into her reticule.

'There.' Mr Benson finished, pushed one set across the desk to each of them and handed his own pen to Maude. 'If you will read them through and sign, then exchange copies.'

Maude Augusta Edith Templeton, Maude wrote in her strong flowing hand. It was not a ladylike signature, her governess had complained, trying vainly to make her produce something smaller and altogether less assertive. She initialled the other pages as she had been taught and handed them to Eden, taking his in return.

Eden Francesco Tancredi Hurst, it said in writing equally as black and considerably more forceful. Maude signed below it, the sudden image of a marriage register flashing through her mind. 'Francesco Tancredi?' she said before she remembered the rumour about his father. It must be true.

'Augusta Edith?' he retorted.

'Great-aunts.' He did not respond with any explanation of his two very Italian names.

'I will call at the bank and arrange for the transfer of funds.' Mr Benson was on his feet, pushing his papers together. 'May I take you up, Lady Maude?'

'Thank you, no. I have my carriage.'

He bowed over her hand before clapping on his hat. 'My lady. Mr Hurst, I bid you good day.'

Eden stood while she sat down again. 'Would you like to see around behind the scenes now?'

'Yes, please. But first—' But first she wanted to speak to him alone and there was the small matter of one attentive lady's maid sitting like a watchdog in the corner. 'I would love a cup of tea.' Eden reached for the bell. 'Anna can go and find that little maid—Millie, wasn't it? Run along and ask Doggett at the stage door where to find her, Anna—and no gossiping with anyone else, mind.'

Trained obedience had the maid on her feet and halfway out of the door before she realised the conflict in her orders. 'But, my lady, Lord Pangbourne said—'

'And you are doing very well, Anna,' Maude praised. 'I will be sure to tell him so.'

'Yes, my lady.' Beaming, she hurried out, closing the door behind her.

'So, your father has set a watchdog to guard you? Not a very fierce one.' He strolled round the desk and hitched one hip on the edge, looking down at her.

'No, she is not, although she is very serious about it. I wanted to say thank you for Monday night.'

He did not pretend to misunderstand her. 'The counterfeit English gentleman?'

'The perfectly genuine one,' she retorted.

'Oh, yes?' He smiled down at her, the first time she had seen him really smile. His teeth were very white, very even and, like the rest of him, looked as though they would bite. Hard. 'You expected the earring, or worse, didn't you?'

'Yes,' Maude admitted. 'Actually, I rather like it, but it might have raised eyebrows.'

'I will confess I was very tempted to go completely to the other extreme and give you my version of the old-school actor-manager.'

'Why didn't you?' she asked, intrigued.

'Because, upon reflection, I found I did not want to scandalise your father to the point where he forbade you to interfere with my theatre. You are my grit, remember? I expect us to produce pearls.'

He was being deliberately provocative. Interfere, indeed! She refused to rise to it, let alone react to being compared to a piece of grit. 'Describe how you would have turned into the old-school actor-manager,' she said instead.

'A shirt with enough ruffles to make you a ballgown, very tight evening breeches and a wasp-waisted tail coat with exaggerated satin lapels.' He sketched the clothes over his body with his hands. 'I would have raided Madame's dressing room for a large diamond ear drop and her curling tongs.' He twirled a lock of shoulder-length hair between his fingers. 'A touch of lamp black to line my eyes and the oil, of course.'

'The oil?'

'Olive oil. I would have oiled my hair and my skin. Your father would have thrown you over his shoulder and swept out of the theatre, believe me.'

'I believe you,' Maude said appreciatively. 'I would like to see that look, one day. But oil?'

'I will give you some. I import it for my own use. It hardly gets used for cooking here in England, although it should be— for both cooking and salads. But Madame bathes with it, treats her hair with it. It is excellent for dry skin in winter weather.'

'But doesn't it smell horrible?' Maude wrinkled her nose, imagining all the sorts of cooking oil she had come across. The image of Eden, his naked body glistening, kept sliding into her imagination. Much better to think of nasty, smelly grease.

'Here.' He reached down into a wooden crate standing by his desk and produced a bottle full of greenish-golden liquid. 'A consignment has just come in.' The cork popped. 'Hold out your hand.'

As Maude hesitated he reached out and lifted her hand. The oil was cool as it trickled into her palm, forming a tiny pool no more than a gold sovereign's width across. 'Smell.' He set the bottle down, glimmering in the light from the window like a bottled lake of enchantment.

Her hand still cupped in Eden's, Maude dipped her head and sniffed. 'Earth and fruit and…green.'

'Taste it.'

'No.' She shook her head as though he had asked her to drink an enchanter's potion.

In response he bent and licked the little pool of oil straight from her hand. His tongue sweeping across her palm was hot, strong and utterly shocking. Maude gave a little gasp and tried to pull away, only to be held firmly. 'Careful, you will mark your gown.' He pulled a handkerchief from his pocket and wiped her palm clean. 'Are you sure you do not want to taste it?' His mouth was so close to hers, his lips slicked with the golden oil. Of course, he *could* mean he would pour her a little more.

And, yes, she wanted to taste it, warm on his lips. Summoning up reserves of willpower she had no idea she possessed, Maude said calmly, 'This is why Papa insists upon a chaperon, Mr Hurst.' He was looking deep into her eyes, his own amused, mocking. Hot.

'Wise man, Maude.'

She had dreamed of hearing her given name on his lips. Caution, tactics, pride made her stare at him haughtily. 'I have not allowed you to address me so familiarly, Mr Hurst.' She spoiled the effect somewhat by tugging at his restraining hand. 'Will you please let me go!'

He released her and went back to his own side of the desk. 'But we are partners, Maude.'

'Business partners,' she said reprovingly as the door opened to admit Anna and the maid Millie with her huge tea tray. 'Thank you, Anna. Why do you not go with Millie and find some refreshments of your own?'

The girls had placed the tea tray in front of her, so she began to pour, trying to think of some topic of conversation that would neither be stilted nor provocative.

'Your cook uses the olive oil, then?'

'My cook regards it as a foreign frippery, not to be compared to good English lard.' He took the cup and saucer, shaking his head at the proffered cream jug. 'If I want Italian food, I must cook it myself.'

'You cook?' It was unheard of.

'Country food,' Eden said with a shrug, but he was smiling with remembered pleasure, not defensively.

'*Italian* country food?' How much could she ask without revealing she had heard the rumour about his parentage? 'How very unusual.'

'I lived in an Italian palazzo until I was fourteen,' Eden said. 'In the kitchens and the stables, I should say, because that was where I was consigned. Both my cooking and my Italian are on the coarse side.'

He had grown up in his father's house, then? But with the servants? The use of the word *consigned* was both unusual and bitter. But she could risk asking no more. His face as he drank the cooling tea had become shuttered.

'May I take that tour behind the scenes now?' Maude asked. 'Or have you other business to take care of?'

'I always have business.' But Eden's grimace as he extended a long finger to ruffle the pages of the notebook that lay on the desk was amused. This was far more than an occupation for him, she realised. He loved the work, the theatre. 'And some of it can be done while we go round.'

Maude set down her cup and saucer and stood up, aware of his eyes on the sweep of her almond-green skirts. This was going so much better than she had dared hope. This was the man Jessica had described as an icicle, and yet he had let her into his theatre, allowed her a glimpse of his early life and surely, unless he was a complete rake and licked olive oil from the palm of every lady he met—surely a flirtation way out of the ordinary?—he was attracted to her. Yes, he was admiring the hemline, or perhaps it was the glimpse of ankle…

'I would suggest something less suitable for morning calls

the next time you visit,' Eden remarked, holding the door for her. 'That pale colour is highly impractical here.'

So much for him admiring the gown she had selected with such pains! But then she had somehow known it would be an uphill struggle, breaking through to the real Eden Hurst she sensed behind the façade.

Maude followed through a maze of passageways, up and down steps, trying to keep her sense of direction.

'The dressing room for the chorus.' Eden opened a door on to a deserted rectangular room, a long bench running down the middle. It had stools on either side, a row of mirrors and everywhere there was a feminine litter of pots and jars, brushes, lopsided bunches of flowers in chipped vases, stockings hanging over looking-glass frames, pairs of slippers, scraps of paper, prints and letters stuck to the walls or under the pots. It reeked of cheap perfume and the gas lighting, greasepaint and sweat. 'It is organised chaos an hour before curtain up,' he commented, closing the door again. 'The other dressing rooms are further along.

'Mrs Furlow is in here,' he added as he opened the door into the room. 'The room used by visiting leads. Madame's dressing room is just beyond.'

Maude realised there was something amiss the moment she stepped into the dressing room in front of Eden and heard the sounds. It was gloomy, with the shade drawn over the high window. In the half-light the gasps were even plainer, more disturbing than if it had been broad daylight.

Confused, Maude peered at the far side where bodies were tangled on what seemed to be a makeshift bed. Someone was being strangled—she started forward to go to their aid, then she realised that it was a couple making love, that the choking cries were a woman in the throes of ecstasy and the curved shape she could see were the naked buttocks of the man between her spread thighs.

'Out!' Eden seized her around the waist, lifted and dumped her bodily into the corridor before stalking back into the room. 'Merrick!' There was a feminine scream, a thump. Shaken but shamelessly curious, Maude applied her eye to the crack of the half-open door—then closed it hastily. A young man was pulling on his breeches. He was also gabbling something she could not catch. Cautiously Maude opened her eyes again.

'Be quiet.' That was Eden. 'I will see you in my office in half an hour.' Maude glimpsed him as he turned to face the bed, his face hard. 'Miss Golding, you will pack your bags and be out of here at once. I will have your wages made up to yesterday and sent to your lodgings.' There was a gasp, a girl's voice protesting. 'You, Miss Golding, are easy enough to replace, Merrick less so. Oh, for pity's sake, stop cowering under that sheet, girl, and get some clothes on. I am quite unmoved by your charms, believe me.'

He stepped back out into the passage, shutting the door behind him with a control that was as chilling as the look on his face. 'I am sorry you had to witness that.'

'So am I, but not half so sorry as I was to hear what you have just said,' Maude snapped. 'That poor girl you have callously dismissed—what is going to become of her now?'

Eden's dark eyes rested on her face with indifference. 'She will find a place in the chorus somewhere. Or a position on her back if that fails.'

'On her—' The crudity took Maude's breath away. Behind Eden's back the door opened and Merrick eased out, his coat bundled in his arms, and hurried away. From the room came violent sobbing. 'Poor thing, let me go and speak to her. He is just as much to blame as she—why does the woman have to take the blame?'

'No.' Eden reached out and shut the door, cutting off the sounds of distress. 'Come, back to my office; it is better if you leave before I have my interview with Merrick.'

Yes, the middle of the passageway was not the place for this conversation. Maude gathered up her skirts and stalked ahead of him in the direction he indicated. Eden Hurst was going to have an interview with her before he got anywhere near the delinquent juvenile lead.

Chapter Seven

'That was cruel and unfair.' Maude stood with her back to the desk, her fingertips pressed to its surface behind her. It was easier to confront him standing up, with some support. 'That young man probably coerced her.'

Eden came in and stood in front of her, close enough to touch, close enough for her to see the coldness that turned his eyes almost black. 'Fairness has nothing to do with it. I am running a business here. If Merrick goes, I will probably lose Susan Poole, his mistress, who is our soubrette. I can ill afford her loss at this stage in the Season, but ingénues like Harriet Golding are two a penny.' He shrugged as though that settled the matter.

'But Miss Golding is just a girl, alone. Don't you care that she might become a prostitute as a result of this?' She admired this man, was convinced she loved him. Surely he could not be this cruel? Could she have so misjudged him?

'Her choice. Merrick was not forcing her, nor has he seduced her. I have been watching them for a few days now.'

'Then you should have done something before now, she was your responsibility.' He was close, too close. Maude resisted the instinct to bend back, put one hand firmly in the middle of his chest and pushed. 'And don't crowd me, you bully.'

It was like pushing the wall. Apparently oblivious to Maude's hand planted on his chest, Eden dug into his pocket and produced his notebook, flipped it open and turned it so she could read what was written on the page.

Under *oil lamps* the definite black letters said *Merrick/ Golding/Poole*. 'Oh. Well, you should have done something sooner. Will you *please* move!'

'If I wanted to crowd you, Maude, I would get a great deal closer than this.' Eden tossed the notebook on to the table, seized her wrist and removed her hand from his waistcoat without any apparent effort. He then took one step forward. Maude tried to retreat, came up hard against the edge of the desk and swayed back. Both big hands came down on the leather, bracketing her hips, a knee forced hers apart and then he was standing between her thighs, leaning over her. 'Now *this* is crowding you.'

Maude struggled for balance, gripped his shoulders and stared, furious, up into his face. 'Let me go.'

'When you admit you were exaggerating,' he said calmly.

Maude, braced to fight, blinked. *'What?'*

'You accused me of crowding you, bullying you. This, I agree, is both. But before, no. You accuse me of unfairness and yet you spent an hour this morning with your attorney making certain this theatre was run as a business.

'I am not running the Unicorn as a recreation, Maude. I am not a gentleman, although you appear to be having trouble grasping that. This is my life and my business and I will not be indulgent with *anything* that threatens it. Harriet Golding is not some little innocent I am tossing out into the cold—she knew exactly what she was doing when she spread her legs for Merrick.'

The fact that he was standing between her own parted thighs was not lost on Maude. Nothing was, not the heat of him, the smell of him, the tightly contained anger nor the discomfort in her back, bowed over the desk. And most of all, more mortifying than all the rest, the knowledge that she wanted to pull him down to cover her body and make love to her here and now and as wantonly as those two actors.

'Very well.' She swallowed. 'I may have been a trifle… emotional about the situation, I admit. Will you please let me up now?'

Eden stepped back and she came with him, pulled by her grip on his shoulders. When she found her feet Maude let go, brushed down her skirt and walked, as steadily as her aching, shaking, legs would allow her, to pick up her hat, gloves and reticule. She had something more to say to him, but she did not know how she was going to find the courage; it was far too close to her own feelings. Yet, how could she not do her best for the girl?

She set the hat on her head, tied the ribbons beneath her chin and then drew on her gloves as she walked back to where Eden Hurst stood in front of the desk, watching her from under lowered brows.

Maude found her mouth was dry and her throat tight. She made herself look up into his face. 'Mr Hurst, have you considered that she may be in love with him?'

'No.' There was a flicker of surprise at the question, that was all. 'There is no such thing as love, Maude. There is lust, there is sentimentality, there is neediness, there are the transactions people make for all kinds of reasons. But there is not love. It does not exist, it is merely a romantic fantasy.'

'Of course love exists.' She stared back, aghast. 'Even if you do not believe in love between adult men and women, surely you acknowledge family love? Parents love their children, children love their parents—I know, I love my father and he loves me.'

'Society and convention makes family units,' he observed. 'Nature influences mothers to tend to helpless infants. And some of them,' he added with chilling flippancy, 'even heed that influence. Familiarity, dependence, desire—you can call it love if you want to.'

'Oh.' *Poor little boy.* He had betrayed so much hurt in those cynical words. She stood there feeling the tears start at the back of her eyes. But this was not a damaged, abandoned child in front of her. Not any more. This was a grown man with scars to cover those wounds. Scars that so obviously hurt. 'You poor man,' she murmured. Then she turned and walked out, knowing that if she stayed she would take his face between her palms and try to kiss away all the years of neglect and loneliness those words betrayed. Would this man ever allow her to try to do that?

Eden stood looking at the door Maude had closed so gently behind her. She pitied him because he denied the existence of love? What sort of foolish feminine fancy was that? He had so much—his independence, work he lived for, wealth, achievement and the sense not to give up his heart and his soul to be toyed with and then discarded by some damn woman. He had made all this out of the stony soil of a mother who had left him for years until it suited her to *find* him again, an uncaring father who refused to acknowledge his son and fourteen years of neglect in the servants' quarters of an Italian palazzo.

It was not even as though Prince Tancredi had maltreated him physically. He could have endured that, for at least that would have been a recognition of sorts. No, the magnificent father who dazzled him with the longing for a look, a word, had simply refused to acknowledge that he was anything but a liability, like a feeble old servant that duty did not allow you to cast out. If a man who had everything—wealth, title, position, looks—could not spare a kind word for his own son, then that son had to learn a hard lesson and open his eyes to the realities of the sentimental nonsense people spoke about love.

And Lady Maude Templeton had the effrontery to pity him? Not apparently for being outside the *ton* or for having no family he could acknowledge, but because he did not believe in the mind-sapping dependency of a foolish emotion. *Dio!* What had he tied himself to? This was as bad as fighting off Corwin's daughters. Worse.

The tap on the door sent him back to his chair behind the desk. 'Come! Ah, Mr Merrick.'

'Sir.' The young actor had tidied his clothing and brushed his hair and now stood bashfully, giving a very acceptable performance of troubled penitence. Yes, he was a good actor, even if Eden would never gratify him by saying so. All the more reason to keep him. 'I'm very sorry, sir, it won't happen again.'

'No, it will not because Miss Golding will be leaving us. Is Miss Poole aware of what has been going on?'

'No, sir.'

'You are lodging with her still?'

'Sir.'

'Then you had better think up an explanation for why you are not getting paid this week, Merrick.' The young man looked up sharply, the boyish charm slipping. 'I will add your wages to what I owe Miss Golding.' That, at least, ought to please his sentimental new partner. If she ever came back.

'Be very clear about this, Merrick. I am keeping you only because of Miss Poole. She's a better actor than you'll ever be and I doubt she'd have the lack of judgement to expose her spotty buttocks to my guests either.' That produced a furious blush, but Merrick held his tongue.

'Nothing to say? I need hardly add that if I find you involved with any other female in this company I will ensure that Miss Poole is fully aware of it. I'll even hand her the blunt carving knife. Now get out of my sight.'

Methodically Eden opened his notebook, crossed out the line about the three actors and added a note about Merrick and Golding's wages and the need to cast another ingénue, then went to open the door. 'Millie!'

'Yes, Guv'nor?' She appeared round the corner, her face screwed up in her usual earnest scowl. 'Post, Guv'nor.' She thrust several envelopes into his hand.

'Thank you. Go and make sure Mrs Furlow's dressing room is in good order.' The maid scurried off and Eden leaned back against the doorjamb, his eyes unseeing on the deserted passageway, wondering if he was coming down with something. He felt decidedly odd. After a minute he scrubbed his hair back with both hands, rubbing his eyes until he saw stars.

There was no time to be ill and no excuse for indulging himself by looking for symptoms either. Eden went back into his office and glanced at the clock. An hour to the afternoon rehearsal. Time to read his post, send Millie out for some food and decide what to do about finding a replacement for Harriet Golding.

There was, almost inevitably, an invitation from the Corwin household. This time it was for a soirée, two evenings hence. Having survived one of Mrs Corwin's soirées before, he was not over-eager to repeat the experience. Did he still need Corwin's money? He was reluctant, but the man had not asked for any involvement with the theatre, not like Lady Maude, and money, wherever it came from, was money.

The other invitation emerging from the pile was unexpected. Lady Standon requested the pleasure of his company, again for a soirée, again in two evenings' time.

It had not been uncommon for him to receive invitations from members of society since his arrival in London, especially those of the faster set. His wealth, and the rapidly growing popularity of his theatre, accounted for it, he supposed, in the same way as prominent bankers or merchants would receive invitations if their manners were sufficiently refined. Such outsiders showed a hostess was daring and completely secure in her own position.

Occasionally he accepted when one of his particular friends pressed the point or when an evening's entertainment included a celebrity singer or writer he was interested in. But he was wary, for he realised that, for some of the female guests—and on one occasion, not just the females—his person was the attraction. As a decorative exotic it seemed he was a desirable accessory on a lady's arm and in her bed. He was not averse to a brief dalliance with charming ladies whose husbands were either tolerant or neglectful, but he liked to make his own choices. He was aware it had given him a certain reputation.

But Lady Standon did not appear to be the kind of lady who thought that slumming it with men from beyond her social circle would be amusing; in fact, he rather suspected she was unfashionably attached to her husband, a man who looked as though he would kill anyone who so much as laid a finger on his wife. Maude would doubtless say they were *in love*. So there was a strong possibility that, after meeting him in Maude's box, she had simply included him on her guest list with no ulterior motives.

Eden pulled the notepaper towards him and began to write, one letter an acceptance, the other a regretful refusal due to a prior engagement. As he sealed them he smiled, amused at his own choices.

Millie poked her head round the door. 'I've done the room, Guv'nor. You want me to take your letters?'

'Yes, send one of the lads to deliver them now.'

Eden was not surprised to find Corwin waiting in the office when he came back after rehearsal. Millie had provided the merchant with tea and he sat in front of the desk, seeming, to Eden's resentful eye, to occupy more than his reasonable share of the space.

'Well, my boy,' he began. Eden showed his teeth in what might be construed as a smile and sat. 'As you can't come to Mrs C.'s soirée, there's a little chat I think we should have.'

'Indeed?' Eden injected polite boredom into his voice.

'Mrs C. is that disappointed, I can't tell you,' Corwin remarked, stirring a heaped spoon of sugar into his cup. 'Bessie, I said to her, it's about time I settled matters right and tight with Mr Hurst, then we'll all know where we are and he won't be bashful about accepting invitations. Why, I said, he won't need them!'

Eden raised an eyebrow. 'I would regret causing Mrs Corwin disappointment, but I am afraid my refusal is due to the fact I will be at the Standons' soirée that evening, not to any bashfulness.'

'Lord Standon? Well, that just goes to show what I said to my Bessie was right—you're just the man we need, sir.'

'For what, exactly?' Eden asked, knowing all too well what the answer would be.

'Why, for our girls!' Corwin took a swig of tea.

'All of them? I fear that is illegal in this country.'

'Ha! You'll have your joke, sir.' The merchant did not look as though he found it funny. 'No, whichever of them you choose, although Calliope is the eldest. Once one of them's wed to you, the others will get off soon enough, I make no doubt of it, especially with the fine friends you've got, my boy.'

Eden toyed with the options before him, of which physically ejecting Corwin was the most tempting. *Uno, due, tre,* he counted silently, then smiled. 'You flatter me with your proposal, sir, but I must decline.'

He expected anger, but Corwin's face merely displayed indulgent understanding. 'I know what it is, and it does you honour, my boy, but we don't take any account of the circumstances of your birth. Why, Mrs C. herself never knew her father, let alone him being an Italian prince.'

'You would oblige me by ceasing to discuss my parentage, Corwin. What you think of the circumstances does not interest me. I have no intention of marrying one of your daughters and that is the end of it.'

The other man's face darkened and he set his cup down sharply. 'Then you'll not get a penny piece of my money for your damned theatre.'

Eden shrugged. 'Your decision, sir.'

'So you do not intend doing the honourable thing, despite compromising my Calliope?' the other man blustered.

'Ah, so you did know about that very unwise visit, did you?' Eden relaxed against the high-carved back of his chair, aware that when he did so the soaring eagle at the top seemed to rise from his shoulders, claws outspread, threatening. A theatrical effect, but it amused him.

'Corwin, I may be a bastard, in all the ways that word can be defined, but I am not able to compromise one young lady

while she is chaperoned by her sister and, happily, by a respectable third party who happened to be having a business
meeting with me at the time.' The merchant's face fell, ludi-
crously. 'I suggest you go home, tear up whatever draft
contract you have been working on and go and seek your
sons-in-law elsewhere. You'll not find one at the Unicorn.'

'He doesn't believe in love,' Maude stated baldly. With
complete disregard for the skirts of her evening gown she was
curled up at the end of Jessica's bed, her back against the
bedpost, her eyes meeting her friend's in the looking glass.

Jessica swivelled round on the dressing-table stool, her
diamond ear drops dangling from her fingers. 'You told him
you loved him? Maude, of all the—'

'No, of course I did no such thing. He sacked one of the
actresses for having an affair with the juvenile lead actor and
I said, what if they are in love? And he said, there is no such
thing. He is so bitter, Jessica, no wonder he seems like an
icicle. I think it all goes back to his childhood, because he
seems to regard even maternal love as something nature
imposes just to make sure children don't starve. Like birds
knowing they have to build nests. Although I don't think he
got much paternal love either,' she added with a sigh.

'He's a grown man,' her friend said robustly, hooking one
earring into her lobe. 'Ouch, oh, bother this thing. Ring for
Mary, will you?'

'No, I'll do it.' Maude slid off the bed and went to help.
'You've got your hair tangled in it. There. Yes, I know he's a
grown man,' she said, reverting to her preoccupation with
Eden. 'But how we are brought up affects who we are when
we grow up, don't you think?'

'Yes, although some people rise above early hardship and

others fall into despair or bad ways, even though they had the happiest of childhoods. If the man is bitter and cold, Maude, are you so sure you love him? I don't know how you can really, you hardly know him.'

Troubled, Maude perched on the edge of the bed again, absently smoothing out the creases in her skirts. 'It isn't logical, is it? I ask myself, I truly do, whether it is just because of the way he looks. But even when he upsets me, even when I see all that bitterness, I still *feel* for him. And there is something, even when I disagree with him quite violently, that makes me sense our minds are linked.'

'Just so long as he does nothing to hurt you,' Jessica said, rising and reaching for her reticule. 'I was in half a mind whether to invite him this evening—Gareth won't be best pleased when he finds out—and then I thought, he won't accept anyway…'

'He's coming to the soirée? Eden?' Jerked out of her brown study, Maude scrambled to her feet and seized the hand mirror off the dressing table. 'I knew I should have worn the pearls. I look a fright, I—'

'You look lovely.' Jessica removed the mirror and took Maude by the shoulders. 'Maude, I do think there's some hope for the two of you if Mr Hurst becomes known in respectable society more.' She frowned as though she was trying to convince herself. 'If we can play down the theatre and play up his wealth… And it helps that you are now so firmly on the shelf.' She laughed at the expression on Maude's face. 'Only teasing, but it does make a difference that you've been out for so long. People might just accept a love match that seems…eccentric. Your papa is being extremely tolerant, you know.'

'He doesn't know I have any feelings for Eden, he just thinks I am interesting myself in the theatre,' Maude said, leaning forward to drop a kiss on her friend's cheek. 'Thank you for helping.'

'Bel will, too, and Eva when she arrives. Eva can make *anyone* acceptable.'

'Even an Italian prince's bastard son?' Maude asked.

Jessica slipped her arm through her friend's. 'Come on, time to go down. I'll have to think about this. But I warn you, Maude, if I find he has hurt you, I'll set Gareth on him.' She paused at the top of the stairs. 'After I have operated upon Eden Hurst's manhood with my embroidery scissors.'

Chapter Eight

'He is not going to come,' Maude said to Jessica as they met at one end of the long reception room. The party had been in full swing for over an hour, the rooms were full of people, all talking at the top of their voices and drowning out the string quartet that was playing valiantly on a dais halfway down the room.

Young ladies just making their come-out were giggling together or blushing up to their hairlines if addressed by a young man, groups of middle-aged gentlemen stood around discussing politics and sport, the chaperons were exchanging politely barbed compliments on each other's charges and in one of the side rooms some of the older guests were playing cards.

Gareth, who took the view that there was no point in entertaining if you did not do it properly, had ordered only the best wines to be served and the guests were already anticipating one of the Standons' famous buffet suppers.

'Don't give up on him,' Jessica urged, 'It isn't late yet.'

Maude was already shaking her head. Then instinct sent a shiver down her spine as tangible as the trail of a cold finger running slowly over every vertebra. 'Eden is here.' She scanned the room, searching for his arrogant carriage and dark head. 'There. By the door.'

He was causing a small stir, heads turned. It was not exactly disapproval, Maude realised, more surprise at his presence at such a very respectable soirée. She remembered what the others had told her about his reputation, the fact that he had been seen at some of the more dashing gatherings, the way he attracted not a little attention from the more adventurous ladies. Whether he really fell for their lures she had no idea; people did not mention such things within the hearing of un-married girls.

Probably, for the man was hardly a saint. Bel was no doubt right. But she was curiously unmoved by the thought of Eden's past *amours*. It was his future fidelity she was interested in.

'Seeing him like this,' Jessica murmured in her ear, 'you can understand the rumours about his father. He's a Renais-sance portrait come to life.' Then she added, her tone puzzled, 'And yet, there is something about him that is familiar.'

But Maude hardly heard her. She was already moving, drifting nonchalantly down the room on the opposite side to Eden, wafting her fan, smiling at acquaintances. She stopped opposite where he was standing, deep in conversation with a group of men she recognised. They were all in their thirties, titled, fashionable, known for their sporting pursuits. And Eden, she realised with interest, was already familiar with them. The way they were together spoke of easy acquaintance. But she had dined at their tables, attended the parties their wives gave, and had never met Eden there.

Yet here he was, obviously comfortable in their company and dressed, just as they were, in the height of elegant male fashion, as he had been the other evening in their box at the theatre. So, he was admitted more comfortably into male society, was he?

'We must hold another charity ball, Lady Maude.' Maude focused her attention on Lady Wallace who had appeared at her side, the aigrette of feathers in her coiffure a danger to everyone within three feet of her. 'Or some other fund-raising event, don't you think so?'

'For the soldiers? Yes, indeed. Last year's ball and the picnic were very profitable, were they not? I was wondering whether we should not try for something a little different this year, but I confess, I have had no ideas yet.'

She had lost Lady Wallace's attention. 'My goodness, there's that Mr Hurst, such a surprise to see him here. So decorative, don't you think? And such lovely long legs. Not that I should be saying so,' she chuckled richly, 'Seeing that he must be young enough to be my son. And of course, there's no *family*, so he's not exactly one of us. To say nothing of that reputation.'

'Really?' Maude held her breath, praying that Lady Wallace would not suddenly recall that she was speaking to an unmarried woman. 'Do tell.'

'He is notorious for bedding married ladies.' The aigrette dipped so low that it almost put Maude's eye out as her companion leaned closer to whisper.

'That is hardly unique,' Maude commented drily, glancing around the room. She could see any number of young matrons with a certain reputation. Once they had provided their spouses with the obligatory 'heir and a spare' they had no shame in engaging in heavy flirtation, or worse, with attractive gentlemen. Anything was possible, provided they were discreet.

'But they do say that he never returns to the same one twice,' Lady Wallace confided, startling Maude. She had assumed that Eden would indulge in an *affaire* with the same lady for some time. 'He invariably loves them and leaves them after the one night, despite their pleas for him to return. And given that, by all accounts, his performance in bed is quite spectacular— oh my goodness, I quite forgot you are not married, my dear. You must forget I said anything about—' She broke off, her pale blue eyes opened wide in alarm. 'Mr Hurst!'

'Lady Wallace.' Maude turned to find he was standing just behind them, looking quite unmoved at being confronted by two ladies, one of whom was goggling at him as though he was a pantomime demon emerging from a trapdoor, the other, Maude was only too aware, who was blushing like a peony. 'Lady Maude.'

'Sir.' It was as much as she could manage to articulate. *Quite spectacular performance? In bed?* She had desired him all year, she still tingled all over when she thought of his kiss, but somehow she had never let herself imagine in detail what it would be like to be taken to bed by Eden Hurst. She knew, in theory, what happened, but it had all seemed a rather hazy concept. Rather daunting, if truth be told, and something she put off quizzing Jessica about. Now, so close to the long frame she knew was hard, muscled…

'Maude?' Lady Wallace nudged her foot with one pointed shoe. She appeared to be more than a little flustered to find herself actually in conversation with such a notorious character. 'I was just saying to Mr Hurst how much I enjoyed the new production of *How to Tease and How to Please*. You have seen it, have you not?'

'Yes, of course. So amusing, and Mrs Furlow was in fine voice. Papa invited Mr Hurst to our box during the interval.' Best to establish early on that they had met in innocuous circumstances.

'Oh, so that is what you meant when you mentioned the theatre at our meeting the other day.' Lady Wallace smiled nervously at Eden, who was looking politely mystified. 'Excellent.' She rallied and tapped him firmly on the arm with her fan. 'You can do so much good, young man.'

'I haven't asked Mr Hurst yet, Lady Wallace,' Maude said, smiling through gritted teeth.

'I've let the cat out of the bag, haven't I? I had better take myself off and let you work on him.' She gave a little gasp at her own choice of words and scurried off in a flurry of feathers like an affronted hen.

'So, Lady Maude, you have something to ask me, have you?' He was smiling in that disconcerting way he had, which always gave her the sensation that there was a lot more than mere amusement going on inside his head. 'Am I going to regret accepting Lady Standon's invitation when I hear what I am to do for you?'

'What I would chiefly like you to do for me, at this very minute, is to procure me something to drink,' Maude declared, 'and find me somewhere to sit down. This is the most incredible crush.'

'The mark of success, surely?' Eden steered her through the crowd to an empty alcove, reaching it just ahead of another couple. Maude recognised Lord Witchell and his latest flirt, Mrs Bailey. There was an interesting moment while the two men eyed one another, then Lord Witchell bowed sharply and walked off. It did not escape her that, far from seeming put out, Mrs Bailey directed a lingering look back over one white shoulder at Eden. A look that said, as clearly as words, that she knew him. Very well indeed.

'I will not be a minute.' Maude fanned herself and studied the room while she recovered her composure somewhat. She refused to contemplate whether Mrs Bailey knew Eden in the Biblical sense or not. It was more to the point to worry about whether he had heard what, or who, Lady Wallace had been talking about.

'Lady Maude.' He was back, a bottle of champagne in one hand, glasses in the other. 'I thought it likely I would need fortifying.' He seemed either unaware, or uncaring, that it was more than a little fast for an unmarried lady to be drinking champagne like this, especially with him. Maude could only be grateful for the wine—the combination of embarrassment, heat and the close proximity of Eden Hurst were a dizzying combination.

'That is not very gallant, Mr Hurst,' she said lightly. 'It sounds as though you would be unwilling to help me.'

'A few days' acquaintance with you, Maude, has taught me caution,' he observed, pouring the wine and handing her a glass. He lifted his in a salute. 'Here's to our partnership.'

With any other gentleman Maude would be flirting lightly, and unexceptionably, by now. Fluttering her eyelashes at being toasted, teasing him charmingly as a reward for fetching her refreshment. But she could not, without jeopardising her business partnership with Eden, flirt with him. It was too soon.

She contented herself with raising her own glass slightly and smiling at him before sipping. 'Lady Wallace, Lady Standon and I are on the committee of a charity founded by Lady Dereham to find employment for soldiers disabled by the war.'

She glanced at him, hoping for a nod of encouragement at least, but he was regarding her steadily, his eyes serious. Why she had the impression that he was thinking about something entirely other than the charity, she had no idea. 'We have bought several inns that are run and staffed by our men, placed others in trades or service, but we are always looking for new opportunities. It occurred to me that you might have some vacancies at the Unicorn.'

The dark brown eyes focused on her; he was back from wherever his mind had been wandering. 'I don't suppose you have an ingénue amongst them?'

'No. Do not be frivolous, if you please, Mr Hurst; this is serious. Surely you can use carpenters and scene painters, doormen and so forth?'

'I am rebuked, Maude. I presume I am still not forgiven for that particular decision?'

'Not unless you have changed your mind.' She should back down on the subject of Miss Golding, she knew. It was unbecoming to argue with a gentleman and, besides, there was nothing in their agreement to allow her rights of veto over Eden's employment decisions. But the cold practicality of his action still chilled her.

'No, I have not. But I expect I can employ one or two men, if they can pull their weight. I am not carrying passengers.'

Maude nodded. 'They will. Our concern is to restore their independence and self-respect by placing them where they can do a fair day's work, not rely on charity. It is finding those positions that is the challenge.'

'Good, I would support that. On one condition.' He had captured her fan, a piece of spangled nonsense that looked ridiculous in his large hand, and was gently wafting it for her.

'What is it?' she asked, wary of both his easy acceptance of her proposal and of what his condition might be. He was sitting back at his ease on the spindly gilt chair, legs crossed, expression relaxed. Why then did he give her the impression of being poised to spring?

'That you call me Eden.'

'I cannot!' Maude glanced around, concerned he might have been overheard. The sight of one of the ladies on Bel's committee ruthlessly cornering gentlemen and lecturing them until they opened their pocket books for the charity was so familiar that no one, so far, showed that they thought the *tête à tête* in any way out of the ordinary, even if they had realised with whom she was conversing, but for her to address a gentleman by his first name was simply not done.

'Not where we may be overheard, of course. But when we are… negotiating?' He furled her fan and handed it back while he refilled their glasses.

'Negotiating?' There was a caress in the way he said the word, as though they were coming to terms about something far more intimate. Maude swallowed wine without noticing, then started as Eden took the fan again, his fingertips brushing the lemon kid glove that sheathed her hand so tightly.

'But yes. We have, after all, a business relationship, do we not?'

'Of course.' She smiled brightly, refusing to let him see how he was disturbing her. But of course, how could he guess how deep her feelings ran? 'If we are negotiating, then I must state my terms. You may call me Maude and I will call you Eden, in private, if you both take some of the men *and* join our committee.'

'Very well. You do not ask me to take Harriet Golding back?'

'I assumed that to ask you to help her would be a lost cause.' Vaguely she was aware that the noise level in the room had dropped—people must be moving off towards the buffet.

'Not necessarily. I will not take her back, but I could probably get her employment at one of the other theatres.' Eden's attention was on the fan, holding it on his knee while he untangled the ornamental cord, which had twisted around his wrist. Maude found herself studying his face, the thick lashes hiding his eyes, the fine modelling of his cheekbones under the olive skin, the strong line of his jaw, the mobile mouth that looked as though it should betray so much and yet hid its secrets so well.

'Then why don't you?'

He did not look up. 'That would mean asking a favour, putting myself in someone's debt. It would need to be worth my while.'

'What would make it worth your while?' she asked. And then he did look up, straight into her eyes and she could not look away, nor, strangely, did she blush. The look went too deep for that.

'Do you know what decided me to play the English gentleman for your father the other night?' he asked.

'No.' The glass was in her hand and Maude drank as though thirsty, her eyes not leaving his. She had asked herself over and over again why he had accepted her money, accepted her interference in his theatre, troubled to soothe her father's concerns. 'Tell me.'

'Because when you want something, you say so. And if you do not get it, then you put forward reasons, you negotiate. You do not wheedle or whine or pout or flutter your eyelashes. You have no idea how refreshing that is.'

'Oh,' Maude said. 'Thank you.' *I think.* It appeared to be a compliment. He liked her intelligence enough to take her investment. So to continue to influence him, to insinuate herself deeper into his life, she had to ensure she did not deploy any of the feminine armoury of flirtation or persuasion. *Not that I have ever whined in my life*, she added to herself. 'What would make it worth your while to help Miss Golding?' she asked briskly.

'Dine with me after the performance on Tuesday.'

After a second Maude became aware that her mouth was open and shut it. Then she reached out, took the fan from him and began it ply it vigorously. How much champagne had she drunk? Two glasses? Or three? Because she was surely hearing things. '*What* did you say?'

'Dine with me.'

'Impossible.'

'You have a prior engagement?'

'No.' Her appointments book was so full for the next month that she had deliberately kept this next Tuesday night free. Papa would be out so she would have the evening to herself to curl up with a frivolous novel.

'You see, Maude? How refreshingly unusual for a young lady to admit she is not engaged every night of the week. Well?'

'I promised Papa I would not go behind the scenes at the theatre in the evening and you are not, I hope, suggesting I dine at your house?' She felt her voice rising slightly and swallowed. Was she wrong about him after all? Was he simply a heartless rake who would try and seduce her?

'I am not suggesting that, no. I am intent upon getting to know you, Maude,' Eden said, 'not ravishing you.' He grinned, the look of genuine amusement transforming his face, taking at least five years off her estimate of his age.

'How old are you?' she blurted out.

'Twenty-seven,' he admitted.

'I thought you older,' Maude said. 'But that is irrelevant.' *Probably.* 'Where are you proposing we dine?'

'Somewhere private that is not my house and will not cause you to break any promise to your father.' He smiled, tempting her.

'If I agree, it will be because I wish to know you better as a business partner and because I desire to help Miss Golding. You should not conclude anything else about my motives,' she stated, trying to look businesslike and not as though Lady Wallace's words were dazzling her brain like exploding sky rockets: *spectacular in bed…*

'You think I might jump to conclusions?'

'I have heard about your reputation, Eden.' There, she had said his name aloud. 'You are notorious for your liaisons with married women, so I hear.' She could feel the heat in her face, just speaking of such things.

'But you are not married, Maude. Say yes.' There had been a shadow behind his eyes when she spoke of his *affaires,* a fleeting darkness, gone so rapidly she thought she had imagined it.

Distracted, she spoke before she had time to consider properly. 'Yes, Eden. I will dine with you on Tuesday.' It must be the wine, otherwise why had she agreed? *So fast, so much faster than I thought. All my plans scattering like dust. How did I ever think I could make him fall in love with me according to a design? How could I not realise that he would set the agenda for whatever he is involved in?*

'Thank you. And will you be my partner for supper now?' He glanced across the room and Maude followed his gaze. The crush had diminished greatly and the sound of the string quartet was once again clearly audible. 'If there is any left, that is.'

'You have obviously never been to one of the Standons' soirées before.' Maude stood up, still holding her glass. Eden lifted his and the champagne bottle in one hand and offered her his arm. She took it, smiling up at him. 'They are famous both for quality and quantity—you need not fear going hungry.'

The queue into the refreshment room was not great and footmen were hurrying back and forth replenishing the long tables. Eden stretched up, looking over the sea of heads. 'I can see a table for two over there in the far corner. If you trust me to choose for you, you could take it now.'

'Anything except crab,' Maude told him, gathering her skirts ready to slip through in the direction he was looking. 'And lots of marchpane sweets, please. Give me the bottle and glasses.'

A young lady should pretend to have the appetite of a bird, of course, she acknowledged ruefully as she found the table and set out the wine. And, given that she wanted Eden to fall in love with her, she supposed she ought to be employing all the ruses at her disposal to make him see her as attractive.

'Why are you frowning?' Eden enquired, placing a platter laden with what must be a selection of every savoury on the buffet in the middle of the table. He was followed by a footman with two plates, forks and a dish brimming with marchpane sweetmeats. 'Enough?'

'A feast! Thank you, but I couldn't eat a tenth of it.'

'I will help.' He poured more wine. 'Now, why the frown?'

'I was thinking—' Could she tell him? Oh, why not? He professed to like her lack of feminine tricks. 'Any lady will tell you that it is most unbecoming to display any appetite at all. I should be nibbling on one patty, perhaps, and you could then, with much persuasion, tempt me to sample a sweetmeat.'

'I see.' Eden's lips quirked into a smile. 'And you have just given yourself away? I have often wondered—and seeing that we are being so frank, perhaps I may ask—are all young ladies, except yourself, possessed of incredible will-power or are your stays laced so tight there is no room to eat?'

Chapter Nine

Maude burst into laughter. Not a giggle, not a titter, but genuine, uninhibited laughter. Heads turned, one or two grey heads were shaken, but no one seemed too shocked. This was, after all, Lady Maude Templeton and much would be forgiven to the Earl of Pangbourne's charming daughter. Even, apparently, taking supper with him.

Eden watched her, his own amusement fading away to be replaced by something quite unfamiliar: affection and a kind of warmth. Maude, he realised, made him feel good inside. He gave himself a little shake, wondering if he was sickening for something, as he had suspected the other day. But it was a very strange fever that seemed to come and go like this.

'Oh, dear.' She struggled with her reticule and produced a handkerchief, which she used to dab at her eyes. The tears of laughter made them sparkle as she looked at him. 'Stays indeed! No, and it is not will-power either—we are expected to eat a large supper before we come out. Didn't you realise?'

'How should I?' he countered. 'I have no sisters.'

'And little to do with unmarried girls in the Marriage Mart,

I would assume.' Maude studied the platter and pounced on a salmon tartlet.

'Are we back to the married ladies again?' he enquired, wary.

'No.' She shook her head, making the loose curls that spilled from the combs set high on her crown tremble. 'That's just your guilty conscience.'

'I doubt I have one,' Eden admitted, biting into a savoury puff and wondering how far Maude's hair would tumble down her straight white back and gracefully sloping shoulders if he pulled out those jewelled combs. Slowly, one by one.

'Then how do you know what is right?' she asked, puzzled.

'I don't know. Judgement, experience, assessment of the alternatives, I suppose.' It was not something he ever thought about. 'There is no good business sense in being capricious or dishonest. You keep your word because otherwise no one trusts you; you deal honestly, or they don't come back a second time.'

'But in your personal affairs?' Maude pressed, choosing a cheese patty.

Eden shrugged. 'The same thing. One does not get involved with anyone who does not understand the rules, then no one gets hurt.'

'Your rules,' she said, raising one eyebrow.

'Yes, my rules, in everything, business and pleasure.' To have the power to make your own rules and live your life by them, not to be dependent on cold, grudging duty. Yes, that was freedom. 'Except with you, Maude—you set your own rules.' She looked at him, faintly troubled, it seemed, then the long lashes swept down to hide her wide brown eyes and she smiled.

Damn it, there was that sensation of…dislocation again, of things shifting. It wasn't dizziness exactly. Like many very fit men Eden found the prospect of being ill not just worrying, but irritating too. He'd go and get a check-up. He couldn't afford to be unwell.

'Would you like me to let you know when I audition for the ingénue part?' he asked abruptly. 'It will be next week, the advertisements have gone out.'

'Thank you, yes, I would be most interested.' She sipped some wine, then began to study the sweetmeats with close attention. 'I must only have three, you understand, more would be greedy, so I have to choose carefully. Do you have your notebook, Eden? I imagine you never move without it.' Maude popped a strawberry-shaped morsel into her mouth and regarded him limpidly.

'Yes, I have my notebook.' Was he that predictable? He dug in his breast pocket and produced it.

'Then please make a note to help Miss Golding find another position.'

'You, Lady Maude, are a very managing woman.' He made a note and pushed the book across to show her.

'And you, Mr Hurst, never do anything you do not want to,' she retorted, closing the notebook and handing it back.

'No,' Eden said slowly, feeling the light brush of her fingers as he took it, inhaling the heady scent of gardenia and warm woman. 'Not always.'

The sudden jolt of physical desire took him aback. She was single, unobtainable, quite out of his reach in *that* way and he had thought, now he knew her, his own self-control would have ensured he was safe from the heat that licked like flame across his loins. He had learned the hard way not to yearn for what his birth debarred him from, to take his pleasures where he was in control without the inconvenience of either attachment or snubs.

When he glanced at her, Maude was cheerfully waving at

an acquaintance across the room. Hell, she'd flee screaming if she had any idea what he was thinking about. Then he recalled their very first encounter. She had not fled then; instead, she had dealt with the situation calmly and with humour. Which, Eden decided, resolutely ignoring the rising tension in his groin, meant she did not consider him a threat in that way, any more than she would fear that any of the professional men in her life—her doctor, her attorney, her banker—would press their amorous desires upon her. That was, he had to believe, a very fortunate circumstance.

'He has agreed to join the committee.' Maude swept into Bel's drawing room, cast her bonnet and gloves on to the side table and bent to kiss Bel and Jessica, who were seated side by side on the sofa studying a pile of silk brocade samples.

'Who?' Bel enquired, with a wicked twinkle.

Maude wrinkled her nose at her. 'Eden, of course. And he will take some of the men.'

'Excellent,' Bel smiled. 'Another really forceful man on the committee besides Ashe and Gareth will be so useful. And we can set him on all the rich widows to seduce money out of them.'

Jessica raised an eyebrow. 'Eden? Are you on first-name terms now, then?'

'I agreed to call him Eden, and to allow him to call me Maude—in private, of course—in exchange for him agreeing about the charity,' Maude informed them smugly.

'So he is moving the relationship on to more intimate ground, is he? Oh dear, Maude.'

'I thought it was a step forward,' she protested. 'But I have discovered what he likes about me, and it is hardly particularly flattering.'

'What?' They both regarded her with gratifying interest.

'He likes my lack of feminine wiles. Apparently I do not wheedle or pout when I want something.'

'Perhaps surrounded by thespian temperaments he appreciates something less dramatic and easy to deal with,' Jessica suggested. 'It is encouraging, I suppose—if you are really set on this. So, what is the next step?'

Maude had been agonising over whether to confide in her friends about the dinner. It would be the sensible thing to do. The prudent thing. But they would doubtless try to talk her out of it. 'I am to attend the auditions for a replacement ingénue for the company.'

'Fascinating,' Bel drawled. 'Of course you'll *love* that. Who in their right mind would want to go shopping, or driving or making calls when they can sit in a dusty theatre watching auditions?'

'Me,' Maude stated. And realised it was not just the prospect of Eden's company that made her so eager—she was looking forward to watching him at work. Would he listen to her opinions or would he tolerate only her presence? 'I enjoy shopping too,' she added, in case they thought she had undergone a complete change of personality. 'What do you think of this hat?'

'Delicious,' Jessica pronounced, leaning over to pick up the black straw bonnet with its high poke, tall crown and row after row of looped and ruched green ribbon. 'You don't wear this sort of thing to go behind the scenes at the Unicorn, do you?'

'No, there's dust everywhere and people rushing about with pots of paint, or gesticulating with a handful of greasepaint sticks.' And she did not want to look too obvious. Eden was going to wonder at it if she turned up in the latest fashions. 'I'm wearing last year's walking and carriage outfits mainly.'

'Oh, *those* old things,' Jessica teased. 'You won't catch a man by wearing last year's fashions.'

'You caught one dressed like a governess,' Bel pointed out.

'And I changed into garments fit only for a courtesan very soon after we met. I have a strong suspicion that Gareth rather preferred the latter.'

'I am not sure Eden notices what I wear,' Maude said, anxious. 'He seems not to be interested in unmarried ladies.'

'Really?' Both Bel and Jessica looked relieved.

'No, nor actresses, as far as I can see. But according to Lady Wallace he goes through married ladies like a knife through butter, just as you said.'

Her friends regarded her with wide-eyed interest. 'I *knew* I was right about his reputation,' Bel said. 'What else does Lady W. say?'

'That he only stays with them the once, however much they plead. And that he is…um, spectacular.'

'Spectacular?'

'In bed,' Maude mumbled, wondering just what *spectacular* involved in practice.

'*Really?* Rich, handsome and a spectacular lover—you certainly have good judgement, Maude,' Bel remarked.

'He is also in business and illegitimate,' Jessica reminded her tartly. 'And the last thing we want is for Maude to be seduced—however wonderful the experience—and then abandoned after one night. Do we?'

'Well, no, of course not. But Maude is very levelheaded…'

Jessica snorted. 'Not about this man, she isn't. You forget, I was there when she first saw him. We were standing in Mr Todmorton's shop and in he walks, looking like a dark angel from the chillier regions of Hell, and Maude just stood there gawking.'

'I *am* here, you know,' Maude interjected, annoyed. 'You do not have to speak about me as though I was somewhere else. And I didn't gawk, I was merely struck dumb with desire.

Dark angel, my foot!' The fact that it perfectly described Eden when he was in one of his frostier moods was neither here nor there; she refused to believe that was the real person. Behind that façade was someone much warmer, someone who needed her love as much as she needed his.

'Yes, exactly: desire,' Bel said seriously. 'You do know what happens when a man makes love to you, don't you, Maude, because we don't want you being swept out of your depth through ignorance.'

Maude retreated into one corner of the sofa, clutching a cushion against her stomach defensively. 'Of course I understand what's involved. And I have been kissed and—'

'I mean the bit between him kissing you and the point of no return.'

'Not *precisely*.' Maude rather suspected that the point of no return would be reached rather rapidly if—*when*—Eden kissed her again, but she was not going to say so or her two friends would probably insist on chaperoning her everywhere.

'Are you going to talk to her about it, or shall I?' Jessica asked Bel. 'Someone ought to, she doesn't have a mother—'

'I am going,' Maude declared, leaping to her feet and snatching up her bonnet. 'You are talking about me in the third person again and I have no intention of sitting through a hideously embarrassing lecture on lovemaking. I will work it out as I go along.' Bel moaned faintly. 'I am serious, you know,' Maude said, halfway to the door. 'I love him. I always knew there was someone, somewhere, who was right for me; that's why I wouldn't marry Gareth, even though I love him dearly. It isn't the right sort of love. I know I might not ever be happy with Eden, I know what the obstacles are, but I am not going to give up without even trying.'

Her friends were on their feet, hurrying across the room to

embrace her and reassure her. Maude let them fuss, allowed herself to be drawn back into the room to be seated on the sofa and apologised to, and all the time a little voice was nagging in her mind. *What if he does not learn to love you? What if he never does?*

Tuesday night approached with the speed of a runaway horse when Maude was worrying about it, and like treacle when she talked herself out of the megrims and started to look forward to it. There was no excuse to go to the Unicorn before Tuesday, try as she might to think of one, and no word came from Eden to tell her where they would dine together.

Maude drove Anna distracted on Monday by having all her evening clothes out, trying on one gown after another, and then declaring that she had not got a thing to wear.

'For what engagement, my lady?' the maid asked after an hour.

'A dinner party,' Maude said fretfully, staring down at the heaps of gauze, tulle and flounces. She wanted to look wonderful for Eden, but she did not want to look as though she was trying too hard and she did not want to stand out, wherever they were going.

'There's the dark blue watered silk,' Anna suggested, lifting it out of the back of the press. 'Only you don't like the under-sleeves.'

They spread the gown on the bed and studied it. It fell into full folds from a high waist, the skirt ornamented by swags and bows in a matching tulle. The neckline was boat-shaped, front and back, with cream lace peeping out to add a little modesty, and full white silk under-sleeves reaching to the wrist from beneath the short puffed sleeves.

'Can you cut them off? They make me feel like a bishop.'

Then it would be perfect, Maude mused. Elegant and charming, it would show off her bosom and the whiteness of her arms while at the same time it was dark and simple enough for discretion. 'I will need it for tomorrow night,' she added, hoping Eden had not changed his mind.

The note came that afternoon. *I would appreciate your opinion on some changes we have made to* To Tease, Eden had written. *I trust it is not too late for you to find suitable companions to accompany you tomorrow evening. I would, of course, be more than happy to arrange for them to be escorted home afterwards so your carriage would not have to make any detours.*

So, they were to go on after the play. Maude frowned in thought. Who to invite? She could hardly sit in the box alone and Jessica or Bel would be impossible to shake off. Of course, Miss Parrish! Maude took her old governess out every month, but she had not invited her to the theatre for some time. This would be perfect, if she could just manage to work out how to get them both there, and Miss Parrish home again afterwards, without worrying Paul the coachman.

In the event everything worked so smoothly that Maude had an uneasy twinge of conscience. The primrose path was certainly straight and even…

Miss Parrish was delighted at the thought of the play, Paul Coachman quite reassured by Maude's explanation that he should take the governess back to Somers Town afterwards while she went on to supper with friends who would send her home in their own carriage, and Papa departed for his own meeting at his club with jovial good wishes to pass on to Miss Parrish.

Her old governess, now employed from her own home teaching young ladies French and Italian, was pleased, as always, with the luxury of the box and the refreshments Maude had ordered. Her enjoyment of the entertainment was so great, her affectionate thanks for the treat so fulsome, that Maude was positively wincing with guilt by the time she had seen her off and slipped back up to the box.

It was strange, watching the theatre change after the audience had gone. The boxes emptied, as did the stalls and galleries, the noise ebbing away until only the murmur of it from the entrance reached her. Maude sat in the shadows and watched while the curtain was hauled up and stagehands began to restore the set to order for the morrow. The cleaners, she knew, came in first thing; soon she was going to be alone in this echoing space.

One by one the gas lights dimmed and went out, leaving only a few. Where was Eden? The tap on the door behind her brought her to her feet, unsure whether to shrink back into the hangings or call *Come in!* As she hesitated, the door opened and a complete stranger walked in.

'Good evening, ma'am. I'll just sort the furniture out if that's all right with you.' Without waiting for her response he gathered up all but two of the chairs and walked out, to be replaced by two men struggling with a small table and a third laden with a pile of linen and a basket of flatware, porcelain and glasses.

They were going to dine in the box? Maude felt the delighted laughter bubbling up and bit her lip to contain it. How clever of Eden—she was not breaking her promise to Papa not to go behind the scenes at night and she was somewhere private where they could dine with discretion.

And still the men hurried in and out, now with flowers, wine bucket on a stand, bottles, candles… And were as suddenly gone. Now what? Where was the food going to come from?

The door opened and there was Eden, regarding her in the soft glow of the dimmed lamps and the flicker of the candlelight. He was still in his dramatic black evening clothes with the theatrical ruffles and the watery glint of diamonds at ear and throat. Maude realised, with a sickening jolt in her stomach, just how nervous she was and then, just how happy she was also. The laugh escaped as a half-suppressed gurgle and he smiled, and everything was all right.

'What amuses you?'

'You really should have a drum roll to announce you, you look so dramatic in that costume.'

'And you look—' He broke off, frowning, then came fully into the box and closed the door behind him. 'You look quite lovely.'

'Why, thank you, sir.' He held the chair for her and she sat, studying him candidly as he took the place opposite. 'This is a very clever solution to the problem of where to dine.'

'I enjoy problems.' He seemed content to sit and watch her, his long fingers interlaced on the white table cloth, his relaxed body elegant in the dark clothes.

'But I was wondering where the food was going to come from.'

'You are hungry? You have not already eaten one supper so you may pick daintily at what I provide?' he enquired, mock-serious.

'No, I have not. Do not tease me, Eden, I am positively ravenous. You have no idea what an effect nerves have on my appetite. I know they should put me off my food, but I seem to react quite differently. If I am subjected to much more stress, I will end up as round as Prinny.'

Eden smiled and shook his head at her exaggeration. 'Are you nervous, Maude?' He seemed not displeased that she should be, which puzzled her for a moment until she realised that he saw it as a purely feminine response to being alone with him. And that, she thought, aroused and flattered him. Not that there were any overt clues to that. It was more something she sensed, something just glimpsed in the dark intensity of his eyes as he watched her, the deep purr of his voice.

'Of course,' she said lightly, smiling to hide the effect the thought of his arousal had on her. 'It was not easy to arrange to be here like this.'

'You may relax now, then, and eat. My cook is ferrying an entire dinner from my house and, provided there has been no accident to the carriage, we may expect it at any moment.'

'Eden, that is—ridiculous! You cannot expect the poor man to cook dinner and then deliver it hot and in one piece after driving halfway across London.'

'How do you know where I live?' He seemed interested.

'A figure of speech,' Maude said repressively. She knew exactly where he lived, had caused her carriage to be driven past his home, now and again, but she was certainly not going to admit it to him.

'And the *poor man* is highly paid to produce my dinner when and where I want it, so you may save your sympathy. Ah, here we are.'

The door opened to admit two footmen bearing a tureen, small dishes and a basket of rolls, which they deposited and bowed themselves out.

Eden lifted the lid of the tureen. 'See? Steaming. All done with hay boxes.'

Maude sipped and exclaimed, 'This is delicious!'

'I am glad it meets with your approval. Maude, may I ask you something?'

'Of course.' She put down her spoon, happy with any

excuse for looking openly at him, and found his eyes dark and thoughtful on her face.

'You are very frank with me. You let me into the secret of young ladies' lack of appetite, you share your opinions about matters that I know full well we should not be discussing. Are you as frank with any man?'

Chapter Ten

'I am not sure I quite understand.' Maude's heart sank. He thought her unattractively fast? She had thought him amused, if anything, by her unconventional attitude. But perhaps he merely found her eccentric.

'I have heard that ladies are extremely indiscreet with their hairdressers. Are you simply refreshingly free from silly notions about what is proper, or do you regard me in the light of your hairdresser?' *He is smiling, thank goodness. In fact, he is teasing me…*

'I can assure you, Eden, I most certainly do not regard you in the same light as Monsieur Maurice, as I hope you would realise if you ever met him. Unless…' she frowned thought-fully at the crow-black wing of hair he was pushing back from his forehead '…unless you too wear a toupee?' His snort of laughter answered that. 'When I am with young men at balls and dinners I act as they expect, because they do not have the flexibility of mind to cope with anything else.'

'And I do?'

'I hope so.' She added more seriously, 'I hope you realise that I am not dining with you alone like this because it seems amusing to be scandalous, or because I am fast and would do so with any man who asked me. It is simply that, with you, I find I can be myself.'

Another man would have been taken aback by that comment, or teased her. Eden merely looked thoughtful. 'Why is that, do you think?' he asked, the piece of bread in his fingers crumbling, uneaten, as he studied her face.

'Because I enjoy your company and I feel quite safe with you.' *And I wish I did not...*

'Despite the fact I kissed you the way I did, nearly took you in the corridor on our first encounter?' he asked outright, almost making her choke on the spoonful of soup she had just lifted to her lips. And the reminiscent gleam in his eyes made her reconsider exactly how safe she felt.

'It was an error,' Maude managed to say calmly. 'And if I had been someone you intended to kiss for the usual reasons...' his lips twitched at her choice of phrase, but she pushed on, managing not to stare at them '...I imagine matters would have concluded in your office and not in the corridor. That was most excellent soup.' She had not seen the little bell until Eden lifted it and rang. The footmen came in, cleared and replaced the tureen with more dishes.

'Lobster, a fricassee of chicken, various vegetables. May I serve you?' Maude nodded and waited while the plates were filled and white wine was poured. 'So, you like my flexible mind, you admire my chef's cooking, you covet my theatre and you are able to disregard my reputation. Is that all that brings you here?'

'Are you fishing for compliments, Eden?' Maude enquired, lingering a moment to savour the meltingly tender chicken. 'You are also aware that you are considered a very handsome man. Perhaps that is why I am here.'

'Thank you.' He smiled as she shook her head reprovingly at him for assuming it was her opinion also. 'I have looks that appear to strike some women as attractive. For which I must thank my father—it is hardly an attribute for which I can claim any merit. But you, I think, are not looking for something so superficial, or a trophy to shock your friends.'

'Exactly. So you are quite safe,' Maude said prosaically. 'We may discuss matters of mutual interest and you need not worry that I am about to fling myself into your arms or tear off my clothing.'

'I am sure I ought to say that is a relief,' Eden said, cutting into his lobster. 'But you must be aware that any man who is conscious and under the age of ninety would wish to find you in his arms, so you must give me full credit for my restrained behaviour.'

It was the nearest he had come to open flirtation. Maude lowered her eyes to her glass to keep her expression hidden while she controlled the impulse to beam at him. 'I do,' she said after the merest pause. 'You mentioned your father just then. Are you very like him in character as well as looks?'

For a moment she thought he would not answer her. 'I hope not.'

'You did not get on well together?'

'He never spoke to me. If it was necessary to decide something, he would speak of me in the third person to one of the servants.'

'Perhaps he wasn't very good with children,' she suggested, chilled. 'Some people aren't.' Eden merely looked at her, but the expression in his eyes said everything. 'Oh.' She swallowed. 'Have you ever gone back, since you became a man?'

'You are wondering if I created an ogre in my mind and it would do me good to confront him? Yes, I went back, once.

I suppose I thought it would be amusing to see what he made of the scrawny little kitchen rat now I'd grown up to look like him, with good clothes and money in my pocket.'

Maude flinched. 'And?'

'And I found it…interesting to see what I would look like in thirty years time, although I wondered if I would ever learn the self-control to stay that calm, that distant, in the face of an arrogant twenty-year-old. Or that contemptuous,' he added, his lips thinning. 'It was a lesson in the perils of sentimentality. I had thought, perhaps, to have made him proud of me; I learned that the only person whose opinion matters is my own.'

'You have found no one else whose opinion matters?' she asked, unable to find anything to say about the rest of that speech. Not and keep from weeping.

'I had thought not,' Eden said. 'Now, let me tell you about the auditions.' His explanations took them through the main course and into dessert. Maude listened and nodded, all the time conscious of the long fingers gesturing to mark a point, the intensity in his eyes when he was serious about something. She did not dare venture into anything more personal again. 'There has been a considerable response to my advertisements, so I expect it to take all day,' he concluded.

'When will you start? I want to make sure I am here to see everything,' Maude said, spooning a syllabub as light and rich as spun silk. 'Mmm. This is *heaven*.'

'You will be bored to death, Maude. I will be starting at nine, but you will hardly want to do more than drop in for half an hour or so, surely?' He reached over and dipped an almond biscuit into the dish in front of her, licking syllabub off the *tuile* with sensual enjoyment.

'You said you didn't want any!' Maude raised her spoon

in mock aggression. 'This is all mine and I will defend it to the death.'

'But that was before I tasted it.' Eden feinted with another little biscuit and Maude rapped him over the knuckles and they both laughed. Then their gazes locked and Maude found she was staring, the laughter dying on her lips as something happened, deep in the dark eyes fixed on hers. 'Perhaps I am not as good with temptation as I thought,' he said slowly. There was a long, breathless moment before he broke the gaze with an almost physical abruptness and reached for the platter of cheese.

Maude got her breathing back under control. 'I will be here for the auditions at nine, then,' she said. 'I would like to give you my opinions and I cannot compare one actress with another if I do not see them all.'

Eden put down his knife, his face showing no signs of amusement or flirtation now. 'The decision is mine. We made no agreement about casting or employment.'

'Yes, of course. I am not claiming any privilege in the matter.' What was it Jessica had called him? *A dark angel from the chillier regions of Hell*—yes, that was it. Well, he was not apparently angry, so Hell was presumably on hold, but his severe masculine beauty and the implacable expression certainly fitted the first part.

She shivered, more unnerved than she liked to admit to herself at his rapid change from amused teasing to icy assertion of his rights. 'I thought I would sit up here and watch, as though I was a member of the audience. My opinion may be of value to you, and if not, you will ignore it.' She did her best to sound neither defensive, nor shaken by his territorial reaction.

'Very well.' Eden could not be said to have relaxed again, for his body had not noticeably stiffened in the first place, yet

Maude sensed the moment of tension had passed. *Don't touch my theatre!* He should have a sign hung up, she told herself, striving to find a lighter note. 'Yes, that will be interesting,' he added, 'to see what you think of each from this vantage point.'

'It is agreed, then.' She risked further provocation. 'And Miss Golding? What news of her?'

'She has found a place at the Sans Pareil in the Strand. They specialise in burlettas; it will suit her well enough.'

'Thank you,' Maude said, warmly. 'I am so happy that you did that.'

'You are happier than Mr Merrick in that case, for he is short one week's wages that I added to what was owing to Miss Golding.'

'So you are not completely heartless, then?' Maude watched his face from beneath her lashes, caught the wry twist of his mouth. 'You did not tell me before that you had done so.'

'It was no loss to me and it served as a lesson for Mr Merrick,' Eden said coolly, disowning any motive of kindness. He must, surely, have a softer side?

'You left me to think you were cruel enough to simply cast her out,' Maude observed, 'and you were not.' Instinctively she reached out, laid her own hand palm down over his. 'It isn't a crime to admit to compassion, Eden.'

He sat looking down at her hand, then turned his under it and lifted until her fingertips were an inch from his lips. *He is going to kiss them...* She could feel his breath, hot on the sensitive skin. Then he raised his eyes, watching her under the thick black lashes as he lowered her hand to the table and released it.

'It is probably as well if you have no illusions about my character, Maude. I am not one of your society gentlemen, running tame in ballroom and parlour. I grew up differently and I know weakness is not gentility, it is danger.' He did not appear to expect an answer to that, instead picking up a knife and looking at her questioningly. 'May I tempt you to some cheese? A glass of port?'

'No, thank you.' Maude shook her head, distracted by wondering how she was ever going to crack Eden's defences.

'Shall I see you to the carriage, then?' She nodded, still not concentrating completely. 'I would like to prolong the evening, but I have no desire to cause Lord Pangbourne any anxiety.'

'Thank you. But he is engaged with friends until the early hours,' Maude said vaguely. 'Still, I should not keep my maid waiting up for me.' Eden came and pulled out her chair for her to rise and she smiled her thanks over her shoulder as she did so.

It happened so fast, came out of nowhere—there was no time to think. At one moment they were formal, she rising gracefully from her seat, he placing the chair to one side so her full skirts were unimpeded, the next she stumbled, her low French heel catching in the carpet rucked by the table, and she was in his arms.

Instinctively her hands went up for balance, fastening on his lapels, and his arms were around her, swinging her away from the low edge of the balcony, folding her against his chest. Her overwhelming sensation was of the scent of him: clean, warm male with a hint of an exotic spice mingling with starched linen and that green earth smell of olive oil.

'You've been oiling your hair,' she said, such a foolish thing to be talking of when she was strained against his body and he was looking down at her as though he was still ravenously hungry.

'Yes,' he said, half-laughing at her, half-serious, with a kind of confusion that seemed alien to him. 'Maude?'

A question, a statement? A plea? She couldn't tell. Nor,

she realised with something like despair, could she pull away. He was going to kiss her. *Too soon...*

Eden felt the sensations wash through him, searching with his mind for his self-control like a man who has dropped something precious into a fast-flowing stream. He was going to have to do this, *he* was going to have to be the strong one, the responsible one. Maude was simply too innocent to realise what was happening here. She probably thought he was going to kiss her, a light good-night kiss, perhaps.

And instead she was a finger's breadth away from being pulled down to the upholstered bench that ran around the box and ravished. He tried not to hold her so tightly, achingly aware of the force of his arousal, aware of the soft skin, the fragrance that rose from it, the primitive need to strip the silks and lawns from her body. What was it about this woman? He had never so much as flirted with a respectable single woman. She was a *virgin,* for God's sake!

Under his hands she quivered and he realised his big hands were gripping her shoulders, the fragile bones trapped under his palms. But she made no sound and the pansy-dark eyes were watching him with something he was quite unable to read.

What had happened? He had thought after that first mistaken kiss that he was simply enjoying her company, the intelligent, amused comments, the sweet femininity surrounding him without any games being played, without any demands being made. Maude was a novelty, a woman he thought might actually become a friend and now—this.

This overwhelming desire came out of nowhere, oversetting him just where he thought he was strongest. He had believed that his will was firm, that his self-control was absolute, that his life was ordered, controlled, planned. And now here was this society chit reducing him to a mass of screaming, mindless need without so much as a flirtatious glance.

And this was not need he could take to some whore to slake. Oh, no, this was need for *her,* for Lady Maude Templeton, and he might as well desire the moon.

He had done harder things than this, Eden told himself, gritting his teeth and forcing his hands apart. Harder things, more painful things, although just at the moment, in the grip of this madness, he could not recall what they were.

Where had this come from? He was a sensual man, he knew that, knew he would never be celibate. But this lust for an innocent young woman he hardly knew? But he did know her, he realised, with the part of his brain that was functioning clearly. He knew her better already than any woman in his life, other than Madame Marguerite.

He managed to let Maude go, then caught her elbow as she staggered slightly, as though her knees were shaking. How long had he been standing there, holding her, drowning in those lovely, wondering eyes? 'I'm sorry, did you hurt yourself when you tripped?'

'No. No, not at all. So clumsy of me.' She stepped away, apparently steady on her feet now, which was more than he felt. That damned dizziness again. 'That will teach me to drink two glasses of wine,' she added, sounding ruefully amused.

Did she not realise what had almost happened just then? Had she not seen how much danger she had been in? It seemed not. And he—what peril was he risking? He could not afford to find himself obsessed with the daughter of a peer, he could not afford the lack of focus that unrequited desire would bring. Or the retribution Lord Pangbourne would bring down on his head if his self-control slipped and he debauched the earl's daughter.

'Time to go home,' Eden said, finding his voice emerged quite normally, not with the huskiness of the desperation he was feeling.

'Yes, of course. My cloak…' Maude gestured towards the shadows, then stood while he swung the heavy velvet around her shoulders. 'Thank you. Now, where did I put my reticule? Ah, here it is.' She seemed to Eden's bemused eye to be quite calm, which could only mean she was very innocent, despite her assured air and her age, or completely impervious to whatever dubious attraction he had for other women, or both.

He held the door for her, then followed her out into the wide passageway, resisting the urge to take her arm, knowing he could not trust himself to touch her. She did, however, seem unusually quiet. Perhaps some sixth sense was making her uneasy. Eden walked beside her, racking his brains for conversation and finding none. And finding no possible excuse for not sending her away, breaking their contract, never seeing her again.

Eden seemed unusually silent, Maude thought as they made their way along the wide, deserted corridors and down the sweep of the stairs to the front lobby.

She looked up, seeing the hard line of his jaw, the dark shadow of his beard just beginning to show. Beyond she could see the head of the unicorn, thrusting out of the wall, its horn lowered, its nostrils wide. It had never seemed fierce to her before, or threatening, but now it did.

Someone materialised from the shadows, opened the door and whistled. Eden stepped out into the night, still not taking her arm, and the cold air struck her skin, making her realise just how heated she was. There were the sound of hooves on the cobbles and a carriage drew up.

Eden snapped his fingers at the groom, who jumped down

and hurried to let down the steps and help her enter. 'Eden?' she queried.

'I will ride on the box.' He shut the door and she was alone. Shivering slightly, Maude fidgeted with her cloak and tied the cord at her neck. There were gloves in the pocket and she pulled them on, feeling the need to cover as much skin as possible, as though that flimsy warmth would stop the fine tremor running through her.

Now she was alone she could think about those few crowded moments after she had stumbled and he had caught her in his arms. What had happened? She was not sure. She was not certain even how long he had held her, his strong fingers locked around her shoulders. She had stumbled, Eden had caught her—and for her the world had stopped on its axis.

But for him? He had been so still, his eyes so intent, his breathing hard. Had he felt the sensual shock that had gone through her? Or was it simply that he had found himself, late at night, with his arms full of young woman and it had taken a moment for him to control a man's natural reactions?

But she did not want him to feel only desire, flattering though that was. She wanted his emotions involved, not his instincts. When they made love—she closed her eyes and shivered—she wanted it to be because he loved her. But Jessica and Bel had warned her that was not how men thought. And it seemed they were right.

Maude was still wrestling with her desires and her ignorance as the carriage slowed and stopped. When the door opened Eden was standing there, his hand held out to help her down. It seemed he was prepared to touch her now. The groom was already climbing the front steps to knock.

She made herself hold Eden's gaze for a long moment, then pulled up her hood and put her hand in his. 'Thank you.'

'Thank you, I enjoyed your company very much.' He kept his voice low, conscious, as she was, of the driver up on the box.

'And I, yours. It was a delicious meal; please thank your chef for me,' she responded, as though they were parting after a normal society dinner party. 'I look forward to the auditions.'

One of the footmen had come to open the door. Maude inclined her head to Eden with a smile and walked with perfect poise across the pavement, up the steps and into the hall. 'Thank you, James. You may lock up now. His lordship will be very late and he has his keys.'

She kept her back straight all the way up the stairs, along the landing and into her room, even though there was no one to see her. Anna came in answer to the bell and chatted cheerfully as she unlaced Maude's gown, put away her jewels, unpinned and brushed her hair, unperturbed by her mistress's silence.

When she had gone Maude sat up in bed and watched the dying fire and contemplated, for the first time in her life, a problem she did not know how to solve.

Chapter Eleven

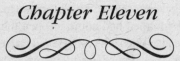

Maude was up there, in her box, although it was scarcely half past eight. He could sense her as clearly as if the scent of gardenias had wafted down to the bare stage and driven away the stink of gas, greasepaint and dust. Eden took the list of hopefuls for the audition from the stage manager and scanned it, although he already had it clear in his mind.

'Who have you got to play opposite them?'

'Tom Gates.' Howard, the stage manager, ran his hands through his grizzled brown curls and frowned at the stage. 'What props do you want, Guv'nor?'

'Table, chair. Throw a shawl over the chair, put something on the table—give them something to use.' He could feel himself turning to look up at the box and swivelled back, despising himself. He had dealt with his frustration, but he had not been able to force himself to think of just any woman. Instead, his mind had been filled with the image of Maude, her supple body, her soft, warm mouth, and he had groaned aloud, the sweat standing out on his brow. 'Here.' He thumbed through the pages of the play in his hand. 'Give them all this scene.'

'Right you are, Guv'nor.' Howard turned back to take the

pages. 'Her ladyship's here.' The man lowered his voice and jerked his head towards the tier of boxes up on the right. 'Been here since eight. Said not to disturb you.' Eden allowed himself a grunt of acknowledgment. 'I sent Millie up with some coffee and sweet rolls.'

'Good.' At least he wasn't fantasising, Maude really was up there. Perhaps there was nothing wrong with him at all, except lust, and slender brunettes with heart-shaped faces and haughty little noses were what it took to reduce him to this state of distraction.

His doctor had patiently examined him, peered into his eyes, listened to his heart, performed whatever mysteries medics did over a urine sample and pronounced him as fit as a racehorse. The man had offered to bleed him should the strange dizzy spells recur, advised laying off the port and drinking more Burgundy instead and recommended a few early nights. 'Not that there's a damn thing wrong with you, Hurst,' he'd added. 'Still, I expect you want some advice for your money.'

Eden stalked off to straddle a chair set stage right, his back to Maude's box, without acknowledging that he was aware she was there. It was ungracious, he knew. He dumped the papers on the small table set beside it, pulled a pencil out of his pocket and tried to make his mind go blank. And failed.

And it wasn't just the physical attraction, it was the way she looked into his eyes as though she wanted to touch his soul and asked him questions and he found he was betraying his innermost thoughts, his weaknesses, the sore areas he tried to ignore.

Try common sense... The more you avoid thinking about her, the more obsessed you will become. There are two options—make love to her or get used to her. The first was patently impossible, which left the second.

Eden stood up, moved centre stage and shaded his eyes to look up at the boxes. 'Lady Maude?'

'Mr Hurst.' He could see her easily now. Maude had taken off her bonnet and she was resting her elbows on the velvet padded rim of the box, a coffee cup cradled in her hands. 'Thank you for my breakfast.' She could pitch her voice to reach him without shouting, he realised, professionally impressed at the clarity.

He should, of course, acknowledge that it had been Howard's idea to send up the refreshments. 'My pleasure.' He wrestled with the conscience that he had assured her he did not possess. 'But you must thank Mr Howard, our stage manager, for that.'

'Thank you, Mr Howard,' she called, waving, and the man produced a rare smile and raised a hand in acknowledgment. *Now she is going to charm the entire company*, Eden thought, resigned to hearing Maude's praises sung by all and sundry.

'Right.' He looked at his pocket watch before laying it beside the script. 'Let's get on with this.'

Maude bit the end of her pencil and concentrated. Mr Howard had given her a list of the hopeful ingénues and she was making careful notes against each. Not very clear… Moves awkwardly… Over-dramatic… Too old… Moves beautifully, but couldn't hear her…

When Eden stood up and announced a break for luncheon, she had come to the conclusion that there were only three so far who seemed right. 'Mr Hurst!'

Eden turned, looking up, and she was almost tempted to launch into the balcony scene from Romeo and Juliet. She repressed the urge; her acting would reduce the audience to fits of laughter. 'Would you care to take luncheon up here?'

She had managed, with some success during the day at least, not to think too much about those moments in Eden's arms that night. Now he seemed to hesitate and she felt her poise slipping.

'Thank you, but, no, Lady Maude. Perhaps you would join Howard, Gates and me down here?' He must have thought her silence meant she was doubtful, for he added, 'With your maid, of course.'

'Thank you, we will be right down.' It was not doubt, Maude thought, managing to keep the smile off her face with difficulty, it was delight. For if he was inviting her to join them, then it meant he was prepared to listen to her ideas.

With Anna at her heels she made her way on to the stage to find hands were transforming the make-shift set into a dining room and putting chairs around the table. Millie bustled on with a tray and began to lay out plates of cold meat, a raised pie, bread and cheese.

'Have you ever been on stage before?' Eden asked her as she stopped, centre front of the fore-stage, and looked out over the ranks of seats.

'Only in small private theatres in country houses. This is breathtaking. It feels so much bigger than it looks from the box.' She glanced at him and saw he was standing, studying the view from the stage with the same look on his face as she sometimes saw on her father's countenance when he came home to Knight's Fee, their Hampshire estate. This was not just Eden's work, not just a tool of his trade—this theatre belonged to him in a way that went far beyond deeds of ownership. What she could see was passion and possession and pride.

'You have good projection and pitch,' he remarked, turning back to the table and taking the jug of ale from Millie. 'Are you sure you cannot act? Think what the appearance of Lady Maude Templeton on the stage would do for the box office.'

'Empty it,' she said, laughing, and took the chair he held for her. Anna, looking alarmed, was seated next to Tom Gates and Howard took the foot of the table.

'Help yourselves.' Eden waved at the spread before flattening his notes next to his plate and pouring ale. 'Can you drink this, Lady Maude?'

'I expect so,' she said, cutting the pie and serving it out. 'It is thirsty work, listening.'

'Right, then. The first one.'

It took about three minutes for the men to forget who she was and to absorb her into the discussion. Elbows appeared on the table, notes were scribbled with one hand while the other waved a slice of bread to make a point, slices of meat and cheese were heaped on her plate without ceremony and Gates clinked his mug against hers. 'Cheers.'

Anna sat, quiet as a mouse, eating steadily, while Maude listened. So far, everyone was agreeing with her impressions, although their analysis of faults and talents were far more detailed and technical than her own.

'Number ten,' Eden said, spearing an apple with his knife. 'No projection. No presence.' The others nodded. Maude looked at her notes.

'I don't agree.'

The three men reacted as though the loaf of bread had addressed them, she thought, amused. 'I beg your pardon, Lady Maude.' Howard stopped gaping at her. 'She wasn't good technically.'

'She looked charming, she is graceful and she reacted well to Mr Gates's lead,' Maude stated. 'Can't you teach her to project her voice better?'

'She should know how,' Eden said.

'But she's young, she cannot have much experience. Won't you call her back?'

Gates looked at Howard. Howard looked at Eden. Eden poured more ale. Maude could almost hear their thoughts. His theatre, his company, his decision—and if he let her override him, would it diminish his authority?

'Why didn't you say anything about the others?' he asked.

'Because I agreed with you about them.'

'Ah. Well, Lady Maude, you are our expert in the audience. Howard, put number ten down to call back.' Face studiously blank, the stage manager made a note. 'Number eleven?'

By mid-afternoon Anna had fallen asleep on the padded bench and was snoring softly, but Maude was still engrossed. She had three more possibles on her list and was finding her judgements easier now she had heard the men's opinions over luncheon. Finally, at half past five, Eden called a halt and she went back down to the stage, leaving Anna sound asleep in the box.

'Well,' Eden said. 'Show me your lists. Lady Maude, gentlemen.' He spread them out on the table side by side. 'It would appear we are unanimous. There's six for you to call back tomorrow, Howard.'

'You mean I got them right?' Delighted, Maude bent over the table, tracing the notes with her finger.

'I'm impressed.' Eden was standing close beside her, the others had walked off; in the distance she could hear Howard calling the names of the afternoon's selection. 'Are you tired?'

'No,' Maude said, then found she could not stifle a most unladylike yawn. 'But I do have a thick head. All that concentrating, I suppose.'

'And no fresh air. These gas lights are all very well, but it is not a good atmosphere to be in all day.'

'We could go for a walk,' Maude suggested, watching as Eden stretched like a big cat, all supple muscle and long limbs.

'It will be dark. This is February, remember.' He stood, turning his head as if to ease his neck, then sat to gather up the papers.

'Is your neck stiff?' she asked as he rotated his shoulders. His attention was on the sheets in his hand; she doubted he was even aware that he was doing it.

'My neck? Yes, a little. I am usually on my feet more.'

'Let me.' Maude moved behind him, put her hands on his shoulders and dug her thumbs into the hard muscle. 'I do this for Papa when he's been in the House all day.' Under her hands Eden's shoulders stiffened. 'Am I hurting you?'

'No.' She wasn't sure if she believed him; his voice sounded more than a little constrained. But it was such a delight to find a perfectly innocuous excuse to touch him. No one could object to having their shoulders massaged, surely?

'Thank you. That is much better.' He moved restlessly and she lifted her hands away. 'I will call your carriage.'

'I love the streets after dark. Walk me home, Eden?'

Eden had been turned away from her, now he swung round. 'It is too far.'

'To Mount Street? Half an hour, I should think. But I will send Anna home in the carriage, she is tired.'

'You cannot walk through the streets with a man and no chaperon,' Eden said firmly.

'I have a veil on my bonnet and they are all perfectly respectable streets.' Maude contemplated him, wondering what argument would work. 'I have a headache. It will be much better for me to cure it with fresh air and exercise than having to dose myself with something when I get home.'

'Is it a thick veil?' Eden asked. She could almost hear the sigh.

'Very,' Maude assured him. 'Will you ask Mr Howard to send Anna home in the carriage when she wakes up?'

'Yes.' Eden looked resigned more than cheerful at the thought of the walk. 'Come along, then.'

'I will meet you in the front lobby,' Maude said. 'It is after four, so I cannot go back stage, remember?'

'I assume your father was attempting to safeguard your reputation when he imposed that condition.' Eden regarded her with a jaundiced eye. 'No doubt it never occurred to the poor man that you might want to take to the streets with me, unchaperoned?' As he strode off stage without waiting for her answer, it appeared to be a rhetorical question.

The evening was cold but dry; the air, even full of the smell of horse manure and smoke, was refreshing after the close atmosphere inside. Maude slipped her hand through the crook of Eden's left arm and breathed deeply as they made their way along Long Acre towards Leicester Square.

The streets were crowded, bustling and, in this part of town, thoroughly vulgar. 'I love this,' she confided. 'Look at how much *life* there is going on here.'

'Indeed.' Eden sounded less enchanted by the sight of barrow boys, ladies of dubious virtue on street corners and groups of working men noisily making their way to the nearest tavern. 'And a couple of streets further north and we're into the St Giles rookery, so hold on to me and don't go wandering off or you'll experience more life than you've ever dreamt of.'

'As if I would,' Maude said demurely. 'Oh, look, Eden, hot chestnuts. May I have some?'

Eden bought a cone of old newspaper, filled with blackened, fragrant nuts and began to peel them as they walked, hampered a little by Maude on his arm, although he gave her his gloves to hold. She laughed at his muttered comments as he struggled. 'You'd curse if it were your fingers being burned,' he grumbled at her when he finally freed the hot kernel. 'I suppose you want the first one too, don't you?'

'It would be the gentlemanly thing to offer it to me,' Maude observed, amused by the glimpse of Eden fumbling with the nut like any schoolboy. 'And don't tell me you aren't one,' she added as he opened his mouth. 'But *I* am definitely a lady, so I think you deserve the first fruit of your labours.'

'Thank you.' He popped it into his mouth, then mumbled, 'I'dths too hot!'

'I know,' she said, laughing. 'Why do you think I let you have the first one?'

He grinned back at her teasing and began to extract another. 'Here, open your mouth, it will mark your gloves otherwise.'

Eating in the street, let alone having a man popping food into her mouth, was thoroughly unladylike behaviour, Maude knew, lifting the edge of her veil just enough for Eden to deliver the chestnut between her parted lips. But as they walked down Cranburn Street into Leicester Square the people they were passing weren't ladies and gentlemen, but people with far fewer inhibitions about enjoying themselves, and their chestnuts were not the only things being consumed. Regaining proper speech again, Eden tossed the rest of the parcel to an urchin. 'Here, catch.'

'Oh, look, Stagg and Mantle's are still open,' Maude said, veering sharply off to the left as soon as they got into the square, only to be brought up short by Eden digging in his heels.

'Over my dead body are you dragging me into a linen draper's,' he stated, with more firmness than gallantry. 'And,' he added as Maude studied his face for any signs of yielding, 'if you so much as flutter an eyelash at me, I will call a cab and that's the end of our walk.'

'All right.' She tucked her hand more firmly into the crook of his elbow. 'It is your turn anyway.'

'For what? Mind that coal cart!'

'For a treat.' Maude looked up at his austere face. 'I had the chestnuts, now it is your turn.'

'I wasn't aware that walks involved treats.' Eden sounded amused—or was he simply bemused?

'My governess started it, and then my girlfriends picked it up and it has become a tradition. So—your turn to choose.'

'I can't think of anything I want. Nothing, that is, that it is reasonable to want on a crowded street,' he added as they walked down Coventry Street towards the bustle of Piccadilly.

'Hatchard's?' Maude enquired hopefully. Once she had lured him into a bookshop, there was the prospect of browsing together companionably, finding out what kind of books he liked, edging him towards the poetry…

'I have far too much reading waiting for me, without adding any more. Aren't you tired yet?'

'Certainly not, this is a mere stroll. At home in Hampshire I walk miles. Oh my, look at that quiz of a hat.'

'It probably cost twenty guineas. The family estate in Hampshire, no doubt?'

'Yes, Knight's Fee. I love it. So does Papa—bone deep. You know, this afternoon, when I saw you looking out from the stage at the theatre, you had just the sort of expression he does when he looks out at the land.'

'Bone-deep love? Yes, I suppose that is what it is. The first time I stepped into a theatre I was fourteen years old and the magic got hold of me and has never let me go. I had never possessed anything before that was my own creation. The theatre let me create and then I was able to buy one, and another, to put on plays. But none of them were right—but I knew I would know when I found it. And in the Unicorn, I have.'

She held her breath, willing him to go on, to let her see more, to understand more. But he had caught himself up, she could sense it.

'And you, Maude—you couldn't live without your country estate and your town house, your balls and your charities, could you?'

'I could if I still had my friends and I could still visit Knight's Fee. Women have to get used to the knowledge they must leave their childhood home, at least, unless we give up all idea of marriage.' It made her slightly breathless, actually speaking of marriage to Eden.

'And you haven't given up, despite your advanced years?' He sounded serious, despite his joke about her age.

'No, of course not. I have always said that there was the right man out there for me and I would know him when I saw him. Just like you and your theatre. I will remain a spinster all my life, rather than compromise on that. That's what gave me the strength to stand up to Papa when he wanted me to marry Gareth.'

'Standon?' He sounded surprised. 'So that is who you were telling me about. But you are good friends, are you not?'

'Excellent friends and we have been for years. It would have been like marrying my brother. Oh, look—' Maude pointed up Dover Street '—that's where we first met.' *Oh, Lord! I blurted that out without thinking…*

'What, you and Standon?'

'No.' Nothing for it. 'You and I. In Todmorton's perfumery shop. I was with Jessica—Lady Standon—you had come in to collect something.'

Eden stopped, ignoring the pedestrians who bumped against him, then began to flow round them as though they were a rock in a river. 'I knew I had seen you before.' He frowned in concentration. 'Sponges. Why do I think of sponges?'

'Because Jessica and I were tossing little ones to and fro and you walked in and had to catch them. We were being foolish and you were looking exceptionally severe.'

Eden ignored that. 'You were wearing green. Moss green and a bonnet with a big satin ribbon and ruching all under the brim.'

He remembered her! And Jessica had said he hadn't noticed them at all. 'That's right,' Maude confirmed happily until she realised with a jolt that she should have pretended not to recall any detail at all. 'It was brand-new. I remember Jessica commenting on it as we went into the shop.'

'And there I was, thinking every detail of the day was burned on your memory because that was the day we met,' Eden said, creating an inner turmoil that made her feel light-headed. If he only knew!

'Well, it was not burned on yours,' she retorted as her scrambled wits reasserted themselves. 'I had to remind you.'

'I could hardly stare at a beautiful young woman, chance met in a shop, now could I?' he asked reasonably, beginning to walk again. 'I saw the gown, the bonnet, a glimpse of your face. I knew you were familiar when I saw you at the theatre.'

Maude could have told him every detail about what he had been wearing: the highly polished Hessians, the buff pantaloons, the dark blue coat, the cane with the silver head, the high-crowned hat in his gloved hands. She could have described in minute detail how his hair had curled over his collar, his words to the shop assistant, the almost physical blow to her senses that seeing him had been.

'Nearly there now.' They were turning into Berkeley Street,

up the side of Devonshire House. 'It seems we were fated to meet again,' he added, almost to himself.

'Yes,' Maude agreed, striving for a tone of bright amusement at the coincidence.

'One could almost say that passing the shop again this evening was an omen,' Eden mused. They had reached the narrow alleyway that ran between the end of the Devonshire House garden boundary and the length of Lansdown House's high wall. The lighting was poor there, contrasting to the open space of Berkeley Square a few yards ahead. 'Do you know, I think I know what I want for my treat.' He stopped and stepped into the mouth of the alley, almost too narrow for them to stand side by side.

'You do?' He was drawing her into his arms, bending his head until his mouth was just above hers.

'I left that shop wishing I could kiss you.'

'You have. Outside your office.' It was an inelegant squeak, but the best she could manage.

'It was hardly my best effort,' Eden said thoughtfully. He lifted her veil back, then his hands bracketed her face, his thumbs caressing lightly against her cheeks.

'Eden—we are on the street!' Her breathing was all over the place and her hands, without any conscious volition, had come up to rest against his lapels.

'Safest place,' he said, sounding rather grim for a man about to kiss a woman. And then he kissed her and Maude stopped thinking about his tone of voice at all.

Chapter Twelve

The pressure of Eden's mouth on hers was light—a caress, not a demand. He did not draw her closer, or try to master her, he simply let his lips stray over hers, tasting, caressing, until finally his tongue-tip slipped between her lips and she could taste in her turn.

His gentleness made her shyer than his force had done; his restraint ensured that every move she made would be very plain to both of them. Maude's fingers closed around his lapels, rather than slide into his hair, which was what she wanted; she stood still rather than pressed herself against him, which was what her body wanted.

The kiss was over almost before it had begun, before her legs could begin to tremble, before her mind became completely blurred with sensation. Eden released her, dropped a kiss on to her forehead, adjusted her veil, then drew her out into the open, her hand once again tucked chastely into his elbow.

'Thank you,' he said seriously. 'That won't happen again.'

'It won't? I mean, why did it happen at all?' Maude asked, flustered and not at all certain she was not angry with him. That brief caress had agitated more than it had satisfied, confused her more than answered any of her doubts and questions.

'It happened because I needed to get that out of my mind,' Eden said. 'I needed to be sure I would not reach out for you when we were alone together. Shall we just say, I was satisfying my curiosity?'

'You may if you like,' Maude retorted. Yes, she was angry. 'Why here, now, in the street?'

'Because it is a very safe place. Even I am not going to go any further than that out here.'

'Even you?' she demanded, coming to an abrupt halt on the corner. 'What do you mean by that?'

'I have a certain reputation,' Eden said, looking down at her. It was hard to see in the poor light, but she thought he looked as grim as he had sounded just before he kissed her.

'For liaisons with married ladies. Very short-lived liaisons,' Maude retorted. 'I hadn't heard that you went about debauching virgins.'

'And I do not intend to start.' Eden strode along the short end of the square, forcing Maude to do a hop and a skip to keep up.

'Excellent. Because I have no intention of being debauched. It sounds horrible. Seduction sounds much better. With the right man, of course.' And if Eden had kissed her like that, that night in the box after dinner, then she could not fool herself— he could have seduced her with no difficulty whatsoever.

He stopped again on the corner of Curzon Street and looked down at her. The sound he made might have been a huff of laughter. 'Hold on to that thought, Maude. Am I forgiven?'

'Of course. It was very pleasant, and instructive, if brief. I could have told you to stop, could I not? And,' she added, risking a smile, 'I did not limit what your treat could be.'

'No, you didn't.' Eden's smile was genuine, if fleeting.

Then he was serious again. Maude wondered if she was imagining the look of bleakness in his eyes, then decided it must be a trick of the torchlight flickering from the flambeaux outside the houses on the corner.

She was making progress with Eden, Maude decided, pouring the earl's morning coffee as a dutiful daughter should, and closing her ears to his robust, if muttered, comments on the government's taxation policy.

Eden was obviously attracted to her, or he would not want to kiss her. And it must be something more than mere desire, because he was so gentle with her. And he had remembered what she had been wearing in the shop that day. And he had listened to her views at the audition. It was slower progress, though, than she had daydreamed of. Foolishly she had expected him to take one look and fall in love with her—or at least manage to do so after a short acquaintance.

And just as obviously the fact that she had fallen in love at first sight did not mean it must be mutual. She sighed, remembering the gentleness of his kiss, the total control. He was very obviously *not* out of control with desire for her.

'You are up very early, my dear.' The sigh had obviously penetrated the barrier of the *Morning Post,* which lowered to reveal her father's face. He frowned, causing his bushy eyebrows to waggle. 'Bad night?'

'Mmm. I couldn't sleep.' Mysteriously, light and gentle kisses appeared to wreak the same havoc on her internal organs and her nerves as passionate, forceful ones. Maude's sleep had consisted of feverish dreams interspersed with long periods tossing and turning and thinking—fruitlessly—of tactics to make Eden fall in love.

'Well, rest today in that case. I don't want you burning the candle at both ends with all those parties and that committee of yours. How's your theatre doing?'

'My theatre? It is very much Mr Hurst's theatre, Papa, even though he does not own it. I am reminded of a big dog with a juicy marrow bone—no one may have so much as a nibble without express permission.'

'He is insolent?' The earl folded his paper and slapped it down beside his plate. 'I'll not have that.'

'No, Papa. Not at all. It is simply that…' She groped for the words to explain. 'It is like you and Knight's Fee. You tolerate the advice of your bailiff and steward and Mr Lambert at Home Farm—but it is you, and you alone, who makes the decisions. Only you inherited the estate; he has created everything himself and I think he can never shake off the fear that he could lose it too.'

The eyebrows rose. 'Territorial, is he? A fine thing for a theatre manager, I must say.'

'He is a powerful and intelligent man, Papa.' He narrowed his eyes at her, suspicious, as she hastened to add, 'You need have no fear my investment is at risk.'

'Humph. Glad to hear it. Ah, now here's the post. Thank you, Rainbow. Good gad, what have we here?' He poked a long finger at the pile.

'Invitations for Lady Maude, my lord.'

'Yours, yours…' Maude scooped up the pile her father extracted and began to slit seals. She was going to have to get her diary out and study it. It was already full, and some of these were events she wanted to attend.

'Papa?' The earl was staring at the sheet of paper in his hand, an odd expression on his face. 'Is anything wrong?'

'Someone your mother and I knew a long time ago is very ill.'

'I'm so sorry. Will you visit?' Maude got up and went to take the chair next to him.

'Visit? No, she lives in Scotland. By the time I got there… Anyway, she was more a friend of your mother's than mine. Almost became your godmother, in fact.' His gaze was unfocused, as though he looked back down the years.

'Really? Why, almost?'

'The old earl, your grandfather, did not feel she was… suitable. And in those days,' he added with a mock-scowl at her, 'one did what one's parents advised.'

'Would I have ever met her?' Maude asked.

'No. Never. Pity she's going.' He sighed. 'Lovely woman. Very talented. Ah well, I must be off to the House.'

Papa's obvious sadness at the news of his long-ago acquaintance subdued Maude's mood and left her the subject of a not-unpleasant melancholy by the time she settled herself in her box again. Anna appeared to have decided that it was quite safe to leave her mistress after yesterday's long, and as far as she was concerned, highly tedious, proceedings.

'May I go down and see Millie, my lady? Only she said she'd show me the costumes and it's ever so interesting.'

'Yes, of course.' Maude waved her away with a vague hand and settled back to brooding on hopeless love, the futility of pleasure, the fleeting nature of existence…

'And lo! What light…'

Maude jerked upright and peered over the edge of the box to find Eden looking up at her. 'Hello. I was indulging in a comfortable fit of melancholy.' Seeing him again after last night should have been awkward, but he appeared his normal, rather cool self, despite the joking quote from *Romeo and Juliet*. Maude reminded herself that they were supposed to be working. 'Sorry, I am paying attention now.'

'In that case, your ladyship, we will begin.' He stalked back to his chair and sat, his back to her. Was he cross with her? Did he expect her to be looking out for him, eager to see him after last night? Or was he angry with himself? Or merely impatient to get on with the job in hand?

Maude cupped her chin in her palm and indulged herself by studying Eden's back. He had discarded his coat and was in shirtsleeves, waistcoat and breeches, an outfit which made him look even more powerfully masculine than usual.

'Miss Jones, hurry up, if you please!'

The first actress hurried on stage, Tom Gates at her heels, and proceeded to say her lines. Maude saw Mr Howard prowling about in the stalls, listening from various positions. She scribbled notes.

Eden called the girl over and began to speak to her, apparently taking details of her past experience. With nothing to do, Maude watched Tom picking up small objects from the table and beginning to juggle. In contrast to his acting, his juggling was positively amateur, she thought, watching him fumble a small jar.

Then it hit her, her wonderful idea for the charity event. Maude scrabbled amongst her papers, found a clean sheet and began to write.

'Next!' Bother. She found the name of the second candidate and made herself concentrate.

By the time all six had been seen it was almost one o'clock and Millie was setting the table again with, Maude was amused to see, Anna helping her. She sorted her notes and went down onto the stage.

Eden and Howard were pacing up and down arguing, Gates at their heels trying to get a word in edgeways.

'Jones or Thomson,' Howard was saying.

'Thomson, possibly, but Miss Lewis was far and away better overall,' Eden asserted.

'Miss Jones picked up cues…' Tom started and was ignored. He saw Maude and grimaced comically.

'I like Miss Jones too,' she offered, but went unheard as the two men began flourishing sheets of notes at each other. Maude marched up, ducked under the stage manager's arm and bobbed up between them. *'Gentlemen.'* They fell silent. 'I liked Miss Jones best.'

'That's three of us then, Guv'nor,' Howard was unwise enough to say.

Eden eyed him coldly. 'Have I said or done anything to give you the impression that this theatre was run as a democracy, Mr Howard?' he enquired.

'No, sir.'

'Lady Maude?'

'No, Mr Hurst.' She smiled sweetly at him. 'But you did say we would discuss this. And I would like my luncheon.'

Eden pulled out a chair for Maude. 'Let us eat, then. And discuss.'

She smiled again as she sat and he had to fight not to smile back. As if he needed any other cue than the gathering heaviness in his groin when he had seen her that morning, her face solemn and a little sad, her chin propped on one cupped hand. Kissing her again had not done a damn thing to stop him wanting her. It had been a thoroughly bad idea, one he had justified to himself at the time and which he now saw as simple self-indulgence. In fact, to call it an idea was crediting himself with an illusion of decision-making when he had to accept the fact that, as far as Maude Templeton was concerned, he simply could not think straight.

They were all sitting waiting politely for him to speak, passing the food around amongst themselves in silence. Maude was even—God help him!—placing food on his plate and buttering his bread for him as if he was her father, or her husband or something.

'Thank you,' he said curtly, wanting to snub her. Clear brown eyes met his for an instant and then the corners crinkled into a smile. Now she was feeling indulgent with his megrims, no doubt! Why wasn't she reacting to what happened last night? He had kissed her, in the street. Down an alley like a whore, he flagellated himself mentally. She should either be angry with him, or bashful, or flirtatious this morning, but, no, Lady Maude Templeton was none of those things. That kiss appeared to have made no impression whatsoever.

Well, it had on him. Damn it, he felt like a seventeen-year-old in the throes of his first infatuation. 'Pass the Stilton,' he said, perversely choosing the platter furthest from him. It was duly passed, he cut his cheese, then looked up. The three of them were regarding him solemnly, like children waiting for grace to be said. His sense of humour, like a cat twitching its tail, came to life.

'Lady Maude,' Eden said politely, his face perfectly straight, 'perhaps you would be so good as to give us your impressions of Miss Jones?'

'Me?' As he had hoped, she was somewhat discomposed by being asked to start.

'Ladies first.' She shot him a glance that told him she knew he was playing with her and unfolded her notes.

'Her voice projected well, she moved gracefully, she responded well to Mr Gates and her timing of the comic lines was perfect. She also looks young enough to play the ingénue for some time to come, unlike Miss Lewis. Oh, yes, and she was the first to go on, you barked at her, and she did not lose her nerve.'

'You base your assessment on the fact that she is not terrified of me?'

'Well, it helps, I should imagine,' Maude replied. 'Awe and respect are doubtless essential, but terror would be a handicap and you make Miss Lewis's knees knock.'

Eden swept the table with a glance, vowing to sack whichever of the others betrayed so much as a glimmer of a smile. Howard had his mouth full of pie and Gates, an actor to his toes, projected nothing but earnest attention. Awe and respect indeed! Little cat.

'Well, do either of you have any comments to make on the stability of Miss Lewis's knees?' he enquired dangerously and was answered by hastily shaken heads. 'I'll take them both, Jones and Lewis, on a month's trial. Satisfied?'

All three nodded and Maude smiled; not, he noticed, a smug feminine smile of triumph, just one of approval. 'What a good idea.'

They finished the meal more comfortably, Howard and Gates relaxing enough to exchange gossip about colleagues at Drury Lane. Maude, he noticed, had fallen silent again. Eden looked up and caught her watching him, uncertainty in her eyes.

'Mr Hurst, might I have a word with you? In your office?'

Ah, so here came the recriminations for last night. Knowing perfectly well he had no grounds on which to defend himself, Eden followed Maude's straight back down the corridor. He did not want her to leave, he realised. If he had driven her away, it was going to leave something perilously like a gap in his life. Which was ridiculous. It implied a weakness, an unfulfilled need, and he had neither of those things.

'Maude.' He waited until she was seated, then went round

to take his own chair. It felt as though he was taking refuge behind a barrier.

'I was thinking about the charity event I have volunteered to organise for the committee,' she said, extracting even more notes from the bundle of sheets in her hands. 'Eden?'

'I'm sorry, a moment's inattention.' A charity event? Not tearful distress, not angry recriminations?

'We've had a ball, and a garden party, but I wanted to do something different this year. And I thought we could hold it here, in the theatre.'

'A charity performance, you mean?' Eden pulled himself together and reached for a pen and paper.

'Not exactly. I wanted to rearrange the stalls and the galleries, set tables out for dining and the acts would all be amateur ones, from members of the audience. I would encourage people to dress up as their favourite characters as well. We'd need a string band and a pianist to accompany those people who wanted to sing and to provide interval music, of course…'

'How many guests?' Eden asked, suppressing his instinctive refusal. Turn his theatre into a cross between country-house theatricals, Astley's Amphitheatre and a vast dinner party?

'Two hundred invitations?' Maude ventured. 'We must make it exclusive.'

'Rip out the stalls?' He was losing this before he'd even begun to object, he knew it. But somehow she was mesmerising him and all he wanted to do was please her.

'Take them out, carefully. We've got some carpenters amongst the men, they'll help your team. The theatre won't need to be closed to the public for more than one night.'

He ought to say no. That was the sensible, prudent thing. He did not support charities, yet somehow she had inveigled him on to her damn committee. He did nothing to compromise the commercial success of the Unicorn and here he was, contemplating an exercise that would cost him goodness knows what. He had a reputation as a hard man and yet he was yielding to a woman who did not even *try* to wheedle concessions out of him. This was dangerous insanity and he was going to refuse.

'Yes, all right. When?'

Maude jumped to her feet and for one, breathless moment, he thought she was going to come round the desk and kiss him. 'Oh, thank you!' She sat right back in her chair again, Eden told himself he was a fool, and Maude drew out her memorandum book. 'Is three weeks too soon?'

Eden studied his own diary. It would give them a break in the run of *Her Precious Honour*, but that was no bad thing—it would give the cast a rest. 'No, that is fine. But can you do it in time?'

'Making things happen is my *forte,*' Maude said with a smile that became, he thought, a touch wry. 'I nearly always achieve what I set out to do.'

'Only nearly?'

'I—' She broke off and the sadness he had seen in her face that morning came back, touching her beauty with a haunting shadow.

'Maude.' Eden reached out a hand, not knowing why and she put out hers to meet it. Their fingers clasped across the stacks of paper on his desk, curled into each other, held. 'Maude, I—'

'Darling!' The door banged back on its hinges and in she swept, Madame Marguerite, scarves flying, gems glittering, her timing, as always, perfect. 'Eden, you absolutely must— oh. And who is this?' She produced one of her carefully graded smiles, this one for lovely young women who might be a threat, but on the other hand, might simply be admirers.

'Lady Maude, may I introduce Madame Marguerite? Madame, this is Lady Maude Templeton. I told you she is investing in the Unicorn.'

'Lady Maude, I'm so pleased to meet you.' One of her less haughty greetings, thank goodness. Apparently she was moved to be pleased. Eden helped her to a chair and resumed his.

'Lady Maude has asked me to join the committee of her charity, if you recall, Madame.'

'But of course. So worthy—you must add my name to the donations list,' she said airily.

'Thank you so much, Madame.' Maude whipped out a notebook and pencil. 'For how much?'

To Eden's vast amusement she sat there, pencil poised, smiling at Madame, who, he knew full well, had intended to forget all about it the moment she was out of the door. He was sorely tempted to sit there and see what happened, but for the sake of peace and quiet suggested, 'Twenty guineas? I'll arrange it, Madame.'

'Thank you, darling.' She smiled at him, her famous blue eyes wide and glorious. 'I can always rely on darling Eden,' she added as an aside to Maude.

'I am sure you can, ma'am. May I say how very much both my father, the Earl of Pangbourne, and I, admire your performances?'

'I am charmed to hear it. I must, however, be on my way. Eden—'

He got up to open the door. 'You came in to say there was something I must do?'

'Oh? Did I?' she said vaguely. 'Never mind, darling, I am sure I'll remember.' She swept out on a cloud of Attar of Roses and a rustling of silk.

Eden went back to his place behind the desk. 'That,' he said superfluously, 'was Madame Marguerite.'

'I was very pleased to meet her,' Maude said. 'She's your mother, isn't she?'

Chapter Thirteen

'My mother?' There did not seem to be any point in lying about it. It was not as though he was ashamed of it, exactly, more that he found it much easier not to think of Marguerite as his mother. There were no expectations then. 'Yes.'

'It is not widely known?' Maude did not appear shocked. But then, she was a lady, and ladies were bred to disguise their feelings.

'Not known at all. How did you guess?'

'I can glimpse a resemblance. Not in colouring, of course. Your presence, perhaps. And yet you both remind me of someone else—I do wish I could think who.'

'She prefers it not to be known,' Eden said, his voice as neutral as he could make it. 'I am somewhat old to be comfortably acknowledged as her son. People would do the arithmetic, you see.'

'But in private—'

'No.' He shook his head. 'Outside the theatre we lead separate lives.'

'Oh. I am so sorry.' That was the second time she had expressed pity for him, and pity was not something his pride would accept from anyone, even if, for some reason, he wanted to pour the whole story of his childhood out to Maude and have her, in some way he could not imagine, make it better.

Eden shrugged. 'She is exhausting enough as it is.'

'Yes, but—' She must have seen something in his face, for she broke off, hesitated, then asked, 'Your father—she married him in Italy?'

'La Belle Marguerite,' he said, inserting the shield of irony into his tone, 'has never found any man worthy of marriage.'

Maude frowned, as though she was untangling a puzzle, not, oddly, as if she found herself disgusted to be having this conversation with a bastard. 'So your father—' She tried again. 'You said he would not speak to you, but did he not even—?'

'He refused to acknowledge me.' She might as well have the lot, see just who her business partner was. Or, more to the point, was not.

'Bastard,' Maude commented. 'Him, I mean. Is it true he is a prince?'

'So you had heard the rumours? He was. He died last year. When I was fourteen, Madame decided I might be of some use to her. She descended on the palazzo, swept me up against very little opposition—as you may imagine, his wife was happy to see the back of me, even if I was relegated to the stables along with the rest of his by-blows—and set me to learn about the theatre.'

'She had just left you with him?' Maude looked more appalled at that than anything else.

'She was sure I would be much better looked after there rather than being dragged around Europe in the wake of her career. And I learned fluent Italian—so useful.'

'And a baby and then a small child would be such an in-convenience with her career and her lovers, I suppose,' Maude said savagely, startling him. 'How she could!' She sat in silence for a moment, staring down at her tightly locked hands. 'I beg your pardon, I should not speak so about your mother.'

'Don't apologise. I do not love her, she does not love me. I am her business manager, she is my leading actress. It is business. I understand her very well; she, I think, understands me not at all.' Maude simply stared at him, her face appalled. 'What?' he flung at her. 'Are you shocked? Do you think I should have loved her, so that she had the power to break my heart?'

'Of course she broke your heart,' Maude said fiercely. 'Of *course* she did. Do not tell me you do not believe in love, just because it hurts too much. It hurts because it is important. It hurts because it is all there is. Don't pretend to me you are not capable of love.'

Eden stared at her, furious, confused, disorientated by her attack. He had told her the sordid truth about his birth and somehow he was at fault for dealing with it well? Then he saw her eyes, the sparkle of unshed tears, and something inside, something cold and hard that he had thought impregnable, cracked. What did she want from him? What was hurting inside him? Something trying to get out, or the pain of emptiness? Her heart seemed big enough to grieve for him— didn't she realise that he had built a wall around his? That he had nothing to give her? *Only more pain*, he thought as he went to her.

'Maude. Maude, don't cry.' He crouched down beside her chair and put his arm around her shoulders. Hell, she was so determined, so positive, she seemed sturdier than she was. Under the weight of his arm her shoulders were fragile. 'Don't cry. I won't know what to do if you cry.'

Tantrums, scenes, furious tears, manipulative tears, crocodile tears. He knew what to do with those, he had enough practice. But these unshed tears, tears she was fighting not to let spill, these almost unmanned him.

'You…you could give me a handkerchief,' she suggested shakily. He pulled a large one from his pocket and handed it to her. 'Thank you.' She blew her nose like a boy and scrubbed at her eyes. No, these tears weren't for show, weren't to manipulate. Her nose had gone pink and her eyes were bleary and she was not sparing a thought for how she looked. 'Sorry. I don't cry, you know.'

'No, of course not.' He did not know whether to get up and leave her to compose herself or not. He wanted to stay, he ought to go. Eden remained where he was on his knees beside the chair.

'It upset me,' she explained, looking at him directly at last. 'I hate it when people are cruel to anyone who is helpless— children, animals, our soldiers when they were too sick to fend for themselves.'

'I'm not helpless,' he said.

'Not now. Our soldiers have scars, limbs missing, eyes gone. We can see their scars, do something with them. Where are yours, Eden?'

'I am not one of your charity cases,' he said, not answering her, rocking back on his heels because otherwise he would kiss those tear-filled eyes, stop her looking at him like that.

'No.' Maude nodded. 'No, you are not. You have done all this, all by yourself. You do not need charity. But don't tell me not to pity the child that you were, or feel anger for him, because I do. And don't tell me not to try to convince you about love, because I will not stop trying.'

'Are you going to get out your Bible and preach to me, then?' he asked bitterly. The priest at the palazzo had done that often enough.

'No.' Maude folded up the handkerchief and regarded him

solemnly. 'It is up to you what you do with your love, and you can put some of it into religion if you want to. I simply intend to convince you it exists.'

'Why?' Eden got to his feet and stood looking down at her. This was dangerous, this could tear him apart.

'Because you are right in front of me, and we are friends and partners, so it behoves me to do something about you,' she said firmly, getting to her feet too and beginning to shuffle her papers together.

'Just like that?'

'Yes.' She nodded, tapping the edges of the pages on the desk to align them. 'When I see something that needs to be done, I do it.'

'And I have no say in the matter?' Eden found he was smiling at her. He received a watery smile back.

'Of course you do. You get to have free choice what to do with your love when you find where you have buried it.' *I know where it is, I have walled it up where it cannot hurt me. Or you, Maude. Oh God, I could hurt you so much.*

She picked up her memorandum book. 'Are you going to the Hethersetts' ball in three days' time?'

Conversation with Maude was like fencing lessons, you never knew where she was going to attack next. 'No,' Eden said baldly, a wary eye out for the next feint.

'But you have been invited?'

'Yes.'

'Excellent. We have a committee meeting tomorrow afternoon—I did tell you, didn't I? We need to discuss our plans for the theatre event and also tactics for taking advantage of the ball. It is very useful having another handsome man on the committee; you can woo all the rich widows, they are impervious to Jessica, Bel and me.'

'*Our* theatre event?'

'Ours. The others are going to be *so* pleased with us. Now, don't forget, the Standons' house at half past two. Goodbye.' He was still standing regarding the door panels when she popped her head round again. 'And don't forget to accept Lady Hethersett's invitation.'

'Mr Hurst is attending today's meeting,' Maude remarked, standing in the Standons' hall while Jessica supervised the footmen hanging a portrait.

'Excellent,' Jessica responded, her attention on what the men were doing with the heavy frame. 'Careful! Don't let the cloth slip off until it is up there, I don't want to risk damaging it. It is Gareth's papa,' she added to Maude. 'There's his mother, behind you. They were in the country house, but not well displayed, and absolutely filthy. I had them cleaned and I think they will look good here.'

Maude turned to study the portrait of the late countess, severely lovely in piled white wig and sky blue satin. 'Beautiful.' She turned back as the footmen pulled at the swathing cloths on the matching portrait. 'Oh, my God.'

'What?' Jessica blinked at her, puzzled. 'I think it is a very handsome portrait.'

'Yes, it is,' Maude agreed. 'But don't you see the likeness?'

'To Gareth? Well, of course, he's much more like his mother at first glance, but there's something about the way he stands.'

'Have you got a *Peerage*?' Maude asked urgently. Why on earth hadn't she seen it before?

'Yes, of course. Here, I'll show you.' Still looking bemused, Jessica led the way to Gareth's study. 'There, several editions, in fact.'

Maude pulled out the one that looked the oldest and flicked through her pages. 'Ravenhurst, Dukes of Allington…here we are, marriage of Francis, second duke, to Francesca. Son Francis 1750, that's Bel and Sebastian's father, then a big gap up to Sophia, 1761.'

'That's Gareth's mother,' Jessica said. 'Apparently Francesca was quite ill after the birth of the heir.'

'Then Augustus, that's Theo's father the bishop, then… Aha! Margery, 1767.'

'Why, *Aha*? I've never heard of her.'

'Exactly. Let's see what happens to her.' Maude began to pull out volumes, opening them in date order. Finally, when she checked the final one she said triumphantly, 'See? *Nothing* happens to Margery. No marriage, she isn't dead. So where is she?'

'I have no idea.' Jessica perched on the corner of Gareth's desk, apparently set on humouring her friend.

'She's La Belle Marguerite and she's Eden's mother.'

'*What?*'

'He told me yesterday she was his mother. His father is, as the rumours say, an Italian prince. Marguerite—or Margery— abandoned the child with his father, who left him to the servants to bring up. She only claimed him years later.'

'How awful, poor child,' Jessica said compassionately. 'But that doesn't make her Margery.'

'One, she gave him the surname Hurst—half of Ravenhurst.' Maude ticked off points on her fingers. 'Two, he's been reminding me of someone, I just couldn't put a finger on it. Three, when he came into the box that evening you were all there, Papa mistook him for Gareth, when he saw him in silhouette in the doorway, and, four, look at the portrait of Lord Standon in the hall.'

'There *is* a scandalous aunt in the family, I know that,' Jessica said. 'Gareth is mildly curious, but apparently even Sebastian doesn't know the story—the older generation just refuse to speak of it. Do you think Eden knows?'

'He is very unruffled about associating with Bel and Gareth, who are his first cousins, if he does,' Maude said. 'But then, Eden is unruffled about most things, except attacks on his control of the Unicorn. I will ask him.'

'Maude, you can't, not just like that! If he knows, he hasn't said anything, so he wants it kept secret; if he doesn't, think what a shock it would be.'

'Yes, I can. And, Jessica, don't you see, Papa can hardly object on the grounds of breeding—an Italian prince for a father and a duke for a grandfather, for goodness' sake.'

'You are overlooking the minor detail of a lack of a marriage certificate to link the two,' Jessica said wryly. 'It doesn't make it better; in some ways, it makes it worse.'

'True.' Maude swallowed, feeling as though she had been punched in the stomach. For one moment she had thought it would all be fine now. Of course it wouldn't. 'It has been such a big secret, what happened to Margery. Bel and Gareth's parents—all that generation—are going to be furious.' She began to put the books back on the shelf. 'I've got to find some way to make Eden acceptable to Papa.'

'You've got to make him fall in love with you first,' her friend added with brutal honesty.

Maude thought about confiding in Jessica. Perhaps she would understand what that strange, gentle kiss in the darkened alleyway had meant.

'Oh, there's the front door knocker, the committee is arriving.' Jessica hopped off the desk and became, once more, a dignified countess. The moment was lost.

'Go and greet people in the hall. I'll stand under the portrait and try to get Eden to talk to me there so you can see,' Maude urged as the Reverend Makepeace's fluting tones reached them.

Eden was exactly on time. Several of the others, more familiar with the household and less on their society manners, had arrived earlier and were gossiping in the dining room. 'Lady Standon, I apologise, I have kept you waiting.' He glanced towards the open door and the sound of voices as he handed his hat and coat to the butler.

'No, not at all, they are early, Mr Hurst. Ah, there's Maude, she will show you the way.' Jessica smiled, affecting just to notice Maude poised under the portrait. Maude smiled and held out her hand to him, turning so that he was forced to stop and stand in three-quarters profile to Jessica, just like the figure in the painting. Maude saw her friend's eyes narrow and she nodded, just as her husband strolled downstairs.

'Maude, good afternoon. Hurst.' Gareth held out his hand and Maude slipped away to stand with Jessica, regarding the two men standing under the portrait.

'I think you are right,' Jessica whispered. 'There is a re-semblance. Are you going to tell the other cousins?'

'How can I?' Maude murmured back. 'That is up to Eden and I have no idea whether or not he knows.'

Maude found herself watching Eden during the committee meeting. He was managing to control any surprise at Bel taking the chair, although she could read him well enough to see his impatience at Mr Makepeace's long, and rambling, report.

There was no disguising the fact that Mr Makepeace and Lady Wallace were treating Eden with some reserve. Presum-ably neither really approved of his presence on the committee.

'Now then, tactics for Lady Hethersett's ball,' Bel announced. 'She tells me that several ladies who are on our list as potential sponsors, but who have so far eluded us, will be attending.'

'And both I, and Dereham, will be absent,' Gareth remarked. 'So the duty of charming the ladies is, I am very happy to say, all yours, Hurst.' There was the slightest edge to his voice.

Eden's eyebrows rose. 'That sounds hazardous. Might I remind you, Standon, that while you and Dereham are safely married, I am perilously single.'

'We are not asking you to propose to them, Mr Hurst,' Jessica said, with a dimpling smile. 'Just flirt. You can flirt, can't you?'

There was silence, broken only by Mr Makepeace's faint cluck of disapproval. Eden regarded Jessica steadily. How he did it, Maude had no idea, but somehow those cool brown eyes gained heat, the severe lips softened and, 'I never flirt, Lady Standon,' he said, his voice somehow huskier than before.

Jessica, sitting next to her own husband, blushed like a peony.

It seemed to Maude that the committee held its collective breath, then Jessica burst out laughing. 'Mr Hurst, that was outrageous! If you can make the toes of a happily married lady curl in her slippers like that, I shudder to think what havoc you can wreak on Lady Hethersett's guests.'

'Ma'am?' Eden looked blank.

'An excellent demonstration of just what is needed,' Gareth commented, his tone steely. 'I need hardly add that should you make my wife's toes curl again, there will be hell to pay?'

Eden inclined his head gravely, Mr Makepeace looked shocked and Lady Wallace was seized with a fit of coughing. Bel consulted her list again, 'There are also some gentle-men… I will distribute them amongst the ladies of the committee later and we can agree tactics over tea. Now, the next item on the agenda is our fund-raising event. Maude?'

'Mr Hurst and I have a suggestion,' Maude said, blithely ignoring Eden narrowing his eyes at her. 'Mr Hurst is very kindly prepared to allow us to use the Unicorn for a gala evening with music and refreshments. The special attraction is that the entertainment will be provided by the guests themselves.'

She explained in detail, conscious of Eden sitting silent, occasionally jotting down a note as she expanded the idea far beyond the bare details she had sketched out for him. Was she going too far? she wondered, braced for him to protest.

But he made no complaint, sitting calmly while the others exclaimed and praised, enthusiastically joining in to identify those leaders of society who must be persuaded to take part in this novel entertainment in order to ensure that everyone would be clamouring for an invitation. It seemed the novelty of the scheme was enough to overcome their reservations about Eden, at least for the moment.

When they finally finished the meeting and tea was served, Gareth made his way over to where Maude was talking to Eden.

'We have some skilled carpenters amongst the men—I have several employed renovating some houses I own,' he remarked. Maude held her breath, hoping this was an olive branch. 'I can bring them over, Hurst, give your men a hand. I'll supervise, if that will free you up for anything more technical.'

'Thank you.' Eden's voice was cool. 'I would be grateful for the men, but I, and I alone, supervise anything that happens in my theatre.'

'I wonder, then,' Gareth remarked, his eyes flickering to Maude, 'that you tolerate Lady Maude's interference.'

'I do not have to.' Eden sounded, to Maude's anxious ear,

faintly amused. 'Firstly, Lady Maude does not interfere, she makes interesting and constructive suggestions. Secondly, we have established very firm boundaries for our partnership.'

'Amazing,' Gareth drawled, helping himself to a macaroon. 'You must be the first man, including her father, to impose any boundaries whatsoever on Maude.' He sauntered off and began to talk to Lady Wallace.

Maude could feel the tension coming off Eden like the heat from a fire. 'He presumes a lot on old acquaintance, does he not?' he enquired, his dark eyes following Gareth's progress.

'No, not at all, he is simply teasing me.' Maude blinked—a low sound, not unlike a growl, was surely emanating from Eden's throat. It could hardly, since there was no large dog in the room, be coming from anywhere else. 'I told you, we have known each other since childhood,' she added hastily. 'I tease him just as much.' It was not jealousy, that was too much to hope for, but the very fact that he wanted to defend her filled Maude with a warm glow.

'Would you drive me home?'

'Unchaperoned?'

'I happen to know you drove yourself in an open carriage,' she said. 'A curricle, perhaps?'

'And how did you know that?'

'You were cold when you came in. Colder than would be accounted for by being in a closed carriage—I was standing close to you in the hall, if you recall. And you were wearing a caped driving coat, which seemed a little excessive for a passenger.'

'Admirable deduction. I was driving my new phaeton.'

'Then, may I drive with you? It is quite unexceptional to be alone with you in an open vehicle, after all.'

'You will be cold.' But he was smiling, just a little.

'I will borrow Jessica's furs. Wait for me.'

* * *

'What is it, Maude?' She looked down at him in surprise from the carriage seat into which he had just helped her. She was not quite certain, for his eyes were shaded by the brim of his hat, but Eden was amused.

'What?'

'Whatever it is you want to quiz me about in private.' Eden went round and climbed into the phaeton, took the reins from the waiting footman and gave the pair the office to start. 'I can't believe that you have just had a sudden fancy to drive through London in the chill of a February afternoon to take the air.'

'I wanted to ask you something highly personal,' she confessed, watching the street unfold between the pricked ears of the bay leader.

'Ask then.' He glanced sideways. 'I won't promise to answer.'

'Do you know your mother's real name?' There was no point in beating around the bush, and sooner or later, they would have to confront the issue of his family.

'Yes.' The leader shied at a yapping mongrel on the pavement and Eden collected him with his voice and a touch of the whip. 'I suppose you are wondering if I know that I have just been sitting down with two of my cousins? Are they aware of who I am?'

'No, only Jessica. She was with me this afternoon when I saw a portrait of her father-in-law and realised why you so often seemed familiar. I looked in the *Peerage* and found your mother,' she added.

'Will you tell them?' Eden sounded merely interested, as though they were speaking of someone else.

'No, not unless you wish to, and I will ask Jessica not to say anything. She is very discreet.' Maude hesitated. He was not pouring out his confidences, but on the other hand, he had not rebuffed her. 'How did you discover the connection?'

'When we were packing to come to England, I found some papers that made me suspect. I have not challenged Madame on the subject. It would not be worth the effort—she always refuses to discuss the past. I do not think the resemblance is such that it is immediately obvious.'

'No, it is something about the way you move, the way you hold yourself, I think. I know them very well, so perhaps it is more obvious to me.' Still he did not react, yet Maude had the feeling she was walking on eggshells.

'Would you not like some family?' she persisted.

'You think they would acknowledge me? I think not. Besides, the question is irrelevant. Unless Madame wishes to make known her identity, I cannot speak of it.'

'Oh. I had not thought of that.' Maude fell silent, brooding on this latest complication. They were almost in Mount Street. 'Do you dance?'

Eden reined in the pair at her front door. 'Do I dance? There are times, Maude, when I find myself baffled by the workings of your mind. How do we get from my parentage to dancing?'

'We do not. But there is no point in pursuing a topic of conversation you are obviously unwilling to discuss and I want to know whether you will dance with me at Lady Hethersett's ball.'

'Yes, I dance. And, yes, it will be a pleasure to dance with you at the ball, Maude.' The front door opened and a footman appeared. Eden glanced at him and added, his voice lower, 'But do not try to extend your campaign to make me admit the existence of love to a scheme to have me embrace all my family—they would not thank you for introducing a theatrical bastard to their fireside, believe me.'

'They already acknowledge you for what you are, not where you came from,' Maude said. 'The Ravenhursts—the ones who are my friends—are more open minded than perhaps you believe.' He made no response, and besides, James was already coming round to help her down. This was not the time to pursue it. 'Thank you, Eden, I enjoyed my drive.'

Chapter Fourteen

The bays fidgeted, testing his control as though his own tension was reaching them. Eden turned them towards Hyde Park. It would be relatively free of crowds now and he could work out the horses' fidgets and his own unsettled thoughts in privacy.

He had come back to England, settled into the fringes of society, confident that the secrets of his birth would remain just that. Secret. Lady Margery Ravenhurst had fled the family home at the tender age of nineteen—it was safe to believe that none of her family would recognise her now, a woman in her mid-forties.

Discreet observation of the myriad Ravenhurst clan had convinced him that with his Italian looks he had no reason to fear exposure either. Frowning, he realised how betraying that word was. There was nothing to *fear* from the Ravenhursts, not in the material sense. And yet it would hurt his pride, he realised, if there was the slightest suspicion that he was courting acceptance, presuming on the connection.

Eden swung the team in through the gates and let them extend their trot across the scuffed tan surface. Trust Maude to see a likeness that he was not even aware of himself. But then Maude looked deeper into him than anyone else ever had. She thought, bless her, that there was something about him worth humanising, worth teaching to love.

And he let himself be seduced and weakened by her friendship, her concern, just as he was constantly tormented by desire for her. She saw him as a crippled being to be rescued, taught love, sent out again into the world like a bird with a mended broken wing. But she assumed he wanted to feel love, that he was capable of it. Love was something you were born into, grew up with, surely? Not something you could learn.

The leader broke into a canter and was ruthlessly brought back to a trot. If he could control nothing else today, he could damn well control his horses. What would it be like to belong to a family like the Ravenhursts? So many of them and yet such a tight-knit clan, gathering in new members by friendship or marriage. It would be suffocating, he told himself. And weakening. And yet seductively warm.

Warm, like Maude. But Maude was special and he was not, he was all too bitterly aware, worthy of a woman like that. He could only hurt her, they were so different and he so scarred. He should send her money back, end their partnership, he knew that, but still he wanted to hold out cold hands to the glow of her smile and her honesty and her concern. Just for a little while longer.

'Papa? Are you ready?' Maude put her head around the door of her father's study, surprised not to find him waiting in the hall, foot tapping, one eye on the clock.

The earl was sitting at his desk, a letter in his hand, staring at the fire. Maude pushed the door wider and he looked up. 'Sorry, my love. Did you say something?'

'I asked if you are ready to go to Lady Hethersett's, Papa.'

Maude went up to the desk, anxious. 'Are you unwell?' He looked uncharacteristically melancholy and suddenly, frighteningly, older.

'Unwell? No, my dear. Just rather…sad. That friend of your mother's—you recall I told you she was ill? Well, now it seems she has died.' He sighed, folding the heavy sheets of paper under his hands. Maude looked down at them, seeing for the first time how prominent the veins were becoming, noticing the age spots, and placed one of hers over his.

'I'm so sorry, Papa. Let me go upstairs and change and we'll spend a quiet evening together.'

'What! Nonsense, you'll do no such thing. It's years since I saw her, we never corresponded more than a note at the turn of the year. No, I'm just a little melancholy, thinking of times long past, that's all.'

Thinking of Mama, Maude thought, squeezing his hand. 'Yes, but I will—'

'No. You run along and enjoy yourself. I am going to go to the club, I'm not good company this evening, but I'm quite all right.' He beetled his heavy eyebrows at her. 'And I don't want you sitting at home when you could be out there snaring that highly eligible son-in-law for me. You give my apologies to Henrietta Hethersett now.'

'If you are certain, Papa,' Maude dropped a kiss on his cheek. 'But I'm not promising a highly eligible son-in-law, I'm afraid.' Her conscience gave a painful twinge at the thought of just how ineligible the man of her dreams was.

'You're a good girl. Just go and find a good man—I only want you to be happy, Maude.'

Papa really meant it, she knew he did, Maude thought as she climbed, alone, into the carriage. But could he possibly conceive just *who* it might take to make her happy?

* * *

'All by yourself, child?' Lady Hethersett tut-tutted indulgently as Maude reached the head of the receiving line.

'Papa is indisposed, ma'am.' Maude dropped a curtsy and smiled back. ' He asked me to give you his apologies. I will find Lady Dereham or Lady Standon at once,' she added meekly.

However, an airy wave when she saw them on the other side of the great reception room that led on to the ballroom was quite enough to fulfil her promise to Lady Hethersett, Maude decided. Just beyond a potted palm she could see Mr Worthington, an elderly gentleman who was on her list of potential benefactors for the charity. If she added him to her collection, she could relax and enjoy herself for the rest of the evening with a clear conscience.

Ten minutes later she was wondering if she was ever going to extract either money, or herself. 'Disgraceful, the number of sturdy rogues sponging upon the Poor Relief,' Mr Worthington was saying indignantly. 'The charge upon property owners in every parish is outrageous!'

'Exactly,' Maude interjected. 'And so many of these men are returning soldiers from the wars. Now, a very modest donation of one hundred guineas to our charity will prove a excellent investment in removing these men permanently from becoming a charge upon the parishes.'

'Hmm.' He eyed her dubiously. 'Investment, you say?'

'Absolutely,' Maude said. 'Of course, it takes a gentleman of experience and foresight such as yourself to appreciate that…' Her mind went blank. Just the other side of the arrangement of greenery she could see a pair of broad shoulders and hear Eden's trained voice.

'Of course, Lady Lucas, I can offer inducements beyond

my, no doubt, imperfect arguments as to why you should become a patron.'

'Inducements? Why, Mr Hurst, you *do* interest me!' Lady Lucas, the wife of a notoriously indolent and neglectful husband, was a sprightly blonde with a roving eye. And, Maude saw as she shifted her position slightly, those wide blue orbs were fixed on Eden's face. Lady Lucas moved closer and rested one hand on his forearm. 'Do tell—or should we go somewhere more private?'

'No need.' Eden laid his own hand over hers, then raised it to his lips. 'I can rely upon your discretion?'

'Oh, yes, Mr Hurst, I am very, very, discreet.'

Trollop, Maude thought, torn between admiration for Eden's technique and indignation at Lady Lucas.

'If you promise not to tell a soul—' Maude strained to hear his lowered voice '—there is going to be a very interesting event at the Unicorn in a few weeks, and I can make certain that you have the very best box.'

'A private box?' Lady Lucas managed to imbue the phrase with overtones of delicious impropriety.

'Oh, yes,' Eden purred, 'Very private.'

'Two hundred guineas.' Maude started, then realised that leaving Mr Worthington to brood on her words appeared to have done the trick. 'Here you are, my dear, a note for my bankers.' He pressed the paper into her hand. 'No, no, do not thank me. Now I must find Lady Smythe, I have promised her a hand of whist.'

As she tucked the note into her reticule, Maude craned to see what was happening with Eden and Lady Lucas, but both dark head and blonde had vanished.

'What's the matter?' Bel asked, appearing at her side. 'You look as though you've lost something.'

'Eden. I last saw him reducing Lady Lucas to putty with promises of a very private box at the theatrical event. And now they've vanished.'

'And you are wondering if he has been swept off to demonstrate his um…credentials? Don't worry. See—he is over there, flirting desperately with Mrs Hampton-Wilde. He really is very good at it; look at her, she is positively quivering. He throws himself into it with far more enthusiasm than Ashe does when I nag him into trying to charm money out of ladies, poor dear.'

'Eden appears to have a natural talent for it,' Maude said darkly.

'Jealous?' Bel smiled wickedly. 'Never fear, he has not seen you yet; when he does, I am certain he'll have eyes for no one else. That gown is stunning.'

'It is rather, isn't it?' Maude allowed herself to be distracted into contemplating her gown. It was cut perilously high under the bust, and perilously low above it, modesty being preserved only with a yellow rose at the centre and a thin ruffle of lace. The underskirt of soft white satin was quite unadorned, but the overskirt of almost transparent gauze was finished at the hem with a double row of rosettes, each with a rose at the centre.

'I love those short sleeves, so intricate.' Bel studied them. 'I've never seen anything quite like it. But how on earth you are going to stay within the bounds of decency if you dance anything energetic, I have no idea.'

'It's very tight, I won't fall out,' Maude whispered. 'And you can hardly criticise.' Bel was dashing in pomona green with a plunging back and fluttering overskirt with high side-slits.

Bel looked smug. 'Ashe *adores* it. He wanted to stay home when he saw it. Oh, look, Mr Hurst is making her blush. Are you going to drift past and see if you can put him off his stroke?'

'Certainly not,' Maude said. 'I am going to see if I can make *him* jealous. And there's the very man.' She let her eyes widen as she caught the gaze of Major Sir Frederick Staines, then dropped them in apparent confusion.

'Careful,' Bel warned, 'he's the most terrible rake.'

'I know. Perfect.' With a laugh, Bel moved on. 'Oh, good evening, Sir Frederick.'

The major was tall, blond, smoothly good looking and perfect for her purposes.

'Lady Maude. May I say how very lovely you are looking this evening?' She dimpled at him. 'Might I beg the honour of the first waltz? And perhaps something later?'

'I would be delighted.' Maude consulted her dance card. 'The first waltz and the fourth set of country dances, then.' As she hoped, he stayed by her side, his eyes a little too brazen in their admiration of her neckline. 'Listen! The orchestra has started.'

The major promptly offered his arm to walk her into the ballroom. With perfect timing they found themselves halted at the doors to the ballroom by a knot of elderly chaperons who were greeting each other loudly right next to Eden, still in attendance on Mrs Hampton-Wilde.

Maude looked up at Sir Frederick, a slight smile on her lips, and was rewarded by him returning the look with one of cheek-warming intensity. 'Oh, Sir Frederick,' she said lightly, 'you quite put me to the blush, you wicked man.'

Out of the corner of her eye she was aware of Eden's head turning, felt the impact of his eyes on her. As she hoped, the major bent over her, murmuring flirtatious nonsense and she laughed, rapping him on the sleeve with her fan in mock reproof.

'Lady Maude.'

'Mr Hurst! My goodness, you made me jump. Good

evening, Mrs Hampton-Wilde.' The other woman bowed, her lips pursing in displeasure at the interruption.

'Might I ask for the honour of a dance?' Eden asked. Maude smiled and nodded. 'The first waltz?'

'I am engaged to Sir Frederick for that set. Perhaps some country dances later?'

'Might I see?' Eden reached for her dance card almost before she lifted her hand. Beside her the major stiffened. 'The supper set and the last one?' He was writing, E.H., even as she agreed. *Perfect.* And even better was the way he was looking at Sir Frederick with cold, hard challenge. He did not like to see her with the other man, that was plain, even if he was unaware of just what that implied.

Although, Maude mused, as her hand was claimed by Lord Nashe for the first set, a quadrille, it could simply be that Eden was aware of Sir Frederick's reputation and would have been wary of his attentions to any young lady he knew.

Still, even if he was not consumed by burning jealousy, it was a good start to the evening and she could not brood upon it any more now—the first of the figures, the *Grand Ronde*, was underway. Maude smiled at her partner and set herself to follow the complex patterns of the dance.

Eden set one shoulder against a pillar and watched the promenading couples through narrowed eyes. Maude was not, thankfully, dancing with that rake Staines, although she would be, he'd seen the initials on her card. The man wasn't safe for her to be with; he was a regular visitor to the Unicorn, to be found in the Green Room after a show, propositioning the girls of the chorus or in a box with some companions and two or three bits of muslin.

Was Maude aware of his reputation? And what the hell was

she doing here without her father, or a proper chaperon? She
was too damn free and easy, that was the trouble…

He listened to his own thoughts and smiled grimly, hardly
noticing the expression of alarm on the face of a bold young
lady who had been staring at him as she passed. Damn it, he
sounded like her guardian, or her elder brother, which was
thoroughly hypocritical of him, considering he was encouraging her in unconventional behaviour—dining in her box,
walking home through the streets. Kissing in alleyways.

But that was with him. She was safe with him—give or take
a kiss. Thoughts of those kisses occupied him through the
entire set. It occurred to him that association with Maude
Templeton was turning him celibate—in action if not in
thought. Which was, Eden mused, odd. He was well aware
that his appetites, while well regulated, were more than
healthy. So why was he avoiding the usual houses where such
things could be discreetly satisfied?

Maude, twirling in the middle of the set, turned her head,
laughing in response to something her partner was saying to her,
and Eden caught his breath. No, he had not lost interest in sex,
he had simply lost interest in any other woman than Maude.

Hell. This was more serious than he had imagined. There
was a strange sensation apparently lodged under his breast-
bone, his normally clear mind was in turmoil—and she, quite
obviously, had no ideas in that direction whatsoever. She
would hardly been so comfortable alone with him if she had.

Maude knew all there was to know about his parentage, so
she must, being very much a member of the *ton* herself, have no
thought at all of any other relationship than the one they had now.

Eden conjured up, with no difficulty whatsoever, the feel
of her mouth under his, her body against him. It was not that
Maude was not responsive when he kissed her, but she was

most certainly not abandoned to passion. It was almost as though she was curious. Perhaps that was it; a well-bred young woman had few opportunities to experience passion and she thought he was safe enough to experiment with a little.

Painfully, an entire new set of emotions were being born—possessive, protective desire, warm liking, the need to be near her. He had never let himself get close to a woman before and there was no one to ask if these were normal feelings.

He had resolved to simply get used to her being around and that was proving impossible. It was impossible, too, to be unmoved by the sight of Sir Frederick Staines waiting for her as she walked off after the completion of the quadrille. Eden looked at his own card. A waltz. Now he was going to have to stand and watch her revolving in the arms of that man.

Eden glanced to either side and realised he was behind the chairs occupied by a group of wallflowers, half a dozen young women watching with ill-concealed envy as their more fortunate sisters took to the floor. He stepped forward, selected the plainest girl he could see and stopped in front of her.

'I regret we have not been introduced, but may I have the honour of this dance?' It was improper on his part, and outrageously fast on hers, but the young woman, sandy haired, befreckled and gawky, jumped to her feet with alacrity.

'I would love to, sir.' She could, he realised with considerable relief as they reached the floor, dance. In fact, despite her height and her surprise at being snatched from the sidelines, she moved very gracefully.

'I am Eden Hurst,' he said after the first few steps.

'Angela Hunter. I haven't been approved to waltz by a Patroness, you know,' she added, biting her lip.

'It's all right, you can simply say I snatched you on to the floor and you were far too well behaved to resist,' Eden said, sweeping her round a corner. 'Everyone will blame me, I have a shocking reputation.'

'Really?' She grinned. 'What fun.'

Now that he could see Maude, it was a simple matter to steer his partner so that they were dancing close to her and Staines. He couldn't hear what the man was saying to her, but at least if he saw any distress on her face he was near enough to intervene.

And then Maude saw him. Her eyes widened, she smiled, then she saw his partner and she frowned. She was puzzled. Good. He fully intended that she should be, it might take her mind off that blond Lothario.

They appeared to be in perfect unison. *It was a wonder the swine can concentrate on his steps*, Eden thought savagely, *because he seems to be fixated on her breasts*. And that damn gown, the soft satin moulding her long limbs as she twirled, fleetingly outlining every lovely line.

Miss Hunter was mercifully quiet, content, it seemed to dance in silence. Glancing down, meeting her eyes and smiling, Eden decided he liked the girl. She didn't deserve to be stuck with no partners, or used by him as a stalking horse. As the set swirled to its end, Maude still happily chatting away to Staines, Eden felt his partner tense in his arms.

'What's wrong?'

'Mama,' she said grimly, nodding towards a tall matron with feathers in her coiffure.

'Never mind.' He spotted Jessica, standing talking to Lord Dereham. 'Come and meet some friends.' Miss Hunter, looking bemused, allowed herself to be led towards them. 'Lady Standon, may I introduce Miss Hunter?' Over the top of the sandy head, he mouthed *Find her partners* at Jessica.

She picked up the cue and smiled. 'Do join us, Miss

Hunter.' They strolled off and a few moments later Eden saw Jessica introducing Miss Hunter to a lively group of young men, two of whom seemed to be asking her for a dance.

'Who were you dancing with?' He turned to find Maude, charmingly flushed from the exercise.

'A wallflower,' he said, controlling his breathing. 'Nice girl, a Miss Hunter.'

'Oh, that was kind of you.' Maude beamed at him. 'So many men just ignore the poor things and the more they are ignored, the worse it gets.'

It was tempting to bask in her approval. 'Kindness did not come into it,' Eden said, some evil genius prompting him to honesty. 'I wanted to keep an eye on Staines and I had no partner. He is not someone you should be associating with.'

'Indeed?' Maude's chin went up. 'I like him. He is charming, good looking and an excellent dancer.'

'He's a rake and a libertine.'

'You exaggerate. He's a shocking flirt, that is all,' she said haughtily. 'And I am well able to take care of myself, thank you.'

'He propositions the chorus girls and he brings birds of paradise into his box at the theatre,' Eden snapped.

'Oh, my *goodness*!' Maude assumed an expression of exaggerated shock. 'How *dreadful*! I am sure you have never so much as *spoken* to one of the muslin company yourself— have you, Mr Hurst?'

'I—damn it, Maude I'm only—'

'Interfering?' she enquired sweetly. 'Really, Eden, anyone would think you were jealous. Ah, there's my partner for the next set. Do excuse me—and please, do carry on your good work amongst the wallflowers. I am sure they will be most grateful.'

Jealous? Eden stood staring after her as she walked towards the young gentleman who had come to claim her hand, the skirts of her exquisite gown swishing slightly with the sway of her walk. Jealous? He certainly felt possessive, and foolishly hurt and— But if he was jealous, that had to mean that this was more than desire, more than friendship. That strange new sensation was making his chest tight again.

He turned his back on the dance floor and walked out, along a passageway, through the doors at the end and on to the cold deserted terrace. Was he developing a *tendre* for Maude? No. No, he could not be doing anything so foolish. He had no idea how. He might as well wish for the moon.

Chapter Fifteen

Well, that was either a big step forward, or a total disaster, Maude thought, joining hands across and promenading down the set. She had certainly succeeded in making Eden embarrassed and angry, but whether he was jealous, and if he was, what he would do about it, she had no idea. He seemed to have vanished from the ballroom.

By the end of the country dances, and the set that followed them, there was still no sign of him and the next set was the supper dance, the first he had put his name to on her card. Some of Papa's choicer expressions ran through Maude's mind. Well, she had plenty of married friends she could join for supper, but as for this set, she may as well go and sit with the wallflowers.

'Lady Maude?' She let the pent-up breath sigh out of her before she turned around. Eden was unsmiling, but at least he was there. 'Our dance, I believe?' He bowed.

'Sir.' Maude dropped an entirely proper curtsy and held out her hand. 'You are freezing!' Even through the fine kid of her white gloves, she could feel it.

'I apologise.' He placed the other hand at her waist, lightly, as if he did not want to press the chilly palm against her. She had forgotten this was a waltz. 'I was out on the terrace.'

'Why?' They began to move in unison with the other couples close around them. 'It is so cold tonight, foggy.'

'I was recovering my temper,' Eden said, his tone conversational.

Maude studied the diamond pin in his cravat. 'Oh?' She did not want to bicker, she wanted to be quiet, in his arms, moving to this loving, lilting music.

'I have never been accused of jealousy before,' he continued, spinning her so that their thighs touched momentarily and her swirling skirts flew around his legs and then away, like seaweed caught by a wave.

'No?' It was a very beautiful diamond. And she could smell him, his cologne, the scent of clean linen, cold skin, hot man. She shifted her gaze upwards, as far as it felt safe. Up to his chin, close shaven, up to his mouth. A mistake. It was too sensual, too masculine, too tempting. 'I am sorry,' she ventured. 'I was mistaken, of course. Why should you be jealous? I just wanted to hit back because you were criticising me.'

Those tempting lips curved—almost a smile. 'You were not mistaken, Maude.'

'I was not?' She looked up, startled. Eden was definitely smiling now, more than a little ruefully.

'No. I am jealous, but, of course, I have no right to be.'

'I…I do not mind, if you are,' Maude ventured.

Eden looked down at her, the smile fading, his eyes fathomless. Somehow they were still dancing, had not collided with anyone; somehow he must be concentrating, which was more than she was capable of.

His lips moved. 'Oh God, Maude.' Was that really what he had said? He sounded desperate. Her heart thudding against her ribs, Maude held her breath. Eden tightened his hold and swept her round, across the flow of the dancers and then off the floor and through the door at the end of the room.

'Eden?' They were in a deserted passageway. Without responding he lifted a branch of candles from a side table, took her arm, guided her along the passage and out into the cold, foggy night air. She shivered as he released her to cup his hand around the wildly guttering flames.

'It is warm in here.' He flung open one of the glazed doors that opened on to the terrace and stepped through. Maude followed and found herself in a small sitting room. Eden dropped the latch on the terrace door, dragged the draperies closed and then strode across the room to turn the key in the door.

'Eden?' He was walking around the room, setting the candle flame to the others on mantelshelf and side tables.

'We need to talk.' He came to stand in front of her, frowning.

'Yes,' she agreed. He looked so grim, but then Eden rarely smiled.

'My feelings for you have become—' He broke off, searching for a word. 'Inappropriate.'

'How?' Maude managed to say.

'I desire you.' He said it as if he was admitting to murder or fraud.

'And I, you,' she confessed. 'I do not find that at all inappropriate.'

'You do not, *Lady* Maude?' he enquired, his voice grating on her title.

'We are both grown up, we can make our own choices.' Desire, that is what he had said. But not love. Did he not love her yet, or not recognise that he loved her?

'Damn it.' Eden turned abruptly away, went to stand with

his back to her, one hand on the mantelshelf. 'You know this is something we cannot choose to act upon.'

'Because you would leave me before one night was out?' she asked softly.

'Because I would not want to leave you at all,' Eden replied, still staring down into the cold hearth. 'It is novelty, that is all it is. It has to be. You are a beautiful woman, a virgin I have come to know as I know no others. I tell myself that of course I want you, and that of course I must not touch you.'

'Because I am a virgin or because of who I am?' If only he would turn around so that she could see his face. But perhaps it was easier to speak calmly, frankly, to his unresponsive back. Whatever she did, she must not blurt out her true feelings for him or he would be gone.

'The former overrides everything else,' he said drily.

Maude bit her lip, wondering what to say, what to do, to reach him. 'I find I am not so attached to my virgin state as I once was,' she said carefully.

That brought him round to face her, at least. But he kept the width of the hearth between them. 'And what if you found yourself with child? Just another inconvenient bastard?'

'If we were so careless, then I suppose I would marry you. A child deserves to be loved by both its parents,' Maude said, calmly, her eyes on his face.

His face stark, Eden took a step back. So, that answered that, the thought of *marriage* produced a physical response of rejection. Feeling slightly queasy, Maude waited to see what he would say.

'You are so tired of your family and your friends that you wish to exile yourself from polite society?' he enquired, one dark brow lifted.

'That was not a proposal,' Maude retorted, stiffening her

spine. 'It was an observation upon a theoretical situation.' From somewhere she found a smile. 'Why did you bring me here if you do not want to be tempted, Eden?'

'Because when I am with you, my rational processes of thought appear to be in as much of a fog as shrouds this house.' He turned his back again. 'I'm a danger to you and to my own peace of mind.'

The bitterness reached somewhere deep inside her. She had been certain that she should not take that first step towards him, should let him come to her, but she could not bear it.

'How could you be a danger to me, Eden?' It only took two steps past a side table to be close enough to touch him. 'You are my friend, you would not hurt me.' She lifted one hand and laid it lightly on his back. At her touch the long muscles went taut and she heard the sharp indrawing of his breath.

Eden turned, so fast that she could not step away, so close that she had to tip her head back to look up into his face, but he did not touch her.

'You are such an innocent. If I make love to you, Maude, you will most certainly be hurt.'

'I am not such an innocent that I do not know what would happen and that, yes, it does hurt the first time.' And very frightening that sounded.

'That is not what I meant,' he said gently. 'I would hurt you here—' he lifted one hand and brushed her temple '...and here.' For a fleeting moment his palm rested over her heart.

'Life hurts.' Maude caught Eden's hand in hers and held it a fraction of an inch above the bodice of her gown. He could have pulled free easily, but he left it, passive in her grip. 'Regrets hurt. My mother said to me once that the things she regretted were the things she did not do, not those that she did.'

And then, just when she thought she could not bear the

suspense a second longer, he kissed her. It was not like either
of the times he had kissed her before, she realised, dazed,
hardly able to comprehend that it really was happening. Now
it was neither an angry assault, nor a fleetingly gentle caress.
He was intent, it seemed, upon reducing her to utter and
complete collapse and she sensed he would devote however
much time was necessary to the task.

Maude tried to keep some hold on reality. Eden had one
hand firmly in the small of her back, the other, still held in
hers, crushed between them. He seemed to be utterly focused
upon what he was doing, carried away by his own desires.
There was a faint thread of common sense that was observ-
ing what was going on and attempting to communicate rationally with her. It was doubtful, it commented, that he was as
completely at the mercy of his senses as he seemed. Certainly he was not as adrift as she was.

Maude gave her commonsense a firm push away. This was
not the time for it. This was the time to strengthen Eden's
desire for her and show him that she wanted him with at least
as much fervour.

Maude made herself relax, allowed herself to feel, gave her
instincts permission to do just as they pleased and discovered,
too late, that they did not need any encouragement whatsoever from her. If she had any illusions that she was in
control, of either herself, or of Eden, she was swiftly dis-
abused of them.

Eden's mouth was an instrument of the most subtle form
of torture. Should kissing be like this? It was at once soft,
sensual, gentle and yet demanding and hot. His mouth was
both hard and sensitive. His lips slid slowly over the seam of
hers, his tongue flickering out to nudge, insistently, at the
join until she opened to him with a little gasp. There was

nothing tentative about the invasion of her mouth—the firm, mobile moist heat of his tongue filled her, probing, licking, teasing. Thrusting.

It was overwhelming that one small piece of flesh and muscle could dominate her, demand, orchestrate her body's response so she began to sway against him in the rhythm of the thrusts. He was thinking about driving into her body, possessing her fully, she realised that. This intimate joining of mouths was simply a metaphor for that total possession.

Jessica and Bel had tried to warn her about this, and she had refused to listen. This was more than kissing—her whole body was reacting, changing. Her breasts ached and throbbed, heavier, fuller, the nipples fretting against the crisp lace trimming, throbbing with a pain that was almost totally pleasure. Deep in her belly, low where her thighs joined, the ache became a pulse, a demanding drum beat. Maude made a little inarticulate sound against Eden's mouth and he lifted his head to look down into her face.

In the candlelight his pupils seemed wide and dark, his face hawk-like, even more beautiful, fine-honed with concentration. 'Maude,' he said, his voice husky. *'Maude.'* He buried his face in her neck, his tongue, then his teeth, fretting at the shivering, sensitive skin as he followed the line down, down to her collarbone, tracing the dip with the very tip of his tongue while she sobbed with the building tension.

She needed *something*, something that would come from this, but she did not know what, did not know how to find it. Did not understand. But he did. 'Eden,' she whispered, her lips against the silky thickness of his hair as he bent lower, found the swell of her breasts, found the low edge of the bodice and ran his tongue under it, touching the straining, hard peak of her right nipple. 'Eden, please…'

Maude clutched his shoulders, shaking, adrift, feeling only the heat and the strength of him. She was leaning back against the table and there was cooler air on her legs. His hand was slipping up under her skirts, stroking up the length of her legs to the mound between her thighs. He cupped it and it felt so right. There was no shame in his touch, only the need to arch against him, seek the point of twisting, aching tension and make it stop, somehow…

He took her mouth again, just as one finger slid through the damp tangle of curls and found the hard knot at the centre of her torment. His tongue thrust, the teasing pressure intensified and everything fell apart into darkness and light and blissful pleasure.

'Maude?'

She stirred, her body limp and heavy and at peace again. 'Eden?'

'I'm here, I've got you.' He was holding her on his lap, sitting on one of the sofas that flanked the fireplace. He lay back against its support, cradling her, and the softness she could feel under her cheek was the linen of his shirt, the solid rhythm, his heartbeat. 'Are you all right?'

'Yes.' She supposed she was. That she would be…eventually. She felt wonderful and strange and very shy. Maude snuggled closer. Eden smelt different. His skin was saltier. There was a faint, intoxicating sensation of musk in the air. Arousal, she realised. Hers, his. Theirs. And his had not been satisfied.

'Eden? What about you? Tell me what to do.'

'No.' She felt the shake of his head. 'We're in enough trouble as it is. We are going to sit here while you collect yourself and then I am going to sit over there until *I* collect myself, and then we are going back into the ballroom.'

Maude rubbed her cheek, cat-like, against his lapel. 'I did not know about that, about what just happened.'

'I realise that,' he said grimly. Eden's body was not relaxed now, holding her. And his voice was no longer tender. Maude felt him shift his grip, felt the exciting bunch and flex of thigh muscles under her and then he stood with an ease that should have surprised her, yet seemed quite natural. This was Eden after all. He could do anything.

Anything but fall easily in love with her, it seemed. He set her down on the sofa and went to take the one opposite. Even in candlelight Maude could see just how aroused he was. To her shame he saw where she was looking.

'These evening breeches are not designed for conceal-ment,' he observed, sitting and crossing his legs. 'Let us sit and discuss unpleasant things for a while.'

The haze of satisfied desire was fading rapidly, leaving Maude staring at reality. 'No doubt you can think of several,' she managed to say.

Too soon, the voice in her head whispered. *Too soon*. That had been desire, pure carnal lust. Not love. Was it even, on his part, much to do with affection either? And she had melted at his touch, all her careful, foolish, strategy in ruins. *I had no idea*, Maude's thoughts whispered. *None*.

Her friends had cautioned her, and in her innocence she had failed to understand. Thinking she could manage a man with the sensual experience and the lack of social constraints of Eden Hurst was like thinking she could ride a wild horse bareback. And now she had fallen. And he had made love to her and remained in control. She had laid her desires open and he had sated them and murmured not one word of affection as he did so. And he had been right—in the morning, when she could think clearly, she knew this was going to hurt a great deal.

Maude clenched her hands together. What had she said to Bel? *I have enough breeding for both of us.* She was Lady Maude Templeton, daughter of the Earl of Pangbourne, and she never, ever, ran away from anything or anyone.

Eden drew in the same deep, calming breaths he used before stepping out on to the stage or dealing with a difficult negotiation, then he conjured up the face of the Earl of Pangbourne and imagined his expression if he discovered that his daughter had been making love with Eden Hurst. That was a start, enough to chill anyone's ardour. If he needed anything else, he could remember that he was the bastard son of a disgraced Ravenhurst and had nothing at all to offer her, certainly none of the things that she deserved.

The trouble was, whenever he looked across at Maude, whenever he drew breath and caught the scent of warm, aroused woman, lust grabbed him again with hot claws.

Why couldn't he resist her? He could resist any other woman on the planet. It was merely sex, he tried to tell himself, an appetite to be controlled just as one would control hunger or anger. But somehow, with Maude, it was mysteriously more.

'That will not happen again,' he said, deliberately harsh, wanting to see her flinch, wanting to repel her.

'No. I can imagine it was very unsatisfactory for you,' she said softly. 'But thank you for being so careful.'

'It was far from unsatisfactory,' he said, charmed into truthfulness. She should be weeping, or having the vapours, or throwing the china at him in reaction by now, not being sweet and understanding and—and Maude. 'It was beautiful to hold you in my arms and to see your pleasure, a privilege that you trusted me.'

That sweet, dazed bliss, the knowledge that he had given her that, overwhelmed the desire simply to take her, thrust into her body, find his own release. It was working now, he could feel the brute nagging lust subside into something that was a warm, regretful glow.

'I think we should go back now, have some supper before we are missed.'

Maude nodded and got to her feet, grabbing at the arm of the chair. 'Oh my, my legs are so shaky!'

Eden reached for her, then snatched his hand back. Better not to touch her, not while they were alone like this. He saw the look of comprehension on her face and winced inwardly. He should have been strong for both of them, but even now, he could not truthfully tell himself he was sorry.

'If you go first,' he said, unlocking both doors, 'and then take the door on the right in the corridor, that opens up into one of the retiring rooms. I'll go out of the door we left by.' He snuffed out the candles as she left with a terse nod. 'Wait for me by the door to the supper room.'

Alone, he stood trying not to think and then found his right hand was pressed to the centre of his chest as if to soothe the pain there. But why was he in pain? Why did he feel as though he had just lost something?

Chapter Sixteen

'Maude? What has happened?' It was Jessica, right behind her. 'Where have you been?'

'What do you mean?' Maude retorted, too flustered to be anything but defensive. 'I'm hungry, that's all.'

'You and Mr Hurst vanished over half an hour ago,' Jessica said. 'And you look…different. Have you—? No. No, I refuse to believe that even that man would do such a thing in the middle of a ball.'

'What do you mean, *even that man*?' Maude managed to keep her voice down to a furious hiss with difficulty.

'The man's a notorious rake,' Jessica hissed back. 'But I never believed he'd debauch a virgin. I should have spoken to your father. I am never going to forgive myself if I find he has—'

'Well, he hasn't. Unfortunately,' Maude snapped, perilously close to tears all of a sudden. 'I had been going to talk to you, ask your advice, but now, I never want to speak of it again to you.'

'Of all the naïve, headstrong, romantic idiots.' Jessica shook her head in disbelief. 'How you—'

'Maude, are you all right?' It was Eden, tall and broad and *here*, just when she needed him.

'No, I am not all right,' she said, taking his arm. 'I would like a glass of champagne, please. And I want to sit down somewhere where I will not be nagged at by hypocritical friends,' she added in a fierce undertone to Jessica. 'I was there when you came back from Gareth's bed at eight in the morning in your evening gown—remember?'

She had never once exchanged a cross word with Jessica and now, here they were, hissing at each other like the start of a cat fight. Unable to bear the expression of shock on her friend's face, Maude whirled round and walked into the supper room.

'Sit.' Eden had found a table. 'Wait there and do not pick any more quarrels until I get back.'

Maude sat, feeling dizzy with reaction and trying to look as though she was having a wonderful time and the only concern she had in the world was what delicacies her partner was going to bring her.

'Here.' Eden put a filled plate in front of her and sat down. 'Eat.'

'I can't. I want some champagne.'

'Eat,' he repeated, filling his own glass and leaving hers empty.

Maude forked something up and chewed it with dogged determination. 'I've quarrelled with Jessica,' she said, sick at heart.

'You'll make it up,' Eden said. 'Please eat some more, you've gone white and it is worrying me.'

A spark of humour surfaced. The poor man was obviously used to dealing with Madame Marguerite's spectacular tantrums, but pale-faced female misery was outside his experience. 'I don't expect this is the usual result of one of your interludes with a lady, is it?'

'No,' he confessed. 'But everything to do with you is

unusual, Maude.' She smiled at his serious face. 'What are we going to do about this?' he asked. She had the feeling the question was to himself, as much as to her.

'Nothing?' she ventured. 'See what happens?'

'Maude.' He leaned closer under cover of pouring her some wine. 'We are having trouble keeping our hands off each other. It does not take much imagination to see what will happen next if things carry on as they have been.'

'We will not meet unchaperoned,' Maude said. 'Then things will calm down again.' From the quizzical lift of his eyebrow she could see that she was not convincing him of that. 'There will be so much work for the theatrical entertainment that we will not have time to think of anything else.'

Eden shook his head, but made no further comment. In silence they ate, sipped their wine and, and, Maude thought sadly, were alone with their thoughts.

'Lady Maude?' She looked up, startled to realise where she was, and found herself looking at the enquiring face of Mr Hethersett, her hostess's elder son. 'We have the next set, but if you are still engaged…'

'No, I have quite finished. Thank you so much, Mr Hurst.' He was on his feet, assisting her with her chair, putting himself between her and her new partner to give her precious seconds to collect herself. 'Thank you,' she whispered again. There was still the last dance to come.

Mr Hethersett, a ponderous young man, was hardly the liveliest of partners for a vigorous country dance. Maude had to concentrate on her footwork, so much so that it was not until she was facing her and had to join hands for a round, that she realised that Jessica was dancing too.

Their eyes met, Jessica's distressed and hurt, before the dance separated them. Maude stumbled over her partner's tardily withdrawn foot and continued down the line, blankly miserable not to have the support of the one friend she had always thought would be with her, come what may. Would Jessica really go to Papa? Somehow that was less important than quarrelling with a dear friend.

The set drew to an end at last, Maude dropped a hasty curtsy to her partner and craned to see where Jessica was. She would go to her now—but, no, at the far end she could see her on Gareth's arm. Leaving.

Maude felt like fleeing the ballroom too, but something—stubborn pride? The need to be in Eden's arms one more time?—kept her there, dancing and chatting and smiling. When he came to claim her hand for the last dance, Maude was ready to drop.

'Do you want to dance?' he asked, pausing at the edge of the floor. 'You look…tired.'

'A gentleman should not say such things to a lady,' she said in a rallying tone. 'We are always radiant.'

'Well, I am not a gentleman and you are not radiant.' He turned back and led her to an alcove. 'Let us stay here, in plain view. Besides, I have something to give you.'

'You have?' He was taking something from the pocket in the tails of his coat, a dark morocco jewellery box. Maude's heart turned over with a thump. 'Eden—'

'I put it in this because otherwise I would be sure to sit on it and squash it,' he explained, placing the box in her hand. Maude opened it. Inside, nestling on red plush, was one marchpane sweetmeat. Her heart thumped back to its normal location. 'You did not eat any at supper,' he explained, his face serious. 'I came away from the jewellers with that box empty because I had taken a pair of Madame's earrings to be cleaned.'

Maude looked down at the small yellow-and-green confection and then up at his face. For one startled moment she had thought he was going to give her jewellery and instead he had given her marchpane.

'Sugar's good for the nerves,' Eden added, his eyes smiling into hers. 'We make sure nervous actresses drink sweet tea.'

'That was very thoughtful, thank you,' she said, meaning it. He had remembered that she liked it. Something out of the corner of her eye made her turn her head. 'Oh dear, people are looking.'

'They think I am about to fall to one knee, perhaps, and they are ready to faint with shock or rush forward to rescue you,' he said sardonically. 'I suggest you eat it immediately, which will confuse them, if nothing else.'

Maude popped the sweet into her mouth, shook the dusting of sugar out of the box and handed it back. The curious on-lookers turned away, some of them smiling. That fast Lady Maude again! She could almost hear them saying it.

'Now, let us dance,' she said, laying her hand on his arm. 'I think we waltz rather well together.'

'You feeling all right, my lady?' Anna placed the breakfast tray on Maude's knees and peered at her. 'You look proper peaky this morning.'

'I didn't sleep very well.' That was an understatement; she doubted if she had slept a wink all night.

'I knew I should have let you lie in, no matter what you said,' the maid pronounced, pulling back the drapes. 'Eight o'clock is no time to be getting up the morning after a ball. You've got dark circles under your eyes.'

'I must see Lady Standon first thing this morning,' Maude said, wrapping her fingers tightly round her chocolate cup for the comfort of the heat. She had to make thing right with Jessica. 'And then we will go to the theatre.'

There was a noise from the landing. Rainbow appeared to be arguing with someone, which was unprecedented.

'Anna, go and see what on earth is going on…' Maude began, but the maid was already round the screen that shielded the bed from the door.

'Oh, Lady Standon! But my lady said she was coming to call on you this morning…'

'You see, Rainbow. I knew Lady Maude would be awake, so you can stop looking starchy and let me in,' Jessica said firmly. 'Anna, I want a private word with your mistress.'

Maude put down her cup and slid out of bed. 'Jessica?'

'Oh, my dear!" Her friend flew round the screen and caught her in a warm embrace. 'I've been perfectly miserable—how are you?'

'Miserable too. Jessica, I am so sorry, I should never have said you were hypocritical, or mentioned that morning, or been cross at all. I know you are worried about me.'

'Oh, I am!' Jessica sat down on the edge of the bed, her arm around Maude's shoulders. 'But I wouldn't tell Lord Pangbourne, I promise.'

'I know. Jessica, I should have listened to you and Bel—it's like riding a tiger, isn't it? How do you get off it again safely?'

'What is?' Jessica was looking bemused.

'Sex,' Maude said bluntly. 'I thought there was kissing. And then there was bed and he'd…you know. I didn't know there was all that stuff in the middle! How on earth do you *think* with that going on?'

'You're not supposed to,' Jessica said, unsuccessfully fighting a smile.

'But I need to think, I need to plan and see what is happening and judge how he's feeling. And when he…we… My mind just turned to jelly.'

'Maude, you can't do this like planning a complicated social event, with a list for this and that and things to be done that will get you a result. Either the man falls in love with you—and Heaven help you both if he does—or he doesn't. Now tell me, what exactly happened?'

Looking back, it wasn't all very clear, but blushing rosily, Maude did her best to explain.

'Oh, my,' Jessica murmured. 'Well, I take back what I said about him—the man has enviable self-control. Now listen, I am going to be very, very frank about things because I do not want you being taken by surprise again. Not,' she added, 'that I hope you ever find yourself in that situation with a man you aren't married to.'

'You did,' Maude pointed out.

'I married him, and very eligible he is too,' Jessica retorted. 'Now listen, and if you do not understand, ask me questions.' She looked around. 'But ring for a jug of chocolate first, I am going to need it.'

'Her ladyship's back, Guv'nor.' Howard put his head round the office door. 'Bloody hell, you look rough this morning.'

Eden growled and put down his pen. 'Send someone with some hot water.' She was here? The day after the ball? After what had happened? 'What's she doing?' he called after the stage manager.

'Prowling up and down the aisles with a tape measure, a notebook and that maid Anna. I'll send Millie with the water.'

Eden stripped to the waist and took his shaving gear from the cupboard. The face that glowered back at him from the glass had a heavy growth of stubble, dark circles under its eyes and hair that had been raked by his fingers into wild disarray. Perhaps he should walk out looking like this, then she would see the real him, the unworthy, uncivilised creature under the veneer.

There was a tap on the door, Millie came in, gave a started squeak, set down the hot water jug and scuttled out. Eden set to work restoring the image he so carefully cultivated: controlled, polished, unapproachable and impregnable. The razor slid through the soap foam on his face, slicing away the whiskers, leaving a clean, smooth track in its wake. If only he could cut away last night as easily. But Maude was under his skin now, too deep to reach without cuts that would be agonising.

When he was finished, hair slicked back, neckcloth tied, he strode out of the room without giving himself time to think.

Maude was on stage, bent over the table, drawing on a large sheet of paper. He walked silently across and looked over her shoulder. It was a rough plan of the theatre. 'Good afternoon, Mr Hurst,' she said, running her pencil carefully along a ruler's edge. He could have sworn he had made no sound.

'Good afternoon, Lady Maude.' She turned her head, her hands still resting on the table, and smiled up at him and he realised what had been making him dizzy all those times he had thought himself unwell. Maude. She looked tired, but the unhappiness had gone from the depths of those big hazel eyes. 'Have you made up your quarrel with Lady Standon?'

'Yes—how did you know?'

'You don't look sad any more. Your friends are important to you, aren't they?'

'Oh, yes. Very.' Eden tried to imagine feeling that desperate at falling out with one of the men he counted his friends. He could not. The only person that touched his emotions in that way was standing right in front of him. How did she manage it, that emotional connection to so many people? It seemed to give her such pleasure and yet, to bring her such pain as well. He thought of the network of Ravenhurst cousins, that big family, and pushed away the momentary yearning to be part of it. Childish weakness.

Maude straightened up, put her fists into the small of her back and stretched. 'I had a note from Bel—Lady Dereham—she has taken your Miss Hunter under her wing, says she does not deserve to be a wallflower and she intends to promote her as an original. Bel also says I am to congratulate you upon your perspicacity.'

'Miss Hunter?' He stared blankly at her. 'Oh, the gawky girl.'

'Yes, the one you picked on as a stalking horse in order to follow me round the dance floor glaring at Sir Frederick,' Maude said severely. 'I shall not disillusion Bel and tell her you ruthlessly scooped up the nearest unfortunate young woman.'

She turned back to her plan, sucking the end of her pencil until he removed it from her. 'You'll make your tongue black. What are you doing?'

'Planning out the tables and so on for the special event. We'll have to think of a name for it. Which blocks of seating may I have removed?'

'Let me see.' He joined her, shoulder to shoulder, at the table. 'I see you have drawn sight-lines in. We could take these and these, put the buffet tables here, the string band in this large box here…'

Somehow, working on such a practical task with Eden, the restraint between them eased. They sat on stage while the work of the theatre went on, sketching, thrashing out problems, occasionally getting up to measure something or go down into the stalls to check the view.

Maude felt warm, happily relaxed with him and he did not

seem to try to avoid touching her, or appear awkward with her. Whether that meant that he simply discounted what had happened and could put it behind him, or whether he was a far better actor than he had let her suspect, she did not know. It was simply happiness to be with him like this, doing something practical, seeing his mind work, watching those big, sensitive hands as he sketched out ideas in the air or on paper.

'We'll need the stage in ten minutes or so, Guv'nor.' It was one of the hands, standing looking up at them from the orchestra pit. 'Got to get set up for this evening.'

'Lord, is that the time?' Eden was sitting on the edge of the table, legs swinging, hair loose on his shoulders, as relaxed as she had ever seen him. A pang of love and longing struck Maude with almost painful intensity. She must have made a sound, for he turned his head to look at her and their eyes locked. There was that look again in the dark depths, the look that made her breath hitch in her throat and her pulse stutter.

'Eden—'

'Late afternoon post, Guv'nor.' It was Millie, balancing a pile of correspondence.

'Put it in the office,' Eden snapped. 'I am working with Lady Maude.' The moment, and whatever it had held, was gone.

'It is all right,' Maude said. 'We have finished for today, after all. Please, make sure there isn't anything important.'

Eden tossed the pile on to the table and sorted through it rapidly. At the bottom, a large letter on thick paper covered in seals crackled importantly. He ran his thumb under the wax, sending red fragments flying, and smoothed it out. Something about the quality of his stillness caught Maude's attention as he scanned the letter again and then a third time.

'Is something wrong?' she asked, unable to bear the suspense any longer.

'Wrong? No, far from it. It is the agents for the Unicorn. The owner has died and they ask if I wish them to approach the heir with an offer to purchase.'

'Who is it?' Maude came to his side and put her hand on his forearm. Under the fabric of the sleeve she could feel a vibration. It seemed to pulse up her arm, infecting her with his tension.

'They do not yet know. The solicitor dealing with the will is to write—they expect to know in a week or so.' He looked up, his eyes burning with a fierce excitement. 'They will sell, surely? Why should they want a theatre? It is something you set out to acquire, not something you keep if it comes to you by accident.'

'You are right, most people would want to realise the asset as soon as possible, especially if they have an inheritance to deal with. Oh, Eden, I'm so pleased for you—the Unicorn, yours, at last.'

'I must not count on it, not until it is certain,' he said soberly, then caught her eye and grinned. 'Oh, to hell with caution! Maude, it is going to be mine, I know it.' And the next thing she knew he caught her around the waist, lifted her in the air and was whirling around the stage in dizzying circles, laughing up at her. 'Yes, yes, yes!'

Maude laughed back, safe with his hands spanning her waist, safe with his strong back holding her up, as dizzy as he was with joy.

'What on earth are you about, darling?' The trained voice from the wings brought Eden to a halt, the laughter dying out of his face. Slowly he lowered Maude to the floor, released her and stepped back. 'Auditioning for the *corps de ballet*?' Madame Marguerite enquired, strolling on to the stage. The feathers in her hat swept down to the shoulder of her deep plum-coloured gown, diamonds winked and flashed at ears and throat, her skirts swished across the boards. She looked, quite simply, magnificent and Maude, her hair in her eyes and her skirts in disarray, felt like a thirteen-year-old romp caught playing with the village boys.

'Celebrating,' Eden said flatly.

'I hardly dare ask what, darling,' Madame said, running a critical eye up and down Maude's tousled figure. 'But it is Lady Maude, is it not?'

'Madame,' Maude rejoined politely, resisting the urge to tug at her skirts and push back her hair. She was not going to react like a naughty schoolgirl, whatever the provocation.

'Well now, and when were you going to tell me this happy news?' Madame Marguerite enquired. 'I do feel, Eden darling, that a quiet word would have been more appropriate—every stage-hand must know by now.'

Oh, my God! She thinks we have become betrothed, Maude thought, hardly knowing where to look. Of all the hideously embarrassing misunderstandings.

'I saw no point in telling you until we know the theatre is definitely on the market,' Eden said. Whether he had understood what his mother had assumed, Maude could not tell, but she could only admire the delivery of the line.

The actress produced an exaggerated start of surprise. 'The *theatre*?' she enquired, in ringing tones, managing to make three dramatic syllables out of the word.

'Yes.' Eden began to gather up the letters. 'The owner has died and the agents are finding out if the new owner will sell.'

Madame appeared momentarily speechless; not a state, Maude guessed, she was often reduced to. It did not last long. 'Eden darling, a word, if you please.' She swept Maude with a look that was assessing and speculative. 'Lady Maude,' she said coolly, before she swept off stage.

'I must be going.' Maude tidied her hair by touch. 'Anna!'

'Here, my lady.' The maid hurried out of the wings with Maude's muff and bonnet. 'I've called the carriage, my lady, seeing what the time is.'

'Thank you.' Maude looked across at Eden, his face as cool and unreadable as it usually was. 'I will see to the invitations, which will take a day or so. Shall we call it *The Unicorn Musicale*?' He nodded, unsmiling. He must be thinking about Madame's false assumption that they were betrothed. He would be feeling trapped by that, coming so close on the re-alisation of how much she desired him.

There was an ache inside her, not just embarrassment, but something else. The sudden change in him hurt, she realised. Whenever she believed they were getting close, Eden brought down an intangible barrier and retreated behind it. Was he truly so unable to love, to make himself open to another person, to trust her enough to make himself vulnerable? She needed love, and she would sacrifice everything for that. But lack of it would kill her spirit, she knew it. It would be better to put some distance between them, just for a little while.

'I…I may not come to the theatre for a day or so, there is so much to do for this. I will send notes, of course. And you will let me know if there is any news?'

'Of course.' *He agrees so readily, he is relieved that I am going.* Her heart sank a little. 'I will see you at the special committee meeting we arranged for planning the event?'

'Next week? Yes, of course. Goodbye, Eden.' Maude paused, tying her bonnet strings. 'I'll be thinking about the Unicorn, and wishing you luck.'

Chapter Seventeen

'Madame?' Eden closed the door of his office behind him and went to sit in the high carved chair. He felt decidedly unfit for dealing with his mother in one of her moods. His body was still jangling with nerves and arousal from being around Maude, the thought that he might have the chance to buy the theatre was threatening to fill his brain to the exclusion of all else, and, on top of it all, his leading lady was leaping to quite ridiculous conclusions.

'What are your intentions towards Lady Maude Templeton?' she enquired.

'Intentions? To continue with my existing partnership with her. Her insights are useful and I find the charity work she has involved me with surprisingly interesting,' he said coolly, instinct warning him against allowing Madame any hint of his feelings.

'Don't try to cut a sham with me, Eden. Any fool with half an eye can see the pair of you are like April and May,' Marguerite retorted. 'Are you sleeping with her?'

'No.' Eden got a tight rein on his temper. 'You are speaking about an unmarried lady of quality.' It was probably not the most tactful of observations to make to someone who had been a lady of quality herself, before she had turned her back on her family and her chances of a respectable marriage.

His mother's eyes widened, and he was seized with sudden doubt. She was a great actress, but could she really counterfeit that flash of pain? Had that scandalous split with her family not been her choice after all? 'I am fully aware of that. And what a catch! Marry the girl, for Heaven's sake, Eden. Think about her dowry, her connections!'

'Think about the Earl of Pangbourne's response when a bastard theatrical manager turns up asking for his daughter's hand in marriage. Horsewhips would feature, I imagine.'

Marguerite shrugged. 'Then get her with child—he won't refuse then.'

If we were so careless, then I suppose I would marry you, she had said. And, *A child deserves to be loved by both its parents.* He eyed his own parent, that uncharacteristic feeling of sympathy quite gone. 'Debauch her, in effect, so I can marry her for her money?'

'A sensible strategy.'

'A despicable one!' he said hotly. The pain of the heavy carving biting into his clenching hands cut through the wave of red anger that her suggestion provoked. 'Lady Maude is a friend.'

'She's in love with you,' his mother said. 'She'll be willing.'

'There may be some physical attraction between us,' Eden conceded through clenched teeth, 'but she is not in love with me. And,' he added before she could say anything else, 'I am not in love with her.'

May I be forgiven for that lie. Even as he denied it, he recognised the emotion that was possessing him. He loved Maude. How had that crept up on him, overwhelmed him without him realising? When had he fallen in love, so disastrously, so hopelessly? With that first kiss? The second? But she, with her gift for friendship, her passionate defence of the wounded and needy, she was simply encompassing him within the fortunate circle of those she cared for. She was not going to give her heart to someone as unworthy of it as he was. And if she did, then she needed protecting from herself. And from him.

'Sentimental fool,' his mother observed, getting to her feet in a flurry of silks. 'I came in today because I was beginning to wonder if you were ever going to visit me. Now I can see why I have been neglected. You will want to start rehearsals soon, I imagine?'

'Yes.' He had been intending to call on her that evening. Not to do so now would be childish and he was not going to add that to the list of failings that seemed to be written in letters of blood on his lids whenever he closed his eyes. And an evening doing a read-through with Madame would most certainly distract his mind from the shattering realisation that he had fallen in love.

But I don't believe in love, the old, hard, cynical part of his brain protested. Everything that he thought he was, was false, it seemed. 'I will bring the script round this evening. May I see you to your carriage, Madame?'

'Thank you, no. You will take supper?'

'Of course. Thank you.' He opened the door for her, then went back to sit behind his desk. After a minute, he put his elbows on the green leather and dropped his head into his hands and tried to think, not to feel, not to hurt. Just to think.

Maude did not love him, of course not. What was there to love? A cold, hard man—out of her world, out of her class. She desired him, as he did her. That physical spark between them had been unmistakable from the very first touch. She was innocent, but not a child—she was old enough, she would say, to know what she wanted. And she wanted him—as a friend and as a lover. Apparently she saw something in him that would be worthy of her friendship, worthy of her attempts to make him admit that love, in its widest sense, existed.

Well, she had done that. He believed in love between a man and a woman now, that was for certain. And in that one sentence asserting a child's right to be loved by its parents, she had, somehow, convinced him about maternal love too. He could imagine Maude with a child in her arms. His child. He could almost feel the love flowing from her. She had shown him how she loved her friends and what misery it plunged her into when they were at odds.

She was every dream he had suppressed for years and the best thing he could do for her, the only way to show her his love, was to deny it and, by denying it, protect her. Honour demanded it, pride dictated it.

Eden allowed himself to imagine calling on the Earl of Pangbourne, telling him he loved his daughter, setting out for him what he could offer her in life. The loss of her status, the loss of her friends, the loss of the brilliant marriage she would one day make. His love, the emotion he had only just discovered, was made null and void by his theatre and the stigma of trade, his bloodlines. It was not going to happen and he was going to have to learn to live with it.

Maude found more than enough to busy herself with over the next seven days. She should have had no time to think about Eden or those moments of bliss in his arms or the sobering reality of his reaction to Madame's assumption of their betrothal.

There were balls and parties and soirées to go to, morning calls to make, clothes to buy, invitations to write for the *Musicale* and there was committee business for the charity.

All in all, she should not have had room in her brain to think of anything else and she should have dropped exhausted into her bed every night. Instead, Maude found herself falling into a daydream about Eden's mouth with half an address written, or worrying about the ownership of the Unicorn in the middle of thinking about a new ballgown or tossing and turning long into the small hours, her body aching for the touch of his hands.

They exchanged notes almost every day, innocuous, practical letters about food and musicians, doormen and footmen, lighting and menus that she would not have blushed to have shown to anyone. Even so, all Eden's notes to her ended up tied with red ribbon, at the bottom of a hat box.

By the morning of the special committee meeting to discuss the *Musicale*, Maude was feeling almost light-headed with lack of sleep and distraction. When she was shown into Bel's boudoir an hour before the meeting she sank down in her usual chair with a sigh of relief, only to be jolted upright by Bel. 'Maude! What on earth is the matter with you?'

'I'm tired, that is all.' She sank back and closed her eyes.

'You are white as a sheet and I could swear you have lost weight. I thought so at the Petries' party the day before yesterday, but the light was so bad I thought I must be mistaken.' Maude heard Bel move to sit next to her, then her hand was lifted and enfolded. 'It isn't just weariness, is it? What's wrong?'

'Nothing—and everything.' Maude opened her eyes and sat up, managing a smile. 'I am busy, but that isn't it. I haven't seen Eden for a week and when we parted it was…difficult. We were celebrating because he thinks he has the chance to buy the Unicorn and Madame Marguerite came in and thought we were happy because we were betrothed. He changed, Bel. I have never seen a man change so rapidly. One moment he was laughing and warm and happy to be with me and the next—cold and distant. He was obviously appalled by her mistake. I said I wouldn't be at the theatre for some time, that I had a lot to do, and he accepted that so easily. And yet, only the night before we…he… Oh, damn! I am not going to cry.'

'You were lovers?' Bel asked, her grip on Maude's hand tightening. So, Jessica had not betrayed Maude's confidence.

'No, not fully. No doubt he regrets even that now.'

'Will he be here this afternoon?'

'He said he would be.' Maude blew her nose briskly. 'Do I look as awful as I feel?'

'Not your best,' Bel admitted. 'Shall we do so something about it?'

'No.' Maude shook her head. 'I don't want to be powdered and pinched. I will smile a lot, no one will notice.'

'I don't know about that,' Bel began, then looked up as the boudoir door opened to admit Jessica, another young woman at her heels.

Maude stared at her. There was something very familiar about the red-haired, elegant stranger. Then she smiled. 'Elinor!' Both Bel and Maude hugged and kissed and exclaimed over the latest Ravenhurst bride.

'You look radiant!' Maude pulled Elinor, whom she had last seen looking the epitome of a drab bluestocking spinster, down on the sofa beside her. 'I wasn't expecting you yet—where is Theo?'

'Talking to Ashe and Gareth downstairs. We only landed two days ago.'

Elinor had married her cousin Theo Ravenhurst in France the previous year and they had embarked on a prolonged Continental honeymoon combined with a buying trip for Theo's art and antiquities business.

Someone else who managed to be in trade and remain respectable, Maude thought with an inward sigh.

'Tell me all the gossip,' Elinor demanded, waving aside Bel and Jessica's questions about the exact state of Paris hemlines and where she had bought her bonnet. 'Talk to Theo about fashions—he makes me buy clothes; he threatened to burn all my old ones.'

At least, with the three others engrossed in their conversation, Maude was able to avoid any more comments about her wan complexion. She slipped out of the room while they were still talking and went downstairs to curl up on a window seat, shielded by the curtains, where she knew she could watch the comings and goings in the dining room unobserved. For some reason she felt shy about seeing Eden again; when the room was full she could emerge and mingle at a safe distance.

As she thought it, he came in carrying a portfolio and a roll of paper, Lady Wallace at his side. His willingness to throw the resources of the Unicorn into supporting the charity seemed to have overcome her suspicions of him.

Maude watched him, indulging in the luxury of just being able to stare unseen. He unrolled what she guessed, from the questions Lady Wallace was asking him, was a plan of the stalls and stage. Their voices just reached Maude from her hiding place at the far end of the long room, Eden's low, rich, sending shivers down her spine, the older woman's bright and chatty.

He anchored the corners of the plan with piles of paper, then looked up, his head cocked to one side, as though straining to hear a distant voice. When Lady Wallace stepped out for a moment, Eden turned slowly on his heel, his eyes scanning the room, then he walked straight towards her. He could not see her, surely? Maude held her breath, dropping the edge of the curtain she had been peeping through and feeling quite ridiculously flustered.

'Hello.' Eden stood in front of her, his mouth quirking at the sight she presented, curled up like the parlour cat on the window seat. 'Move up?'

Obediently, Maude swung down her feet and sat up to give him room to join her, so close she could feel his body heat and inhale the achingly familiar scent of him. 'How did you know I was here?'

'I seem to be able to sense your presence when you are in a room,' he said. 'Maude, are you all right? You are very pale.'

'I'm a little tired,' she confessed, catching at an excuse for her behaviour. 'Elinor Ravenhurst and her husband Theo have returned from France, so I came down for some peace and quiet before the meeting.'

'And now I have disturbed you,' he said, running the ball of his thumb gently along her cheekbone. 'You've lost weight, Maude.'

'Some, I think,' she confessed. 'I've been overdoing it, I expect.' He cupped her face in both hands, looking at her with dark, fathomless eyes. 'You…you haven't disturbed me, Eden.'

'Have I not?' As though drawn by something he saw in her face, he leaned forward and touched his mouth softly to hers. 'I am sure your friends would say that was a good thing. I am quite certain I should agree.'

'I meant,' Maude managed to murmur against his lips, 'that you do disturb me, but I do not mind.'

The lavish folds of green velvet hid them from the room. Outside, the garden was deserted. They could stay here, in their private hiding place, for hours, barely touching, speaking with their eyes—and perhaps she could learn what his were saying.

'Where is Maude?' It was Jessica, answered by Bel.

'I haven't see her since we were upstairs.'

'I have lost Mr Hurst, too,' Lady Wallace added. 'He was here just a moment ago.'

'Leave this to me,' Eden said quietly, emerging from the curtains. 'We are here. Lady Maude was feeling a trifle faint—the cool of the window seat has revived her, I am glad to say.'

He offered her his hand and she stood, feeling quite shaky enough to give credence to Eden's assertion that she was unwell. 'I'm sorry to keep you waiting,' she apologised, taking a empty chair next to Mr Makepeace. Her friends, thank Heaven, appeared to have decided that it was best not to draw attention to her any further and the meeting began.

As the discussion unfolded, Maude began to feel better, although whether it was the praise heaped upon Eden and herself for their work so far, or the gentleness of his caresses that seemed to linger on her skin, she did not know.

'We have had over a hundred acceptances already,' she said, when it was her turn to speak. 'And at least a dozen offers to perform. I do think that members of the committee should each present a piece.' She said it, part seriously, part in jest, but to her surprise everyone nodded their agreement except Eden.

'I will be directing,' he said firmly. 'I never perform.' And nothing could shift him from that position. Watching him from beneath her lashes, Maude had the distinct impression that the thought of performing made him nervous. Which was rather endearing, considering how confident he appeared on stage and how forcible his presence could be.

It seemed that very little now remained to be done. Those things she had thought of and had made a note of to raise in the hope that others in the group would take on, had all been swept up already by Eden and organised with ruthless efficiency. He and Ashe had their team of carpenters, augmented by some of the handier of the soldiers, drilled with military precision to strip down and rebuild the stalls in hours, the theatre orchestra were practising interval music and the pianist was well prepared and confident of accompanying whatever the amateurs might decide to sing.

It seemed that all Maude's excuses to keep her mind busy had gone. Which meant, she realised, that she was going to have to think about what had just happened with Eden and decide what to do next. She was frightened, she realised, as the meeting broke up and transformed into a tea party. Frightened that she would somehow misread Eden's intentions and feelings, might scare him away by revealing her true feelings for him to soon. Or leave it too late.

'Come to the Unicorn tomorrow, Maude,' Eden said to her as they stood to one side, sipping tea. 'I have missed you.'

'And I, you.' She did not look up at him, content to feel him so close beside her, unwilling to confuse herself further by trying to read his expression.

'And we need to talk, I think,' he added, as much, it seemed, to himself as to her.

Yes. Maude drew in a deep breath, down to her toes. *Time for the truth. Courage, Maude.* 'I'll come tomorrow,' she promised.

'Maude, I would like to speak with you in my study, if you have finished your breakfast.' Lord Pangbourne folded his newspaper and fixed her with such a beady eye that her overactive conscience produced an uncomfortable twinge. Could Papa, in some way, guess what she was intending to do today?

'Yes, Papa, of course.' Another white night had produced

the resolution that she was going to tell Eden she loved him and see what his reaction was. Not enthusiastic, she feared. He would see the barriers to their happiness even more clearly than she could—and that was assuming he wanted to marry her anyway and it wasn't all just desire mixed with friendship.

She still had not decided what words she would use. How did you propose, in cold blood, to a man?

Still pondering, she followed her father out of the breakfast room and into his study. She loved that room, dark and full of books and smelling of bay rum, brandy and leather.

'Sit down, my dear.' He took his seat behind the desk and unlocked a drawer. 'You recall me telling you that an old friend had died?'

'Yes,' Maude nodded, wondering what this was about.

'And I also told you that this lady, Sarah Millington, almost became your godmother?' Maude nodded. 'Well, my dear. It seems she has left you a legacy and one that I think will startle you as much as it has me.' Lord Pangbourne lifted a packet from the drawer and unfolded a sheet from the top. 'Here. Read for yourself.'

It was an extract from a will, copied in a heavy black hand. Maude tilted the page to catch the light from the window and read.

To Maude Augusta Edith Templeton, only child of my beloved friend Marietta Templeton, Countess of Pangbourne, née Masters, I leave the freehold and all the curtilage, appurtenances and rents of the property known as the Unicorn Theatre, Long Acre, London…

Maude read it again, half-convinced she was seeing things. But, no—she was the owner of the Unicorn Theatre. Eden's theatre. Her hands shook as she refolded the paper, trying to imagine what this was going to mean.

Chapter Eighteen

'But how on earth did she come to own the Unicorn?' Maude asked, emerging from her muddled thoughts.

'Sarah Millington, as a young woman, left her respectable home to go on the stage. A scandalous thing, of course, but I suspect there was some sad story behind it—a seduction, perhaps.' Lord Pangbourne settled into his chair, his expression unfocused as though he was looking back down the years. 'Your mother, before I was courting her, was stagestruck. She wanted to act and of course, that was quite impossible. But she found ways to meet actors and actresses, Sarah amongst them.

'Sarah became a great friend, but she never forgave herself that she introduced Marietta to a certain young actor and that they fell in love. Naturally, it was quite hopeless. They tried to elope, were caught at Hatfield, and to prevent a scandal her father sent her away to his aunt in Wales. The young man was killed the following year in an accident with falling scenery and Marietta was allowed back to London, where we met. I courted her and she agreed to marry me.'

'I thought…you always seemed so much in love,' Maude

ventured. *Poor Mama! How would I feel if I was dragged away from Eden, just when we thought we were safe? How had she heard the news of his death, so far away from her?*

'I believe we were, although I never fooled myself that I was the great love of her life,' her father said, smiling ruefully. 'We were very happy, and when you arrived, even happier. Anyway, your mother kept in touch with Sarah, but after the near scandal they were very discreet, even after our marriage. Unlike many actresses Sarah was careful with her money, retired at the peak of her modest success and bought property. The Unicorn was one of her purchases.'

'It wasn't the theatre where the young actor was killed?' Maude asked, suddenly chilled. *If I have been standing on the very stage where Mama's love died...*

'No.' Her father shook his head. 'No, I do not think I would be comfortable there either, if that were the case. He was on tour—Norwich, I think. But he acted at the Unicorn, often. That was where your mama first saw him.' He gave himself a little shake and seemed to come back entirely into the present. 'You see why I was not entirely surprised at your interest in the theatre and why I was not inclined to forbid it to you?'

'Many other parents would have seen it as *exactly* the reason to forbid me,' Maude observed, thinking how very fortunate she was in her father.

'I do not expect you to fall in love with an actor,' Lord Pangbourne said with a smile. 'You are far less sheltered than your mama, you have met many more gentlemen and you are old enough not to have fairytale dreams, I am sure.'

Oh, indeed, this was not a fairytale! Maude glanced at the clock. There was an hour before she could reasonably set out to the Unicorn, time to think.

'You will sell to Hurst,' her father observed. 'He'll be delighted. But talk to Benson, make certain the price is right. This is business, not friendship.'

'Yes, Papa. Perhaps I will. Although the rent would be useful.' Oddly, one part of her could discuss this rationally while the other was confused and uncertain.

Her instinctive reaction was against the idea of selling the Unicorn. She loved it, partly because it was Eden's passion, partly for some atmosphere of its own. And now it was *hers*. If she married Eden, it would become his, along with all her property, of course, that was the way the law worked. A stab of anxiety warned her that it was a powerful incentive for him to marry her. Part of her did not want to believe that it might influence him, part knew that she was dealing with a man who had grown up rejecting love, focused only on his ambitions. She must not tell him until she had spoken to him today about her feelings.

But then she would be deceiving him by keeping the knowledge of something so important to him secret. Or she could to sell it to him first and then speak of her love…

But she did not want to sell it. Somehow that theatre had dug itself under her skin and into her affections. And it would have had such emotional resonance for Mama: that was why Sarah had left it to Marietta's daughter. Mama would not have wanted her to sell it, to lose that link to her first love. Yet, she would have wanted Maude to be happy with the man she loved.

But Eden was more important. More important than anything, surely? And he wanted the Unicorn with a passion. And she loved him—so shouldn't she give him what he wanted, unconditionally? Confused, Maude opened the copy of the will and stared at it again as thought the black letters would somehow tell her what to do, what was right. They were absolutely no help whatsoever. One thing she knew: she could not see him today, not with the shock of this so fresh in her mind.

'I want to go down to Knight's Fee, Papa,' she said, suddenly certain that she must get away. 'I've been overdoing it, I feel tired. I'll go down this afternoon, if you don't mind.'

'Of course, my dear.' He smiled his understanding, leaning across to pat her hand. 'I expect this story about your mother has upset you a little. How long will you stay?'

'Just a few days—until Tuesday, perhaps.' That would give her time, surely, to decide what to do. She could not take any more, not with the *Musicale* looming in only eight days' time. 'I'll go and write to the committee, let them know where I am.' And, somehow, manage a note to Eden to account for her absence when it had been obvious that he had wanted to speak to her seriously about something. The excuse of her health would convince him, however reluctant she was to deceive him.

...and so I think the sensible thing is to go down to the country for a few days and rest and get some fresh air. I will be back on Tuesday next week, so do not think I have abandoned you and the Musicale *entirely! Maude.*

Eden looked down at the note, fighting the irrational disappointment. He had wanted to see Maude because he was going to do the sensible, honourable, thing and tell her that he was becoming too fond of her for prudence and that after the *Musicale*, they should keep a greater distance. And here she was, distancing herself. Excellent. That was what he told himself. But it was not true, of course. He should do what was right for Maude, yet he simply wanted to be with her, and to hell with the risks of that proximity.

And yet this note did not ring true. Yes, he could believe that she was tired, perhaps even unwell. Yesterday he had wanted to hold her in his arms, he had wanted the right to carry her to her bed, tuck her up, pamper and coddle her until the

roses were back in her cheeks and she was answering him
back with her usual spirit. But if she was unwell, it was not
because she had been overdoing things. Maude Templeton
was perfectly capable of dancing 'til dawn every night of
the week. There was something wrong and he knew,
in his heart, that it was to do with him.

Eden studied the abrupt signature. There were tiny marks
on the paper as though she had made several false starts at
ending the note. What had she almost said? Had she been on
the point of sending him her love? His hand clenched around
the note, crumpling it as he sneered at himself for such a
foolish dream. More likely Maude had wrestled with endings
that would show her desire to set a proper distance between
them, had failed to find something suitable and had simply
put her name.

She liked him and he did not subscribe to the convenient
fiction that unmarried young ladies were not possessed of any
feelings of passion or desire separate from those of chaste
love, so why should she not want him as a lover? But love?
Did she share that overwhelming feeling he had only just discovered for himself?

Maude knew him too well, had seen into the space inside
him that he had never realised was there and which he now
knew was an inability to care for another person as she should
be cared for. With so much love herself, she must not put
herself into the power of someone who could only take from
her, never give as she deserved.

He looked down at his big, scarred hands holding the scrap
of paper, the hands of a man who worked for his living. She
was a lady. And he was not a gentleman. Somehow, knowing
that he was a Ravenhurst, and yet being outside that charmed
circle, made it worse, not better, and even their cautious friend-

ship would be withdrawn if they realised that a black sheep
from the wrong side of the blanket was compromising Maude.

Of course she could not love him. Carefully he smoothed
out the note and laid his blotter on top of it, then got up to go
and make someone else's life hell. And tonight he would go
and seek some undemanding, uncomplicated professional
female company and put Maude Templeton out of his mind
and his heart and his soul.

'Aah.' Maude let out a long sigh and felt her shoulders drop
as she relaxed. Coming home to Knight's Fee always did that.
The remains of the ruined tower of the long-abandoned castle
poked up from the wood that clothed the hill slope and the old
house sprawled beneath it, dreaming above its water meadows
in the countryside.

Her father joked that each succeeding generation of Tem-
pletons had studied architectural developments carefully, then
had built a wing, or made some alteration, in the least distinguished style of their time. Yet for all its rambling layout and
lack of coherence or sophistication, the whole was a simply
charming, unpretentious home.

Here the smoke and fogs that beset London gave way to
clear skies and the air had a freshness that had Maude itching
to find her boots and go for a long walk.

Would Eden like it here? She had no idea what he thought
of the English countryside, so very different to the land he had
grown up in. Would she ever be able to show him Knight's
Fee, walk with him through the woods where soon the prim-
roses would cluster under the beeches, and bluebells fill sunlit
glades heady with their scent and the drone of the nectar-
drunk bees?

'Mrs Williams, good afternoon.' The housekeeper came

bustling into the hall, her face wreathed in smiles. 'An impromptu visit, I'm sorry I didn't send warning. Now, tell me, how does everyone go on?'

The housekeeper's news kept Maude distracted for a good hour while they sat and drank tea and Mrs Williams made efforts to tempt her to buttered scones and jam.

'You need fattening up, my lady, you're too pale. I'll get you the creamiest milk from the dairy for your breakfasts and tell Cook to make some sustaining dishes. That London life isn't good for a young lady like yourself—you need the fresh air and proper wholesome food to put roses in your cheeks.' She cocked her head to one side like an inquisitive blackbird. 'But I expect all the young gentlemen will be pining if you are away for long.' Maude felt herself blush, and the housekeeper, who had known her all her life, chuckled richly. 'Or just one young gentleman, perhaps?'

'It's all right, darling. It happens to the best of gentlemen, you just lie back, sweetheart, and we'll soon have your sugar stick sitting up and taking interest.' Mrs Cornwallis's latest acquisition, a tall, buxom blonde with big blue eyes and absolutely no resemblance to a certain hazel-eyed brunette, reached out and trailed a hand expertly up Eden's thigh as he sat on the edge of the bed and grimly contemplated an apparently celibate future.

He had chosen this girl—Sally—quite deliberately, as a complete contrast to the woman who was haunting his mind and obsessing his body. Far from being incapable, his state of arousal had been uncomfortably insistent, right up to the moment he started taking his clothes off and was faced with the reality of the woman on the wide bed.

It now appeared that something that felt uncomfortably like his non-existent conscience was preventing him from making love to anyone else but Maude. If nothing else, it was convincing proof that he was in love, Eden thought with grim humour. No one had told him about these inconvenient aspects of the condition.

He took hold of Sally's skilfully exploring hand and placed it firmly on the coverlet. 'Don't trouble yourself, I've just concluded that what I need is a brunette,' he said with a wry smile for his own predicament. 'You'll be paid, never fear.' He felt the bed shift as she came up on her knees behind him, pressing the whole curvaceous length of her torso against his naked back and whispering tantalising suggestions in his ear. 'No, I don't think your brown-haired friend Jeanie joining us would help, either.'

He could only hope, he thought as he found his shirt and pulled it on, that once he had spoken to Maude, had finally put an end to their strange relationship, that he could accept her loss and get back to something approaching normal. He was not cut out for self-denial, that was certain, he decided, tossing money on to the side table and finding a reassuring smile for the pouting Sally. He wasn't cut out either for having his mind fogged with daydreams of unobtainable women, not since he had mooned after Guilia, the cook's seventeen-year-old daughter when he was thirteen.

'Damn it, Maude,' he muttered, jogging down the staircase into the brothel's reception hall, 'why don't you come home?'

Maude woke to sunshine and a soft breeze. A perfect day for a walk to her favourite place for thinking, she realised with relief, cajoling a small picnic basket out of Cook, who grumbled that she'd wanted to make sure her ladyship had three good, solid meals, not mimsy cold stuff, even if it did include her special chicken pie and a big slice of fruit cake.

She then had to fight off Mrs Williams' attempts to send her out with a footman at her heels to carry the basket and protect her from nameless dangers in her own woods. Finally, sturdy boots laced up, an ash stick in one hand and the basket in the other, Maude was able to escape out through the kitchen garden and up the steeply sloping path to the castle ruins.

Panting slightly, she scrambled up the last few feet of rough path and on to one of the slabs of stone that lay scattered around what had once been the little castle the first Templeton had built to lay claim to this land. It was a favourite spot, flat enough to sit, south facing to catch the sun and with a view out over the wide acres down to the river. The sight of it brought a pleasure that was almost painful in its intensity.

Could she give this up for Eden? If he loved her, she would have to, for her own world would shun her and she could not expect him to visit Knight's Fee in a hole-and-corner way, as though she was ashamed of him. Her first euphoria on discovering that he was a Ravenhurst had given way to the realisation that this only made things worse. Their very prominence, her close relationship to them, emphasised all too clearly Eden's circumstances. She had wanted to rush to her friends, tell them all about their charismatic new cousin—now she found herself desperate to keep it secret from them.

Papa would never cast her off, she was sure of that, but he was a man with a position to maintain, prominent friends and associates—he would have to show his disapproval of the match in public.

If Eden loved her: that was the key. She would tell him, she was decided upon that. Tell him, straight out, how she had loved him since she had first seen him, how she had come to the Unicorn to be with him, beg him to tell her the truth about his feelings. If he did not love her, then she would sell him the Unicorn, keeping her identity a secret and... And what?

Maude sat down on the bare stone, drew up her knees and rested her chin on them. Retreat here to Knight's Fee and become a country spinster? A society marriage with both partners frank about the absence of love between them was one thing—to marry one man while nursing a broken heart for another, was something else.

Maude stayed all day, high on the hillside, occasionally stretching her legs to walk through the woods, always coming back to her eyrie. She ate her lunch, more hungry than she could remember being for weeks, then amused herself luring a robin close with crumbs. He proved a willing confidante, cocking his head to listen as she talked to him, flying down with a whirr of wings to hunt through the grass before coming back for another fragment of cheese.

'I can't tell Eden about the Unicorn until I know how he feels,' she explained when the robin flew up to perch on the basket handle, watching with black beady eyes. 'Otherwise how will I ever be certain that it did not influence what he says? He is passionate about that theatre. And ruthless.' It was hard to have to believe that about the man she loved, but this was no time to delude herself about the darkness in him that she so much wanted to overcome. 'Passionate and ruthless enough, perhaps, to marry me to get it.'

The bird was a good listener, but not much use for helpful advice. 'I should wait until after the *Musicale*, don't you think? Or before?' The trill of song from a perch in the hawthorn bush gave no guidance. 'After,' Maude decided. 'If he says *no*, I don't think I'll have the courage to stay in

London. Oh, robin, if Eden doesn't want me, do you think I'd ever find someone as kind as Papa instead, like Mama did?'

Why the tears should come then, Maude did not know, but it seemed she could not stop them, letting them flow unchecked down her cheeks, blurring the view of the valley. 'Eden.' She hugged her knees tighter, bent her face to them, letting the moisture soak into the fine wool. 'Oh, Eden, I love you so much.'

Chapter Nineteen

'You look so much better!' Jessica enfolded Maude in a huge hug. 'It must be all that country air.'

'All that country cooking, to be truthful,' Maude smiled. 'It is a miracle I can get into any of my gowns. How is everything and everyone?'

'Every*thing* is fine, if you mean the *Musicale*. As for every*one*, we are all well, thank you. The only person who is not very well is Mr Hurst.'

'Is he sick? An accident?' Maude could make no attempt to hide her anxiety.

'Far from it. So far as one can tell, he's as strong as a horse. No, it's his temper. I swear the man has not smiled since you left and the slightest error or omission amongst his company, or the men, is dealt with in a manner which brings the Grand Turk vividly to mind. As for the ladies, he endures our shortcomings with a courtesy that will probably induce frostbite before much longer—I cannot begin to tell you how glad we all are that you have returned to tame the beast.'

'Oh.' Maude could not help the smile that spread across her face. 'Do you think he missed me?' Then her fragile confidence dipped again. 'Or, perhaps he is annoyed that I left him with all the work.'

'I rather suspect the former.' Jessica grinned. 'The man thrives on work. No, I think he has been pining, although Eden Hurst's version of that condition ensures that all around share in the misery.' She pulled Maude down to sit beside her. 'Has he said anything to you?'

'Nothing definite,' Maude said with a sigh. 'But he is so gentle with me, so tender—and he seems happy, and able to show that happiness, when he is with me. And then, something happens to remind him of who we are and it all vanishes. Or perhaps it is true, what he says, and he simply does not know how to love and that can never be cured.' She drew a deep breath. 'I am resolved to tell him, Jessica, tell him exactly how I feel about him. But not until after the *Musicale*. May I tell Papa that I will stay on for a while with you that evening?'

Her friend nodded, her eyes not leaving Maude's face. 'Oh, Maude, I really do not know what to hope for the best.'

'Hope for my happiness,' Maude said fiercely. 'Mine and Eden's.'

They sat, hand in hand in silence for a while until Bel breezed in, shedding her furs into the arms of Jessica's butler.

'I have the final list of performers,' she crowed. 'And there are three of the Almack's patronesses upon it! Lady Cowper, Princess Esterhazy and Lady Jersey, would you believe? I cannot prevail upon any of them to tell me whether they will perform together or individually, or what indeed, they intend to do—but such a coup!'

'Maude, darling—I'm sorry, I didn't see you.' Bel swooped for a kiss. 'You look so well. Now, what are you going to do on the night? Jessica, Elinor and I plan to sing together and

Ashe is going to teach Gareth a rousing military song with some of the soldiers as a chorus.'

'I hadn't thought,' Maude confessed. 'Recite something, I suppose.' As she said it, she remembered that moment when Eden had stood on the stage below her box and spoken one line from Romeo and Juliet. Dare she? Could she find a passage that would tell him what she felt and yet be something that she might speak before an audience? 'Shakespeare,' she added, vaguely. She could not act, but she could recite and Eden had said she had good projection.

'So serious.' Bel pulled a face. 'Still, I suppose we have lots of songs and comic pieces. Tomorrow we are going to the theatre to run through the order with Mr Hurst. Will you come?'

'Yes.' Maude nodded. That would be best. She did not trust herself to be alone with Eden and not tell him how she felt, tell him that she owned the theatre and he need no longer worry about it. Her friends would be more than adequate chaperons.

'We cannot rehearse, that is the trouble.' Bel stood in the centre of the fore-stage, a list in her hand, and addressed Eden, who was standing in front of the stalls looking up at her. 'I mean, *we* can, but I can hardly ask some of the guests how long they will take.'

'It doesn't matter,' Eden said. 'Give me the list, with what you've got, and I will work out the timings as best I can and then improvise on the night. If necessary, the orchestra can cut all its pieces—or add things in if we are running short.'

'Mr Hurst, you are quite wonderful,' Bel said, beaming at him.

'And you, Lady Dereham, are offering me Spanish coin,' he retorted.

'Oh, no, Mr Hurst,' Jessica added, laughing at them as she and Elinor joined Bel. 'We all think you are wonderful.'

'*All* of you?' His dark brows rose as he scanned the three of them.

'Lady Maude too,' Bel said, slyly, looking into the wings where Maude was standing, content to be at a safe distance. She had slipped in without Eden seeing her.

'She is here, then?' It seemed to Maude, as she stepped out of the shadows, that Eden's expression lightened, the corners of his eyes creased into a smile, his lips curved, even as he bowed punctiliously. 'I see you are in good health, ma'am.'

'Thank you, yes. Good country air and food and I am quite myself,' she said lightly, moving to join the others. He watched her walk across the stage, his eyes locking with hers as she reached Bel's side.

'You will take tea with me?' Eden asked, still speaking directly to her.

'We would be delighted, Mr Hurst,' Jessica said briskly, her voice cutting across the tension between them.

'In my office, then. Lady Maude will show you the way, if you will excuse me.'

Maude led the way into the square room, amused, despite her preoccupation, at the reaction of the others to the mass of prints and playbills on the walls and the drama of Eden's great carved chair. They flitted about the room, peering at the pictures, the shelves of books, the heavy black opera cloak with its scarlet lining swept around the shoulders of a bust of Shakespeare.

She watched them, standing beside the chair, her hand absently caressing the great eagle that crowned the back. Eden entered quietly and joined her while Bel and Jessica went to help Millie find space for her tea tray.

'You came back,' he said, softly, resting his left hand, the one with the diamond ring, on the eagle's claw.

'Yes. I never meant to stay away for long.'

'There is much I must say to you.' His dark eyes seemed to suck her in as though she was gazing deep into a woodland pool. There was tenderness there, and anger and a haunting sadness. 'I missed you, Maude.'

'And I you.' Somehow their fingers had drifted together, meshed, locked. His hand was warm and dry and she could feel the calluses on his palm, the hardness of the ring. 'Eden…'

Behind them Bel cleared her throat and Eden turned, smiling. 'Would you pour, Lady Dereham?' and the moment had gone.

They had gathered round the tea table and were discussing the final details when suddenly the light flickered, dimmed, almost vanished. 'What on earth?' Elinor gasped. Then, as suddenly as they had faded, the gas lights were glowing as brightly again.

Eden got up and checked the lamps. 'Strange—this has not happened before. I can only assume the gas pressure dropped for a moment. Will you excuse me, ladies? I must check that no lamps have gone out completely anywhere.'

'I don't like the things,' Jessica confided as the door closed behind Eden. 'I know they give a stronger light, but the smell gives me a headache.'

'They must be safer than oil or candles, though,' Bel suggested. 'You can't knock them over like oil lamps and the flame is enclosed.'

'That's true. But then there is the disturbance and cost of having to have the pipes put in everywhere,' Jessica countered. They were still discussing it when Eden returned.

'Inexplicable. If it happens again I will have to speak to the gas company—we cannot risk being plunged into gloom in the middle of a performance.' He looked around the four faces as one by one they finished drinking their tea and began to gather up their possessions. 'Is there anything else I can assist you with, ladies?'

'No, thank you. I think everything has been organised to perfection.' Jessica retrieved her umbrella. 'We will see you on the afternoon of the *Musicale*, then?'

'Lady Maude?' She stopped, biting her lip, then turned with a smile.

'Mr Hurst?'

'Could you spare me a few minutes? There is something I would discuss with you.' Maude's heart seemed to jolt in her chest. Eden looked almost vulnerable, standing there, waiting for her response. But she could not risk being alone with him, not yet.

'I am sorry, but I must go now, the others are waiting for me.' She gestured towards the door as their voices faded away down the passage. 'After the *Musicale*, Eden. We will talk then.'

'Very well,' he said sombrely, as though she had given him bad news. 'You had better hurry, don't keep your friends waiting.' And somehow she forced a smile on to her lips and walked away.

It was like throwing a party to celebrate his own breaking heart, Eden thought as he stood on the stage at the Unicorn and surveyed the ants' nest of activity that was transforming his theatre.

Men in shirtsleeves were everywhere, scarred soldiers, some limping, some with only one arm, mingled with his own carpenters and riggers while their noble lordships, Dereham and Standon, apparently enjoying themselves enormously getting sweaty and filthy, checked their work against Eden's master plans.

Behind him, the scene painters and the scenery shifters

were working to create the backdrop under Theo's direction and in the boxes two dozen footmen, loaned by the various committee members, flapped tablecloths and clattered silverware under the command of his butler.

Backstage the Green Room had been transformed into a base for the caterers, his own cook supervising the men from Gunther's while Millie, white with excitement at the responsibility, was in charge of the ice boxes and their precious contents.

Maude was with her friends, arranging flowers and deciding on where the swags of greenery were to go. She was avoiding him; her smile, when they found themselves close, was strained. He, thankful for small mercies, knew no one expected him to smile at them; he rather thought he had forgotten which muscles were used.

Eden found his mind wandering to Maude again. What did she feel for him? Could she possibly share the emotion that was wrecking his sleep, leaving his body aching with unfulfilled desire and his thoughts flinching away from the knowledge of the pain to come? Would it be better if she did not—or worse? Better, he told himself. Then only he would be hurt. If she loved him, the knowledge could only bring him a second's happiness.

All around him activity was slowing, men were stopping, standing back to eye what they had achieved, slap each other on the back. It was done. Even the ladies seemed satisfied at last, putting down scissors and wire and reaching out for one last tweak at vases of nodding blooms.

Now all that remained was to clear away the tools, sweep up and for the caterers to take over. Eden raised his voice. 'Thank you! I suggest that everyone who is not involved in catering or cleaning leaves now. Beginners…that is, the committee, back here at six, if you please.'

Three hours for them to bathe and dress and rest. Three hours for him to transform himself as his theatre had been transformed and to show Maude, so very clearly, that the notorious Eden Hurst was not a suitable companion for her.

'What on earth are you doing, my dear?' Lord Pangbourne enquired with a chuckle, emerging on to the first floor landing to find Maude clutching the balustrade and muttering.

'Practising my piece for this evening,' she said. 'Oh dear, I wish I had joined in with the others; my singing might be poor, but at least no one would have known if I had just mouthed the words.' But it was not the act of performing that was making her insides tie themselves in knots and her hands shake, it was the thought of what Eden's reaction to what she was saying might be.

'You will be fine,' her father said firmly. 'What are you performing?'

'Just a short piece from Shakespeare,' Maude said vaguely. She had said little more than that to Eden, other than to add, 'It will only take a few minutes. I will go at the very end, before the string band's last piece', before escaping under the pretext of taking delivery of the hothouse blooms.

'Most suitable, I am sure. You look very lovely,' Lord Pangbourne added. 'That soft green suits you.'

'Thank you, Papa.' She had chosen the gown with care, selecting a simple column of green silk over an underskirt of soft cream crepe. Anna had piled her hair high, dressing it with pearls to match those in her ears and circling her throat.

It was, Maude thought, considering her appearance with ruthless detachment, the most elegant and also the most seductive garment she possessed, the low bodice cupping her breasts, the cunningly cut sleeves seeming on the point of slipping from her shoulders. If everything went well, they would slip from her shoulders under the pressure of Eden's hands and his mouth would find the lush curves they guarded. And if she failed, then Anna would unfasten it with care, hang it up to air and then fold it away again in silver paper and lavender—she would never want to wear it again.

Two hours later she was sitting applauding her male friends and their soldier chorus while the Unicorn shook with cheers and clapping. 'It's a wild success!' Jessica was on her feet, clapping. 'Everyone is loving it.' She collapsed back again on to her seat and fanned herself. They were using the Templeton box for their party so they had the best view of the whole theatre. Some people were promenading, others seated, eating. Parties had taken boxes and had crammed them with their friends and the wine was flowing like water.

Ashe had had the idea of charging for champagne, deliberately inflating the price, and guests were vying to be seen buying with a lavish disregard for cost in support of the charity. The rows of bottles in front of parties was becoming a matter for competition, and it was certainly helping the amateur performers overcome their nerves, adding an extra dimension to some of the more comedic pieces as performers literally tripped on to the stage to roars of laughter from their friends.

But the ladies, and most of the older men, were providing enough dignified entertainment to leaven the jollity and Eden was managing the order and presentation of the acts with flair.

He was also playing his role of showman to the hilt. Maude had told him she would like to see his impersonation of the old-school actor-managers and now she was wondering if he had remembered that and had dressed accordingly.

She watched, a fond smile on her lips, as he walked out to introduce the next act. 'My lords, ladies, gentlemen! The lovely, the distinguished, the talented Lady Patronesses of Almack's!'

They filed on, grouped themselves with the elegance of three Greek goddesses at the centre of the fore-stage and bowed. Jessica craned to see the four who had not agreed to perform. 'Mrs Drummond Burrell is sucking lemons,' she reported. 'I am sure she wishes now she had agreed to take part.'

But Maude was watching Eden signalling to the string band to strike up the accompaniment for the song. His hair was glossy with oil, curled, dressed so its length was very obvious. His skin was golden in the gas light, his eyes so dramatically dark that she knew he must have outlined them with kohl. He had never looked so Italian and in his flamboyantly frilled shirt and his jet-black suit of tails she thought he had never looked quite such a dangerous male animal before either. Diamonds winked everywhere, including both ears, and the audience seemed to love him. He exactly fitted their mood for the evening—different, exotic, decidedly scandalous—and his uncompromising control of the stage seemed to steady the nerves of the most anxious performer.

Ashe, Theo and Gareth came in, larger than life after their success, grinning and demanding praise for their act. 'And we have a surprise for you,' Ashe added, flinging the door to the box wide. 'I give you Her Serene Highness, the Grand Duchess Eva, and Lord Sebastian Ravenhurst!'

Maude was so swept up in the excitement of the new arrivals and the need to find chairs, settle them in the box, explain what was going on and demand news, that her planned half-hour of quiet rehearsal, when she had intended to slip away backstage by herself, was quite forgotten.

Eva, magnificent in ruby silk, waved to her friends all

around, in between explaining their unexpected arrival. 'The wind in the Channel was just right, we seemed to fly across, then the children were so good we just pressed on from Dover and arrived at five this evening and of course you'd told us about this in your letters, so we put the children to bed, got changed and here we are.'

'Aren't you exhausted?' Bel asked over the clamour of a demonstration of Scottish sword dancing by three officers of a Highland regiment.

'Not in the slightest,' Eva pronounced. 'Who have we missed?'

'All of us except Maude, and she is the last act.'

The officers left the stage to cheers and Eden walked back on. Eva raised her quizzing glass. 'What a very dramatic young man.' Maude saw Jessica kick Eva's ankle warningly. 'Are we supposed to pretend he doesn't exist?' she asked provocatively with a sideways look at Maude.

'What have they been telling you?' Maude asked, resigned to Jessica and Bel having regaled Eva with the entire story, episode by episode, in their letters.

Instead of teasing her, Eva lent over and touched her cheek in a fleeting caress. 'That you have lost your heart and it is hard for your friends to see how it is not going to be broken.' Maude swallowed, shaken by the tenderness in Eva's voice. The Grand Duchess could be so autocratic and overwhelming that the gentle understanding in her eyes brought tears to Maude's own. 'There are those who said I made an unequal marriage—the bridegroom included,' she whispered. 'But love gives you courage.'

Maude hung on to those words as the evening passed and the moment arrived when the act before her own came on to the stage. 'You had better hurry down,' Bel whispered.

'No, I am staying here,' Maude said, getting to her feet. 'Please can you all move back a little and dim the lamps on that side?'

Puzzled, they did as she asked. Maude stood back in the shadows, waiting. Lady Calthorpe and her daughter came to the end of a charming duet and Eden walked back on stage.

To Maude's eye he was puzzled, obviously wondering where she was, but, with a glance back into the wings, he announced, 'Lady Maude Templeton!'

There was silence, then Maude stepped to the front of the box in the light of the only remaining lamp and spoke Juliet's words, her voice clear across the crowded space.

Gallop apace, you fiery-footed steeds,
Towards Phoebus' lodging…

Chapter Twenty

"...come night, come Romeo, come thou day in night;
For thou wilt lie upon the wings of night,
Whiter than new snow upon a raven's back.
Come gentle night, come loving black-browed night,
Give me my Romeo..."

The theatre was hushed as Juliet's words, the plea of a woman whose lover has been wrenched from her by a cruel twist of fate, who knew all too bitterly the barriers keeping them apart, floated out above them.

Maude spoke them from her heart, her eyes locked with Eden's. He stood, stock-still, looking up at her, his face white.

"...and when he shall die,
Take him and cut him out in little stars,
And he shall make the face of heaven so fine,
That all the world will be in love with night..."

It was almost ended, he was still there, still intent upon her lips.

"O here comes my nurse...what news?"

And Maude stepped back into the shadows and into Eva's arms. The silence stretched on, then the applause broke out and the tension was broken.

'Wonderful!' Bel was openly mopping at her eyes, the others clapping. Lord Pangbourne beamed proudly as Sebastian put a chair forward and Maude sank down, her legs trembling. *Give me my Romeo.*

The string band began to play incidental music, the audience to gather itself, talking at the top of its voice. Laughter rose up to the box as the stalls began to empty. It was over—and it was just beginning, Maude told herself.

'Maude and I will stay on a little, Lord Pangbourne, just to thank everyone who has worked so hard behind the scenes,' Jessica was saying. 'Is that all right?'

'Of course.' He was still beaming proudly. 'And you say you cannot act, Maude. I have never heard better, I declare.'

'Ah, yes, but you were not acting, were you?' Eva murmured in her ear.

'I'll just go down and have a word with Mr Hurst, thank him for managing the stage so well,' Maude said, slipping to the door of the box. She hurried down the stairs, held up every few paces by people wanting to congratulate her upon the evening or her recitation. Finally she made it to the door off the lobby and made her way to the wings.

Eden was there, giving orders to the stage manager and the hands. 'Everyone help the caterers,' he was saying. 'The rest can be dealt with tomorrow. Lord Standon is taking care of the money; someone find him and carry the strong box to his carriage.'

Maude waited, enjoying seeing Eden work, the effortless way he covered everything that needed to be done. Finally the workers trooped off to their tasks and he turned and saw her.

'Maude.' It was there in his face, all the hope and despair and doubt that was whirling inside her. 'Maude, that was…'

'Hurst, my dear fellow. A triumph! I am very impressed, very impressed indeed.' It was Papa, marching across the stage, hand outstretched to wring Eden's. He turned and nodded briskly at Maude. 'Telling him the good news about the theatre, my dear? That's the way to round off the evening, indeed it is!' He dropped a kiss on Maude's cheek. 'Now, don't you and Lady Dereham stay here all hours, will you? You need your rest.'

'What about the theatre?' Eden asked, his voice ominously quiet as the earl disappeared from sight.

'I…I know who owns it.'

'And you were about to tell me?'

Some demon of truthfulness had Maude shaking her head. 'No… I mean, yes, I was going to tell you, but not just now. You said you wanted to speak to me.'

'And how long have you known who owns it?' He made no move to come closer.

'A week. Just over. Eden—'

'Would you be very kind and wait for me in my office, Lady Maude?' he asked with awful politeness. 'I doubt that we will want to edify the stage hands with this discussion.'

'Yes, of course.' Maude walked stiffly past him. He was furious, she could understand why. But it wouldn't last, once he understood…

Eden stood outside his own office, hand on the door. He had made himself stay and organise things until his stage manager could take over and then he had walked back here, still not allowing himself to think about what Maude's knowledge meant.

Gritting his teeth, he walked in, closing the door behind himself and turning the key in the lock. Maude was sitting in an upright chair, her hands clasped in her lap, her chin up.

'You know who owns the Unicorn?' he asked.

'Yes.' She swallowed. 'I do.'

'*What?*' Maude met his eyes defiantly. 'You bought it?' The sense of betrayal was like a blow.

'No, I inherited it from a friend of my mother. She was an actress. I did not know until last week she was the owner.' But she had known last week, had known it and had not told him, even though she knew he was waiting anxiously for that very piece of news.

'Why did you not tell me? You know I want to buy it. You know how much it means to me.'

'I did not think I wanted to sell it,' she said. 'I thought I might keep it, as an investment. Then it would be safe for you.'

'You could have invested the money,' Eden said, furious, something very like fear gripping his heart. 'If you keep it, when you marry it goes to your husband. You know that, it is the law. God knows what *he* will do with it.'

'I wouldn't…' She swallowed. 'I would not marry someone who would do that.'

'Indeed?' Eden demanded, his voice sceptical in an effort to hide the hurt of thinking of Maude as another man's wife. 'You'd put that in the marriage settlements, would you?'

'No,' she snapped, on her feet in a swirl of silks. 'No, because I only want to marry you.'

'You—' Eden knew he was staring, couldn't find the words. He tried again. 'You want to marry me? Impossible.' She couldn't be doing this to him, not on top of that speech this evening, not when he had screwed himself up to renounce anything to do with her.

'Why is it impossible? Are you married already?'

'No, of course not. You know why you cannot marry me. Look at me.' He took a stride forward, seized her arms and pulled her back against him, forcing her to look at their images in the long glass. 'And look at yourself.' The contrast of her simple, lovely pearls, the elegant, understated lines of her gown and the glitter and tawdry tricks of his own appearance. 'You are a lady, of the *ton*, a *virgin*, for God's sake. I am a bastard, a theatre manager, a rake with a notorious reputation. Just because you desire me—'

'I love you.' Maude spoke the words to his image in the glass, her voice steady. 'I love you, Eden. I was going to tell you that tonight. That is what those words I spoke tonight were for.' Then her voice began to shake and she twisted in his grip. 'How much closer could I get to telling you I loved you in front of the whole damned *ton*?'

She loved him? Eden's heart seemed to turn to water in his chest, something—joy?—was struggling to surface against the fear for what this could mean, the impossibility of it. And there was a little nagging voice that would not be silenced. 'When, exactly, were you going to tell me about the theatre?' he asked.

Maude was so still in his arms, her face pale and very lovely as she looked up at him. 'After I told you how I felt,' she whispered. 'Eden, tell me how you feel about me—I can't bear it, not knowing. I have loved you for so long, ever since I first saw you. My love—'

Her words made no sense, he shook his head, grasping the one thing that was clear. 'Why wait to tell me you own the theatre?'

'Because…because I wanted you to be thinking just about us, not to be influenced by the Unicorn.'

'Influenced?' A coldness gripped him. 'You were not sure whether I would tell you the truth about my feelings for you if I knew? You thought I would pretend to love you to gain the Unicorn?'

'I was not certain. You are so passionate about it.'

'And if I said I did not love you? You would punish me by keeping the ownership secret?'

'No!' Maude gave a little push against his chest as though to push away the very thought. 'I would have told the agents to sell it to you and not reveal the owner.'

'I see.' Eden was not sure he believed her—a woman scorned would have to be a saint to do such a thing when she could hold such a weapon against him. 'So, you love me, you say, but you do not trust me.'

'Eden, I have loved you for a year and known you for a few weeks. I trust you, of course I do, with my life, but this is so important to you.'

'If I loved you, Maude,' Eden said slowly, 'and burning down the Unicorn was what it took to have you, then I would light the match myself. If you do not know that about me, you know nothing.'

Her eyes were huge and shimmering with tears she was too proud to shed, her mouth, soft and vulnerable. She was everything he wanted and he had told her the truth: he would destroy the Unicorn if that was the only way to have her, if that was all it would take to make him eligible for her.

But if she could not trust him… And she was right not to. She sensed the haunted darkness inside him, the unworthiness. And then through his misery he saw that she had indeed handed him a weapon, the one he needed to convince her he did not desire her for every reason a man could desire a woman. He tried to feel glad, glad that here was an excuse to break with her, one that would surely cut the tie between them with the sharpest knife.

'I realise,' he said harshly, 'that for a lady like yourself to admit desire for a man like me it might be necessary to dress it up as an elevated emotion, as love.'

'No,' Maude whispered. 'Oh, no, Eden.' Her hand fluttered at his breast and the need to hold her, rain kisses on her, was agony to resist.

'I would enjoy taking you as a lover, Maude, but if you think I am insane enough to entangle myself with a society virgin just for that, you are far and away wrong. I have no desire to find myself called out by your friends, my cousins.'

'You don't love me?' she asked. 'No, I can see that you do not. You cannot find it in you to forgive me my lack of trust.' There was bleakness in her eyes now, pain. 'I will go now and send Benson round in the morning to discuss selling the theatre to you.'

'You want me to buy back your investment as well?' he asked, wondering why he was still able to speak of such matters when he had just denied his own feelings and wounded Maude to the very heart. But talking of business suited the image he wanted her to have of him. It was the true image, after all. In a day or two she would be grateful for her escape, he had to tell himself that.

'No.' She pushed back out of his arms and he let her go. The last time he would hold her. 'I will not come to the theatre again, I will not interfere. I do not think I could bear to return. But should I consider marriage in the future, I will sell my investment back, never fear.'

Maude opened the door. His last chance to say those three words. He was hurting her now; to say them would be to ruin her. This, if ever, was the time to pretend to himself that he was a gentleman. Eden held his tongue. 'Goodbye, Maude.'

She turned, looked back and now he could see one tear sliding down her cheek. 'Goodbye.' Then she was gone.

She should go home, or at least to Jessica's. Maude passed down the passageway like a ghost, her surroundings as insubstantial as a dream, She had told Eden of her love and he had rejected her. She had shown her lack of trust and wounded him—but surely, if he had loved her, he would have told her so, despite that?

Her mind could hardly touch the hurt with thoughts; she knew she could not speak of it to anyone, not yet. Maude came up against a closed door and stopped, disorientated, before she recognised that this was the dressing room where she and Eden had found the two lovers. It would be deserted now, she could sit in there a while. Time would pass and perhaps she would be able to think what to do next, where to go.

How long she sat there in the dark, she did not know, nor what she had been thinking about. Her consciousness just seemed to be full of pain, a dull, bruised ache that stabbed like a knife wound if she let her thoughts drift to Eden.

But her limbs were cramped and she felt so tired. Maude got to her feet and went out again into the silence that seemed to fill the old building. She should go now; the stage doorkeeper, who doubled as a night watchman, would find her a hackney. She felt her way through the darkness until she realised where she was. This was the door to Eden's office.

Just once more, she told herself, pushing it open and finding by touch the box of Lucifers he kept on his desk. She had never lit the gas before, but she had seen Eden do it. Maude struck a light, then turned the tap, jumping as the gas lit with a loud *pop*. His great chair loomed out of the shadows and she went to sit in it, curling up under the grasp of the eagle's claws. She would just rest there for a few minutes, absorbing one last memory.

She was so tired, as though she was ill. Perhaps a broken heart *was* an illness. So very tired. Maude's head drooped and she slept. Above her, the shadow of the eagle on the wall dipped wildly as the gas flame fluttered and dimmed, then strengthened again.

The shouting brought Eden bolt upright in his bed. Hell—had he managed to sleep after all? The noise was approaching his room, raised voices, three at least. The candle on the nightstand had almost burned out, but gave enough light for him to see the face of his watch: three o'clock.

He flung back the covers and got out of bed, stark naked, just as the door banged back.

'You cannot go in there! My lord, my lord, I will have to call the Watch!' Greengage, his butler, was giving ground before the bulk of a much larger, taller, older man whose arm was held by one of the footmen, quite ineffectually, for he was being towed along despite his efforts.

'Sir, I tried to stop him, but he has run mad, I think!' Greengage gasped. 'I'll go for help, sir.'

'No.' Eden had seen who the furious intruder was. 'Leave us.'

'But—'

'Out!'

'Where is my daughter?' Lord Pangbourne advanced on Eden, clenched fist raised. 'Where is she?'

'Not here, my lord.' Eden moved quickly, catching the earl's arm as he stumbled. 'Is she not with Lady Dereham or Lady Standon?'

'No, I went there first, when she was not returned by one. And to Lord Sebastian's house, too. That left only you.'

'I give you my word, she is not with me and I have not seen her since she left my office at the Unicorn.' The older man's eyes were fixed on him with painful intensity and he felt his colour rise. 'I realise that I am not a gentleman, that you may not be willing to accept my word, but I give you leave to search this house, cellars to attics.'

'Of course I take your word, Hurst, damn it,' Lord Pang-bourne snapped. 'Do you think I would allow Maude to associate with you if I did not consider you a man of honour? Your parents may have acted without much; that's not to your discredit. I make my own judgements about men. But where is she?' he asked, suddenly looking desperately anxious and vulnerable.

'We parted…angrily. It may be that she is still at the theatre, I can think of nowhere else. I'll go, right away.' Eden went to drag on the bell pull, his heart pounding. *Maude.*

'I'm coming, too, and for God's sake, put some clothes on, man.' The earl sounded more himself.

Greengage burst into the room, a poker in his hand and the footman on his heels. 'Sir!'

'Put that damn thing down, get a carriage harnessed. *Fast!*' Eden threw open the clothes-press door and began to drag on clothes.

The pair skidded into the theatre yard. Eden was out of the carriage before it came to a halt. 'There is no light in the stage-door office.'

The stench of gas hit him, even before he got the door properly open. In his cubby hole, Doggett lay slumped over the table, his face strangely flushed. The gas lamp hissed, unlit. Eden turned it off. 'Drag him out into the air,' he snapped, his heart turning to water inside him, even as he began to run. 'I'll find Maude.'

He hardly dared think, lest fear freeze him, could not strike a light to search by for fear of igniting the gas. His brain was already clouded by the fumes as he ran down the passageway, into the Green Room. It was empty, its gas lamps turned off. The office, she might have gone there.

Eden ran, shouldered open the door into the dark room, hearing the hiss of gas, choking as the fumes hit him. For a moment, as he turned the tap off, he could see nothing, then the huddled form slumped over the desk came into focus.

'Maude! Maude!' He half-lifted, half-dragged her, a dead weight, out into the corridor. But he could not see, and the fumes were making him choke. Eden pulled her over his shoulder and ran for the yard and the clean, fresh air.

'You have her!' Lord Pangbourne started towards them. Beside the carriage the groom knelt over Doggett. 'That poor old fellow's gone. But she is all right? Tell me she's all right!'

'I don't know.' Eden lowered Maude on to the damp flags. 'She's not breathing. I think she was breathing when I found her.' The fear was washing over him, the despair clutching. She had come back for him, gone to his room, and he had not been there for her and now she was dead. 'Maude! My love, darling, speak to me. Maude!' Desperate, he slapped her face, jerking her head back and forth, but there was no response. Eden bent, covered her mouth with his and breathed hard down into her lungs.

He could taste the gas as he worked, masking the scent and the taste of her. Desperate he kept going, aware of the earl's sobbing breath beside him. It was no good, she had gone. Eden sat back, feeling the tears begin to roll down his cheeks. 'Maude, oh, my love, my love.'

And then she coughed, a pathetic, tiny noise like a half-drowned kitten. Eden snatched her up, pulled her against his shoulder, patting her back hard while she gasped and choked and then, at last, clung to him. 'Eden…' Her eyes were closed, but she breathed.

Lord Pangbourne threw his arms around the pair of them and they rocked together in the chill morning while Eden cried tears of incredulous joy and the older man wept unashamedly.

Chapter Twenty One

'Eden.' Restless, Maude turned her head on the pillow. Her head ached appallingly, her stomach hurt as though she had been sick and somewhere, in the back of her mind, she knew that something was terribly wrong.

'Hush. Try to drink this, dear.' Jessica's voice. Maude opened her eyes on her friend's anxious face. 'There, you'll be all right soon, try to drink a little. Jane, come and help Lady Maude sit up.'

Between them they pulled her up against the pillows and the maid held a glass of barley water. Maude sipped, choked and sipped again. 'What happened?'

'Do you remember being in Mr Hurst's office? The gas pressure must have dropped and your light, and that in the stage-door office, were the only ones lit. The flame went out and when the pressure came back the taps were still open. Gas poured out and nearly killed you. If your father and Mr Hurst had not arrived in time and found you and the stage doorman…'

'Doggett?' Maude recalled his lined, cheerful face. Jessica shook her head. 'Oh, no.'

'He was an elderly man; his heart must have given out.'

'Eden saved me?' She could remember, as though in a swirling nightmare, his voice, her father's presence. She could recall the pressure of his mouth, but not a kiss. She could remember his words. Or a dream of his words.

'Yes, he found you, brought you out, breathed air into your lungs until you started breathing again by yourself.'

'Where is Papa?'

'We made him go home, once it was obvious that you were no longer in any danger. He was very much upset and distressed and the doctor said he must rest. Gareth has gone with him.'

'And Eden?'

Jessica smiled. 'He is here, outside your door where he has been for the past ten hours. I can't move him. Do you want to see him?' Maude could only nod. Her friend got to her feet. 'I should stay and chaperon you, but I really think even the most notorious rake is safe alone with you at the moment.' She opened the door. 'Mr Hurst, Maude is asking for you.'

Maude struggled up further against the pillows, pushing her tumbled hair back from her face. Eden deserved her thanks, if she could only find the words and then, no doubt, he would go.

He stopped inside the door and just looked at her. His face was strained and smudged with dirt, he did not look as though he had slept and the expression in his eyes made her breath catch in her raw throat. Maude held out one hand, silent, and he came, not to take it, but to catch her up in his arms, pull her into a fierce embrace. 'Oh, my God, Maude, I thought I had lost you.'

She clung, then pulled back, staring at his face. His eyes were red, as though he had wept, and in their darkness was emotion so deep she caught her breath. 'Eden? I can remember you speaking to me, calling me back. You said—'

'Maude, my love,' Eden said, with so much sincerity she could not doubt him. 'My love, my darling, my heart.' His mouth, taking hers, was gentle; she felt him tremble under her spread hands and her heart soared.

'You love me? Oh, Eden, I knew, I sensed it. I am so sorry I did not seem to trust you—I was afraid. I love you so much, please forgive me.'

He sat back, taking her hands tight in his. 'It gave me the excuse I needed. Maude, I had to tell you, last night, tell you that whatever it was between us had to end. That I could not—' He broke off, closed his eyes and continued. 'I could not love you.'

'But you do?' Puzzled, she stared at him, cold apprehension touching the edge of her burgeoning happiness. 'Do you mean you did not realise you loved me until I almost died?'

'No. I knew I loved you, I have known that for days. But I know I should not, and I must not. Maude, this cannot be. It was bad enough, loving you, but I knew it would be worse if we both knew.'

'I don't understand.' But she did. Eden did not think he was good enough for her. 'I am old enough to marry without consent, if that is what it takes. Eden, no one can stop us.'

'I can,' he said grimly. 'Do I need to remind you that I am illegitimate, in trade and I have a shocking reputation?'

'And most of the men whom I know had a shocking reputation, until they were married,' she protested hotly. 'I love you Eden; if that means I have to put up with some snubs and a shorter list of invitations, well, to hell with them! They aren't people I want to know in any case.' She looked at his face, set in stubborn lines of absolute determination. 'Eden, kiss me and then tell me you don't want to marry me.'

'Of course I want to marry you,' he retorted. 'I want to live the rest of my life with you. Damn it, Maude. Don't look at me like that. I am trying to do the right thing, not drag you down, cut you off from your friends.'

His kiss was hard, fierce, angry. It made no concession to the fact that she was ill or frail and it spoke more strongly than he ever could of just how he felt for her.

Maude pulled him down to lie with her on the big bed, opening her mouth to him, inciting him to deepen the kiss. His tongue slipped into the moist warmth of her mouth, taking, claiming, and she groaned against the impact, scrabbling to push away the bedclothes so she could feel the length of his body against hers.

She could feel him trying to resist and yet he helped her, his big hand coming up to cup her breast through the thin nightgown, his thumb fretting at the nipple until she writhed against him. The heat was pooling deep in her belly, wanton, excited, and Maude pushed her hips against the hardness of his pelvis. And then he rolled away from her to sit on the edge of the bed, his head bowed, his hands raking into his hair.

'No! Maude, let me retain what glimmerings of honour I possess, what pride I can salvage from this. It would be wrong of me to seek to wed you, I would be blamed, and rightly, for taking you away from everything that is your life and your birthright.'

Shaken, Maude pulled her nightgown into some kind of order. She had lost him and she should be sobbing her heart out, but oddly she was angry, furiously angry.

'Your pride?' she demanded. 'You would stand on your pride and break my heart? You would sacrifice what we are and what we could have because of your damned pride? You would end the lives of the children we would have together before they are even conceived? For pride? Where is the honour in that—or do you truly not have any? You had a hard start in life and you rose above it to become the man I admire and love, but you wear your bitterness like a badge to warn people away in case they hurt you. You did not disbelieve in love—you are afraid of it.'

Eden swung round, his face stark. 'Maude—'

'Go away. I don't want you here. You saved my life and I thank you for it. I will love you until I die, but I never want to see you again if you can throw that away for pride.'

He got to his feet, slowly, as though it hurt him to move. 'Maude, I want only to do what is best for you.'

'What you, in your arrogance, think is best,' she retorted. 'You admired my intelligence, I thought. Well, you do not admire it enough to allow me to use it, or my independence, it seems. Goodbye, Eden.'

The door slammed behind him, every iota of his cold control gone, taking her hopes and dreams and future with him.

Eden spent the next twenty-four hours in a sort of blind fury of shock. By sheer will he got the Unicorn functioning again, Doggett's funeral arranged and his widow and family cared for and then, alone in his bedchamber, he let himself recall Maude's words.

Pride and honour. He had thought them the same thing, but it seemed she did not. She loved him, wanted to marry him, to have his children. He did not deserve her, he knew that, listening again and again to her words in his head.

Gradually something like hope began to penetrate the darkness. If he could marry her without making her give up everything that made her life what it was—her loves, her loyalties—then he could marry her with honour. Doggedly Eden set himself to work out exactly what Maude would need if she were to marry him and to keep everything of her present life that she valued.

First, he must believe what she told him—a few snubs would not hurt her. But her friends meant a great deal to her and the closest of those, the dearest, were the Ravenhursts. If he married Maude, then the hope of keeping his parentage secret would vanish under the pressure of society's intense curiosity. The Ravenhursts would hate the revelations about their aunt and Maude would know she had contributed to that. And they, surely, would never forgive him for the blow to their family and what he was doing to Maude.

And she adored her father. To give Maude what she wanted, what she deserved, he was going to have to sacrifice his pride and lay himself open to the risk of hurt and rejection, the loss of the dream of friends and family he had not ever dared to acknowledge he needed. And he had to learn to forgive. Hope, and her words, must be enough to make this work. He had thought himself able to organise anything— well, now was the time to prove it. Eden pulled paper and pen towards him and began to write.

Promptly at eleven the next morning he walked up the steps to the Earl of Pangbourne's front door. Maude, he knew, was still at the Standons' house. Jessica, bless her, was keeping him up to date with little notes reporting that Maude was physically stronger and was out of bed. *But she is so quiet*, Jessica wrote that morning. *So very still.*

'Mr Hurst, to see his lordship. He is expecting me.' The Templeton's butler bowed him in, took his hat and gloves and then hesitated.

'My name is Rainbow, sir. We are all very fond of Lady

Maude,' he said stiffly. 'His lordship tells me that you saved her life.'

'Yes, but it was my fault she was in danger in the first place,' Eden confessed, wondering at a butler of this superiority unbending to make personal comments.

'I'm sure it will not happen again,' Rainbow remarked, taking Eden aback. 'His lordship is in the study, if you will follow me, sir.'

The earl stood up as Eden entered and offered his hand. 'Come, sit down.'

'You are recovered, my lord?' Two nights ago he and this man had clung together, shed tears together, over Maude. Now he was shaken to find how much he was concerned about someone he hardly knew, how much he felt for him. It was as though Maude had ripped open a locked compartment in his heart, leaving him vulnerable to not just her, but to everyone he met.

'Yes, thank you. My doctor said it was shock and over-exertion, nothing more serious. You said in your letter that you want to talk to me about Maude, hmm? You'll take a glass of brandy?'

'Thank you.' It was early for him to be drinking, but Eden could only feel grateful for a little Dutch courage. He took the glass, sipped, waited for the older man to sit. 'I love Maude and I want to marry her.' The earl nodded, his face giving nothing away. 'She says she wants to marry me. But I cannot take advantage of that, not unless I know we will have your blessing and not unless I am certain that such a match will not compromise Maude's position in society and her relationship with her dearest friends.'

'As the daughter of an earl, there is not a lot that can compromise her standing,' Lord Pangbourne remarked, swirling his brandy.

'Marriage to a bastard half-Italian theatre manager might,' Eden said bluntly. 'Constant whispering, gossip, cuts will hurt her.'

'Very true. I will be frank with you, Hurst. I had you investigated before I allowed Maude to associate with you. I know who your parents are, I know the names of the society women you have slept with, I know as much about your finances as you do yourself.' Eden felt his anger burn, then subside as quickly as it had flared. Of course her father would do anything to protect Maude—so would he in his shoes. 'You're a rake, but you don't seduce virgins, you're a hard man at business, but you don't cheat, and you've a brain in your head.'

He took a swallow of brandy and regarded Eden over the rim of the glass. 'I wouldn't have gone out of my way to pick an illegitimate half-Italian in the theatre business for her though, I'll be frank.'

'Who would?' Eden enquired bitterly, provoking a bark of laughter.

'I'll tell you something about her mother, my Marietta. She was a wild girl—beautiful, intelligent, impossible to handle. She fell in love with an actor, tried to elope, but they were caught and separated. He died in an accident. I loved my wife, Mr Hurst, and she loved me, but I knew that her heart had been broken and it would never be whole again.

'I gave Maude as much freedom as her mother had been denied because that was what her mother would have wanted. I thought I saw something in her eyes when she mentioned you, so I set her boundaries, which I know she's kept to—even if she's bent them as far as they'll go, I'll be bound.' Eden felt a twinge in his newly found conscience, more, perhaps than a twinge, for the older man smiled. 'I see you have the grace to blush, sir! If you love her, and I believe you do, after seeing you the other night, then you have my blessing.'

Eden stared into the golden brown liquid in his glass. He had come prepared to beg, if that was what it took, and this extraordinary man had given his permission without hesitation. He found it difficult to make his voice work. 'I see you set more importance on your daughter's happiness than on society's strictures, my lord. I give you my word, Maude will never have cause to regret marrying me.'

Eden raised the knocker on the Henrietta Street house, aware that Madame would have finally drifted out of her boudoir and would be pecking at a little light luncheon by now.

He was shown through without ceremony and stood for a moment to admire dispassionately the picture his leading lady made. His mother. Coiffed, subtly tinted, dressed in the most feminine of gowns, she was posing even though she thought herself alone, finger at her chin, head tilted as she studied a fashion journal.

'Eden, darling.' She pouted as she became aware of him. 'Has all the fuss subsided at the Unicorn? I cannot be expected to work in such an atmosphere.'

'You mean the natural distress of the company over Doggett's death and the anxiety of getting the gas system to work more safely?' he enquired. 'Yes, all the *fuss* is subsiding.'

He sat and regarded her, wondering, even as he did so, which leading actress he could secure at short notice if what he was about to say sent her off into screaming hysterics. 'That was not why I called.'

'What then, darling?'

'When I was born, did you register my birth at any of the English embassies?' he asked.

'What? Yes!' Marguerite goggled at him, shaken off guard into frankness. 'Yes, of course I did—in Florence. And the chapel register at the palazzo. But I went to the embassy because I wanted you to be able to get an English passport if you needed one.' She stared at him. 'Why on earth are you asking?'

'You never gave me that passport after we arrived in England,' he pointed out.

'Didn't I?' She shrugged. 'It is around somewhere, I suppose.'

'And what name did you put in the embassy register?'

Marguerite became flustered. 'Name? Why, Eden Francesco Tancredi, of course.'

'My surname, Mother.' He could not recall ever calling her that, not since the day she took him from the palazzo and told him sharply to call her Marguerite, or Madame, never Mother.

'Eden, I do not like you to call me that,' she began.

'I do not care what you want, *Mother*.' He smiled, his voice light, aiming to keep her off balance. 'What surname did you put?'

'I… Hurst, of course.'

'I suggest you tell me the truth,' he said. 'If necessary, I will contact the embassy directly, or tear this place apart until I find those passports.'

'Damn you, then.' She flung down her napkin and got to her feet, pacing angrily away from him. 'Ravenhurst. Is that what you wanted to hear? Is that going to make you any more acceptable to that chit of Pangbourne's? I never speak of my *family*.' She said the word as though it were a curse. 'Never, you know that. Why must you upset me, be so selfish, Eden?'

Selfish? He was about to throw the word back at her and then something stopped him. It was hard to know what, exactly. The memory of the affectionate concern he had felt for Maude's father came to him. It had felt good to care about the older man, to receive back his approbation, his trust. This difficult, demanding, selfish woman in front of him was his mother and in the depths of her eyes was, he finally recognised, pain and vulnerability.

'Mother.' It felt strange to say it like that, as though he meant it, as though it mattered. 'Tell me what happened, why you defied your family and left home.'

'No.' But it was half-hearted. Something glittered in her eyes and he pulled a handkerchief from his pocket and handed it to her. La Belle Marguerite took it, buried her face in it, exquisite paint notwithstanding, and wept. He sat, silent, not knowing what she would want him to do. Eventually she emerged, smudged, smeared and suddenly a middle-aged woman, no longer a diva.

'I fell in love,' she said. 'He wasn't good enough for the daughter of a duke, they said. They told him that and he accepted it, promised not to see me again, promised to go to the family estates in the West Indies. Abandoned me.' The handkerchief twisted in her hands. 'I ran away to catch him before he sailed, but I was too late. He had gone, but there in the inn was an acquaintance of his. So kind, so helpful. I couldn't go back, he told me. I was ruined. By the end of that night, so I was. But still I went home. I thought, you see, that I would tell them the truth and they would let me go after my love, out to Jamaica.'

'But they didn't?'

'No. They shut me up, presumably to see whether I was going to make things worse by being with child. When it was obvious that I wasn't, they told me that George's ship had gone down in a storm with the loss of all hands. So I ran away again, fell in with a travelling troupe at Dover—you can guess the rest.'

Eden felt sick with an empathy he had never dreamt he could feel. 'They cut you off?'

'Yes. The old duke made all my brothers and sisters swear they would never speak of me again. I came back to London, a few years later, determined to try to see my mother. Then I saw a report in *The Times* of a marriage in Jamaica. My George. So they had lied to me about that, all of them. It taught me a lesson, at least.'

'That you cannot trust anyone?' Eden queried. 'That you can lock away your heart?'

In answer she turned to him, put her arms round his neck and sobbed as though the heart he had never believed she possessed, would break.

'Mother,' he said gently when she recovered herself a little, 'I love Maude Templeton and she loves me. The Ravenhursts are her best friends, almost her family. If I am to have any hope of marrying her and not destroying everything she holds most dear, then I must tell them who I am and seek their recognition.' She moved convulsively in his arms. 'This is not the generation that lied to you and banished you, Mother. These cousins know nothing about that old story. They admire you for what you are now.'

Marguerite sat up, her face with its ruined make-up stripped bare of artifice. 'Then tell them.' She managed a smile. 'Will having a daughter make me look old, do you think?'

Eden's third appointment of the day was at the very superior town house that Eva, Grand Duchess of Maubourg, and Lord Sebastian Ravenhurst kept for their regular visits to London. He wished, as he was ushered through into the salon, that he was wearing his stage costume, the diamonds in his ears, the ironic disguise he had used all these years to hide behind.

All he had now was his real name, the counterfeit appearance of a gentleman and the love of a woman he would walk over burning coals for. This, as the double doors swung open on to the eight people ranged around the room, felt rather more dangerous.

'Good afternoon.' Lord Sebastian Ravenhurst greeted him from his position by the fireplace. Under the portrait of his father, the third Duke of Allington, he watched Eden with sombre, assessing eyes. 'You wrote to me and asked that we Ravenhursts who are Maude's friends gather here to meet you. Perhaps you would care to explain why, Mr Hurst?'

'Because that is not my name,' Eden said. 'My name is Ravenhurst and I am your cousin. Acknowledging me will bring you scandal and pain. You owe me nothing, certainly not recognition; by our grandfather's decree my mother, your Aunt Margery, forfeited that years ago. But you all, I believe, love Maude Templeton and I am here to beg you, on my knees if I have to, for her happiness.' He looked round, meeting eight pairs of serious, steady eyes in turn and waited on their judgement.

Chapter Twenty-Two

'I am not going.' Maude sat defiantly in her dressing room in an old afternoon dress and frowned at Jessica and Elinor in their full glory of ballgowns, diamonds and plumes. 'I told Bel I was not going.'

'You said that when you were still feeling so poorly after the gas,' Elinor pointed out. 'You can't mean to miss Bel's ball, surely?'

'I still feel poorly,' Maude said stubbornly, feeling not unwell, but harassed. She did not want to go anywhere where she might be expected to smile and flirt and behave as though her heart was not broken. Soon, she would make the effort. Soon, she would do her duty and go and find herself an eligible and suitable husband in cold blood and give her father the grandchildren she knew he longed for. But not yet. Not while there was the slightest danger that she might simply sit down and weep as the sadness and despair swept over her. It felt like a bereavement, not the end of a love affair, and she wanted time to mourn.

'You are perfectly well,' Jessica said briskly. 'It is not like you to be a coward, Maude.'

'I am not,' she retorted, stung. 'I am unhappy. Do you

expect me to plaster on a smile and go and cavort at Bel's ball as though nothing was wrong?'

'Yes.' Jessica sat down with care for her silver net skirts and wagged her fan at Maude. 'It is the big event in the Season for Bel, and you owe it to her to turn up and look as though you are enjoying yourself. Your father is going.'

'I haven't got anything to wear,' Maude said, feeling cornered and guilty and miserable all at once.

'Poppycock.' Elinor jumped up and pulled the bell cord. Anna came in with a speed that showed she must have been waiting outside the door. Was everyone in the plot to harass her? 'Anna, your mistress is complaining she has nothing to wear, which means she is feeling well enough to go. Now, show us her wardrobe.'

Resigned, Maude got to her feet. To resist any further was perilously like sulking and she never sulked. It would hurt, but she supposed it was like getting back into the saddle after a fall. 'Very well. The new yellow gown, Anna.'

'Now that,' Jessica approved, 'is lovely, like autumn leaves. So clever, all those layers and the different colours and the way the hems are cut so it flutters. Your amethyst-and-diamond set with it, I imagine?'

'Yes,' Maude agreed, trying to get into the mood. She had bought this gown expecting that Eden would see her in it, the thought lending pleasure to the choice of every detail. Now it was just another gown.

But she dressed and let Anna pile her hair up into an elaborate knot within the tiara and pretended that she cared enough to make a decision on which side the one long curl should drop to touch her shoulder. She put on her new bronze kid slippers and slid the fine cream gloves up over her elbows and hurried so as not to keep her friends waiting.

Her reward was her father's face when she followed Jessica down the stairs to where he was waiting. 'Papa, I thought you were gone by now.'

'Lady Standon convinced me she could persuade you.' He smiled down at her 'How lovely you look, my dear.' He kissed her cheek. 'I've been worried about you.'

'I know.' From somewhere Maude found a smile and saw him relax a little. 'Now, shall we go and dance all night?'

It seemed to Maude, emerging from the end of the receiving line and hearing her name announced, that it would be some time before any of them reached the dance floor. Eva had attracted her usual crowd of admirers and friends and was holding court in the first reception room, Sebastian, Theo and Gareth at her side and a collection of some of the most notable guests, including four of the Patronesses, drinking champagne with them.

'Honestly,' Maude remarked with the first genuine feeling of amusement she had experienced in days, 'trust Eva to pick up all the best-looking men in the room.'

'Well, she can put mine down, for a start,' Jessica said with a laugh, watching Gareth responding gallantly to one of Eva's outrageous sallies. 'Here, let me help you with your dance card—and if you try to tell me you intend to sit a single one out, I will set Eva on you.'

'Yes, Jessica.' Maude submitted to having the ribbon tied round her wrist. They had been late, almost past the point of fashionable lateness, and behind them the flow of new arrivals had subsided to a trickle. Maude accepted a glass of champagne from a passing footman, having no difficulty ignoring the more conventional choice, for an unmarried lady, of ratafia.

'Lord and Lady Langford! The Marquis of Gadebridge!' the footman announced. 'Mr Ravenhurst!'

'Who?' Maude frowned at Elinor. 'Theo's over there.'

'There's more than one Mr Ravenhurst,' Elinor said, smiling. 'See?'

As she spoke the crowd parted, heads were turning, a buzz of comment swept through the room, overriding the gossip and laughter. And there, in the middle—tall, immaculate and looking exactly like Jessica's description of the dark angel from the chillier regions of Hell—stood Eden. The whispering fell silent; his expression was enough to make anyone think twice about any speculation within his hearing.

Then, just at the point where the silence became excruciating, Bel left her position at the head of the stairs and linked her hand through Eden's arm. 'Well, I think I might safely desert my post now, Cousin.' There was an audible gasp from all around. 'Have you met the Grand Duchess and your Cousin Sebastian? There are so many of us, I quite lose track of who has met who.'

Ashe beside them, she bore down on Eva. It seemed the crowd were holding their breath, then Sebastian stepped forward, his hand held out. 'Cousin.' Eden shook it, bowed to Eva, then was swallowed up in the knot of Ravenhurst men.

'Come on.' Jessica tugged at Maude's arm.

'No.' Her head was spinning. 'No, you go, I am going to sit down.' She waved her hand vaguely towards the ballroom and slipped away into the crowd before Jessica could catch her.

Inside the ballroom, people were unaware of the stir outside. The orchestra was playing a spirited tune for a set of country dances and Maude was stopped several times by friends eager to talk and gentlemen asking for the honour of a dance.

'No, thank you,' she kept repeating. 'I have been a little unwell, I am just going to watch.'

At last she reached the alcove near the end of the long room and parted the heavy swagged curtains that gave a fragile privacy to the space and its gilded sofa and chairs. Later, couples would sit out there to cool off, flirt a little, but now it was empty. Maude sat down and tried to make sense of that had just happened.

Her pulse was racing, her breath came short as though she had been running and she felt dizzy. It was the shock of seeing him, of course, she told herself. She could—she must—regain some control. But what was he doing here, calling himself Ravenhurst, and why had the family accepted him, without any sign of shock or rejection? And what did it mean for her?

The curtains parted, the heavy fringing rustling a warning and Maude plied her fan, trying to look as though she was just sitting out in the cool.

'Ah, there you are.' It was Eden. He let the green velvet close behind him and stood looking at her while she got to her feet without any of her usual grace.

'Eden?' Then he held out his arms and she was in them, uncaring what had gone before, only that he was here, now, and she could hold him. 'Eden.' Her face was pressed into his shoulder, the edges of his waistcoat digging into her bosom, his fob chain pressing against her ribcage, his heart beating as hard as hers.

'Maude.' He set her back away from him. 'My darling, I can't kiss you with that damned tiara on, I'll put my eye out.'

She gave a little gasp of laughter. 'That is not the most romantic thing you could have said, Eden.'

'No.' He was smiling at her and hope began to grow in her breast, like a snowdrop pushing up through the snow towards the sun. 'No, but I hope this may be.' Before she could move, he was on one knee before her, lifting her hand to his lips.

'You accused me—rightly—of letting my pride stand

before our love. I have the consent of your father to address you, I have the support of the Ravenhursts, your friends, in using my real name—their name—despite the fact that it is my mother's also. And I have her blessing to go and find her a daughter to love. I believe that if you will do me the honour of becoming my wife, you can do so without losing any of the friends that you value or the life that you are used to.

'Maude, you have taught me how to feel, how to love and I love you, with all my heart, with my life, with my soul.' He raised his eyes to hers and what she saw in them stopped the breath in her throat. 'Will you marry me?'

'Yes.' Maude tugged his hand. 'Oh, yes. Eden, I love you so much, stand up and kiss me—I don't think I can bear it for a moment longer if you do not!'

He got to his feet. 'There is going to be a hellish amount of gossip until people get used to me being a Ravenhurst. You are certain?'

'For an intelligent man, Eden Ravenhurst,' Maude said, throwing her arms around his neck and pulling his head down to hers, 'you sometimes worry about the most foolish things. People have been gossiping about me since I put my hair up for the first time.'

The touch of his mouth was everything she had been pining for and she opened to him, parched for his love, aching for his touch. The heat of desire flowed through her like licking flames and yet it was this embrace she craved, the gentle question in his caress, the question she could answer with the trust of her kiss, the completeness of her yielding.

Eden overwhelmed her, and this, she knew, was just the beginning of their journey. Maude abandoned herself to the taste of him, the heat and the hardness, the scent of him. Her love, her husband, her—

'Thank goodness!' Bel's voice jerked them both back to reality. Eden swung round defensively, Maude tight to his side. 'We'd lost you,' Bel explained, 'And we didn't know if Eden had found you or what you had said and your father is about to—oh, he's started!'

She held back the curtain and they stepped out to find the orchestra had fallen silent, and so had the guests, all facing towards the podium where Lord Pangbourne was speaking.

'…so I am delighted to announce, with all their friends here together, the betrothal of my daughter Maude to Mr Eden Ravenhurst.' Gasps, cheers, a babble of voices rose. He cut them off with a lift of his hand. 'Maude? Where are you?'

Holding tight to Eden's hand, Maude let herself be led down the length of the ballroom, the crowd parting in front of them, smiling and reaching out to pat Eden on the back, or touch her hand, or simply stare in amazement until they reached the podium.

'Papa.'

'Come up here, both of you.' Eden lifted her up, then came to stand beside her. 'I hope you've asked her,' her father said anxiously to him, provoking laughter from everyone close enough to hear.

'Yes, sir,' Eden said, smiling and lifting Maude's hand to kiss it. 'And she said *yes*.'

'Well, Lady Maude Ravenhurst, are you quite exhausted by your wedding day?' Eden put his arm around her, pulling her close as they looked out from her bedroom window across the darkness of the parkland towards the lights of Knight's Fee, where the wedding guests were still celebrating, late into the night.

'A little,' Maude said, running the tip of her tongue along

her lower lip and watching with interest the effect that had on her husband. 'I might have to lie down in a minute.' Eden had amused her and touched her, in equal parts, by the propriety of his behaviour towards her in the two months since their betrothal was announced. It had not been easy for her. For him, knowing what to expect from lovemaking, it must have been a strain. But she rather thought they were going to reap the benefit tonight.

'Hmm, yes, of course you must lie down,' he said now, deeply serious. 'After all, you should try out this handsome new bed.' To Maude's vast relief Eden had been delighted with Lord Pangbourne's suggestion that they use the Dower House as their own country home and decorating and furnishing it had kept her jittery nerves under control. It could not do much for them now as he took her hand and led her towards the elegant canopied bed with its rose pink hangings and silken coverlet.

'I should leave you,' he added, managing to look concerned. 'You'll want to sleep. At what hour do you like to take breakfast, my love?'

'Eden Ravenhurst,' Maude said, taking a firm hold of his lapels. 'If you do not take all your clothes off, this minute, and then mine, and then make love to me, I am going to scream.'

'I think,' he said, his trained breath control suddenly all over the place, 'that it might be faster if we both undress together.'

It was not faster, but it was, Maude discovered, both fun and intensely arousing. She had not expected to find herself giggling helplessly as Eden hopped from one foot to the other as he dragged off his stockings or that taking off her corset would be such a ticklish endeavour or that they would find themselves suddenly still, the laughter dying out of their faces as they just looked at each other.

It was like learning a language with a complex grammar

and vocabulary, Maude thought hazily, as she let her hands wander over Eden's long, naked body. There was what he looked like, how he felt, the textures of his skin, the contours of hard muscle and arching bone, the crisp friction of hair. There was the way he reacted to touch, to the caress of her breath, the tentative sweep of her tongue, the brave explorations of her hands.

He lay there, exotic and golden and beautiful, letting her touch and caress and wonder, doing nothing to alarm her, watching her with dark, heavy-lidded eyes while the pattern of his breathing changed and while his body stirred into rigid arousal.

'May I touch?' she asked, hand reaching a fraction of an inch above the heat of him.

'Yes.' He sounded as though he was gritting his teeth.

'Oh,' she murmured, fascinated by the soft skin over iron hardness, the movement, the…reaction.

'Maude?' She whipped her hand away. It sounded as though he was in pain. 'Oh, my God, Maude.' And he rolled her over on to her back, the silk slithering beneath her and his weight came down so that her body shifted, instinctively cradling him and his mouth found hers as she sighed and arched. He slipped a hand between their bodies to where she ached, where the heat and the moisture and the need focused in all their intensity, and stroked as he had that night that seemed so long ago.

Muted against his mouth, her pleas and sobs were answered, not as before with his wicked, skilful fingers, but the thrust of his hips. He stopped just inside her and lifted his head. 'Maude, look at me.'

She focused her eyes on his face, and saw every muscle strained with the effort of control, saw the love in his eyes, saw the question, and smiled. 'Oh, yes, Eden, love me.'

Her cry as he entered her was soft and the smile became a gasp of pleasure as he filled her, completed her, thrust long and hard and inexorable into her core until she shattered, sobbing in his embrace and heard his cry, muffled against her breast.

A while later, when she stirred against his shoulder, he shifted her gently on to the pillow and propped himself up on one elbow to look down at her. His hair fell over his shoulder and she reached up to play with it. 'Well, wife?'

'Very well.' She should, she supposed, be feeling shy, but all she felt was wonderful. 'I had understood it was not very…that it took getting used to, at first.'

'So did I,' Eden said, thoughtful. 'Do you suppose we have a natural talent for making love to each other?'

'That must be the case,' Maude agreed, letting go of his hair and using the end of a lock of hers to stoke his nipple experimentally. 'Oh, look.'

'I believe everything is in working order,' Eden said. 'But we had better check again.' He dropped his head to nuzzle into the curve of her neck, and she could feel his mouth smiling. 'How long is it since I told you I loved you?' he asked, his voice muffled.

'Several minutes, I feel quite neglected.'

'Do you?' He sat up, frowning at her.

'No.' Maude shook her head. 'I feel very much loved. Eden, did I ever say how much I admire you for what you did—going to my father, confronting the Ravenhursts, making peace with your mother? I should never have lectured you about pride, I have too much myself, and yet you took my rejection and you forgave my lack of trust and you gave me—this.'

'Because I love you. You taught me how to love, showed me all the kinds of love. I thought that I could never be fit for any woman to love, that all I could give in return was dust and ashes and, eventually, pain. You saved me, Maude, healed me. I would give you my life; all I could give you was my pride.'

'And your love. I have thought of something else you may give me.' Maude reached out and pulled him down so his body slid against hers, fitted as though he had been designed for her. 'How many children would you like, Eden?'

She had been afraid to ask him that, afraid his own childhood would have killed that instinct in him. Then his mouth curved in that lazy, sensual, thoughtful smile that made her blood tingle. 'One for me, one for you, one for us. All to love.' His hand stroked down over the gentle curve of her belly. 'All made from love.'

* * * * *

RICK'S APPOINTMENT with his attorney early Wednesday morning went only moderately better than his meeting with social services the day before. The prognosis wasn't great—but at least his attorney was going to file a motion for DNA testing. Just so Rick could petition to see the child…his sister's baby. The sister he didn't know he had until it was too late.

The rest of what his attorney said had been downhill from there.

Cell phone in hand before he'd even reached his Nitro, Rick punched in the speed dial number he'd programmed the day before.

Maybe foster parent Sue Bookman hadn't received his message. Or had lost his number. Maybe she didn't want to talk to him. At this point he didn't much care what she wanted.

"Hello?" She answered before the first ring was complete. And sounded breathless.

Young and breathless.

"Ms. Bookman?"

"Yes. This is Rick Kraynick, right?"

"Yes, ma'am."

"I recognized your number on caller ID," she said, her voice uneven, as though she was still engaged in whatever physical activity had her so breathless to begin with. "I'm sorry I didn't get back to you. I've been a little…distracted."

The words came in more disjointed spurts. Was she jogging?

"No problem," he said, when, in fact, he'd spent the better part of the night before watching his phone. And fretting. "Did I get you at a bad time?"

"No worse than usual," she said, adding, "Better than some. So, how can I help?"

God, if only this could be so easy. He'd ask. She'd help. And life could go well. At least for one little person in his family.

It would be a first.

"Mr. Kraynick?"

"Yes. Sorry. I was…are you sure there isn't a better time to call?"

"I'm bouncing a baby, Mr. Kraynick. It's what I do."

"Is it Carrie?" he asked quickly, his pulse racing.

"How do you know Carrie?" She sounded defensive, which wouldn't do him any good.

"I'm her uncle," he explained, "her mother's—Christy's—older brother, and I know you have her."

"I can neither confirm nor deny your allegations, Mr. Kraynick. Please call social services." She rattled off the number.

"Wait!" he said, unable to hide his urgency. "Please," he said more calmly. "Just hear me out."

"How did you find me?"

"A friend of Christy's."

"I'm sorry I can't help you, Mr. Kraynick," she said softly. "This conversation is over."

"I grew up in foster care," he said, as though that gave him some special privilege. Some insider's edge.

"Then you know you shouldn't be calling me at all."

"Yes… But Carrie is my niece," he said. "I need to see her. To know that she's okay."

"You'll have to go through social services to arrange that."

"I'm sure you know it's not as easy as it sounds. I'm a single man with no real ties and I've no intention of petitioning for custody. They aren't real eager to give me the time of day. I never even knew Carrie's mother. For all intents and purposes, our mother didn't raise either one of us. All I have going for me is half a set of genes. My lawyer's on it, but it could be weeks—months—before this is sorted out. Carrie could be adopted by then. Which would be fine, great for her, but then I'd have lost my chance. I don't want to take her. I won't hurt her. I just have to see her."

"I'm sorry, Mr. Kraynick, but…"

* * * * *

*Find out if Rick Kraynick will ever have
a chance to meet his niece.
Look for A DAUGHTER'S TRUST
by Tara Taylor Quinn,
available in September 2009.*

HARLEQUIN

60 YEARS

of pure reading pleasure®

We'll be spotlighting a different series
every month throughout 2009
to celebrate our 60th anniversary.

**Look for Harlequin® Superromance®
in September!**

THE
DIAMOND
Legacy

*Celebrate with
The Diamond Legacy
miniseries!*

Follow the stories of four cousins as they come to terms
with the complications of love and what it means to
be a family. Discover with them the sixty-year-old secret
that rocks not one but two families.

A DAUGHTER'S TRUST by *Tara Taylor Quinn*
September

FOR THE LOVE OF FAMILY by *Kathleen O'Brien*
October

LIKE FATHER, LIKE SON by *Karina Bliss*
November

A MOTHER'S SECRET by *Janice Kay Johnson*
December

Available wherever books are sold.

REQUEST YOUR FREE BOOKS!

Harlequin® Historical
Historical Romantic Adventure!

2 FREE NOVELS PLUS 2 FREE GIFTS!

YES! Please send me 2 FREE Harlequin® Historical novels and my 2 FREE gifts (gifts are worth about $10). After receiving them, if I don't wish to receive any more books, I can return the shipping statement marked "cancel." If I don't cancel, I will receive 6 brand-new novels every month and be billed just $4.94 per book in the U.S. or $5.49 per book in Canada. That's a savings of 20% off the cover price! It's quite a bargain! Shipping and handling is just 50¢ per book.* I understand that accepting the 2 free books and gifts places me under no obligation to buy anything. I can always return a shipment and cancel at any time. Even if I never buy another book, the two free books and gifts are mine to keep forever.

246 HDN EYS3 349 HDN EYTF

Name	(PLEASE PRINT)

Address	Apt. #

City	State/Prov.	Zip/Postal Code

Signature (if under 18, a parent or guardian must sign)

Mail to the **Harlequin Reader Service:**
IN U.S.A.: P.O. Box 1867, Buffalo, NY 14240-1867
IN CANADA: P.O. Box 609, Fort Erie, Ontario L2A 5X3

Not valid to current subscribers of Harlequin Historical books.

Want to try two free books from another line?
Call 1-800-873-8635 or visit www.morefreebooks.com.

* Terms and prices subject to change without notice. Prices do not include applicable taxes. Sales tax applicable in N.Y. Canadian residents will be charged applicable provincial taxes and GST. Offer not valid in Quebec. This offer is limited to one order per household. All orders subject to approval. Credit or debit balances in a customer's account(s) may be offset by any other outstanding balance owed by or to the customer. Please allow 4 to 6 weeks for delivery. Offer available while quantities last.

Your Privacy: Harlequin Books is committed to protecting your privacy. Our Privacy Policy is available online at www.eHarlequin.com or upon request from the Reader Service. From time to time we make our lists of customers available to reputable third parties who may have a product or service of interest to you. If you would prefer we not share your name and address, please check here. ☐

HH09R

COMING NEXT MONTH FROM

HARLEQUIN®
HISTORICAL

Available August 25, 2009

- **THE PIRATICAL MISS RAVENHURST**
  by **Louise Allen**
  (Regency)
  Forced to flee Jamaica disguised as a boy, Clemence Ravenhurst falls
  straight into the clutches of one of the most dangerous pirates in the
  Caribbean! Nathan Stanier, disgraced undercover naval officer, protects
  her on their perilous journey. But who can protect his carefully guarded
  heart from her?
  The final installment of Louise Allen's Those Scandalous Ravenhursts
  miniseries!

- **THE DUKE'S CINDERELLA BRIDE**
  by **Carole Mortimer**
  (Regency)
  The Duke of Stourbridge thought Jane Smith a servant girl, so when
  Miss Jane is wrongly turned out of her home for inappropriate behavior
  after their encounter, the Duke takes her in as his ward. Jane knows she
  cannot fall for his devastating charm. Their marriage would be forbidden—
  especially if he were to discover her shameful secret....
  The first in Carole Mortimer's The Notorious St. Claires *miniseries*

- **TEXAS WEDDING FOR THEIR BABY'S SAKE**
  by **Kathryn Albright**
  (Western)
  Caroline Benet thought she'd never see soldier Brandon Dumont again—but
  the shocking discovery that she is carrying his child forces her to find
  him.... Darkly brooding Brandon feels his injuries hinder him from being
  the man Caroline deserves, so he will marry her in name only. It takes a
  threat on Caroline's life to make him see he could never let her or their
  unborn child out of his sight again....
  The Soldier and the Socialite

- **IN THE MASTER'S BED**
  by **Blythe Gifford**
  (Medieval)
  To live the life of independence she craves, Jane has to disguise herself as
  a young man! She will allow no one to take away her freedom. But she
  doesn't foresee her attraction to Duncan—who stirs unknown but delightful
  sensations in her highly receptive, very feminine body.
  He would teach her the art of sensuality!